no one
to hear you
SCREAM

julia Madeleine

ISBN: 0980887429
ISBN-13: 9780980887426
LCCN: 2010915283

Black Heart Books
First Edition

Library and Archives Canada Cataloguing in Publication.

I. Title.

PS8626.A32N62 2011   C813'.6   C2011-900405-4

Printed in the United States of America

ACKNOWLEDGEMENTS

My deepest gratitude to the following people who've taken the time to help me with the creation of this story: Penn Yan Police Chief Gene Mitchell (now retired) for his enthusiastic and invaluable advice on police procedures, weapons information, real estate, and Penn Yan historical information; Charles Oliver Wolff, Esq., for his legal wisdom; Brandy Kroll, piercer extraordinaire of Malefic Tattoos for reading all my drafts and helping me with all those spelling errors; to my father, David Bell, for his encouragement and enthusiasm; and to my husband, Fabien, for always believing in me and for "getting it"; that all-consuming creative addiction.

For My Dad

Chapter
ONE

He spied movement from beneath her skull as a pool of dark red crept steadily across the hardwood. Could it stain? Too late, he realized. He should have planned this better, put down some plastic.

Rory Madden cocked his head to one side and leaned over her body lying on the living room floor, her milk-white limbs splayed out awkwardly. He waited for the woman to inhale and release another agonizing scream, as he searched for the flutter of an eyelid, a twitch of her lips, anything. She didn't budge.

"You left me no bloody choice now, did you?" Rory sucked his teeth.

He inspected the wrench in his hand, knowing he should wash the end of it with bleach, though he didn't see any blood or hair. But forensics had a way of finding the most infinitesimal amount of DNA. One negligent moment could cost a lifetime of freedom—it was best not to be sloppy.

In the kitchen, he cut himself a rough line of coke from the heap on the counter with a bankcard, crushed the larger flakes into a fine powder, and divided it into two tidy lines. Using a rolled up twenty-dollar bill, he snorted each line up a nostril. The drugs crashed through his brain like lightning, inducing both pain and ecstasy, releasing him from the prison of his senses. He awoke to the euphoria surrounding him, as if he had been walking through a dream all of his life and had only now opened his eyes. He went back to work, using the wrench to tighten the seal on a pipe underneath the sink. When he was done he washed the wrench with bleach and hot water, and then tossed it into a toolbox. The clash of metal echoed throughout the empty house.

From the cupboard he retrieved a plastic bag, and from his toolbox he grabbed the duct tape and his painter's drop sheet. He went back into the living room and squatted beside the woman, pressing his fingers on her wrist to search for a pulse. Nothing. He studied the delicate arch of her eyebrow and those bewitching lashes that had so fascinated him.

In this square of light, she looked like a sunbathing Marilyn Monroe, but bruised and broken.

He let out a breath as he gazed down at her and wondered if he would ever find a woman he could respect; love, even. Seemed impossible. Yet he wanted it. He wanted to be able to connect with something real, have something lasting, something more than just his own misery for company.

He pulled the bag over her head and duct taped it around her neck so the blood wouldn't leak onto anything else. Then he tucked the drop sheet underneath her and rolled her body inside, securing it tight with tape. Next, he filled a bucket with soapy water and a little bleach, and cleaned up her blood with a mop.

When he was done he flicked open his Zippo with one hand and lit a cigarette.

"Great. Now what the hell am I going to do with you?" He let out a stream of smoke, watching it unfurl and twist in the sunlight flooding in through the wall of windows.

"Well, I could bury you on the property."

With an index finger he rubbed the stripe of dark beard he shaved into a vertical line from his bottom lip down to his chin. He stroked the stubble on his head, enjoying the velvety feel, as he considered the twenty acres of woods that surrounded his house.

Nobody ever went there; it was private property. What were the odds of anyone finding her if he dug deep enough? Slim to none. It was probably his best bet. The creases in his cheeks deepened as his lips curled upward, stretching over a set of teeth that were perfect with the exception of one slightly crooked upper incisor.

He stabbbed the unfinished cigarette in an ashtray, then lifted the body in his arms the way he had done on more than one occasion under different circumstances, and headed out to the garage. The echo of their angry words screamed inside his brain as he draped her over the back of his ATV and secured a shovel on top of her with a couple of bungee cords.

A hot August breeze waved up and swallowed him as he opened the garage door. In his dusty work clothes and construction boots, he stepped around to the gardens at the front of the house. His dark gaze took in the multitude of white roses with their silken petals and razor green leaves as they stood majestically in the sweltering heat. He cradled one in his hand and breathed in its perfume, allowing it to fill him.

He smiled and released a little moan of pleasure. "Magnificent."

Rory surveyed the expanse of his property—nothing but trees and open fields. His closest neighbor was about two hundred yards down the road and couldn't be seen from his property. That's what he liked about this piece of land: total seclusion; no one to see you coming and going; no one to object to any target practice, or complain if you made a bonfire, or turned your music up too loud. And no one to hear you scream.

Two Rottweiler puppies yelped and jumped up at the chain link fence of their dog run when they saw him come around the side of his house on the ATV. He rode back across the field, the dog's whines diminishing as he gunned the throttle. He looked out at the spectacular southwest view of Keuka Lake. The view is what sold him on this property, high above East Lake Road, just south of Penn Yan in upstate New York, to build his dream home. It was a far cry from the dingy flats in The Hammer, the poorest, roughest area of West Belfast, where he had grown up. But the scenery around Yates County reminded him a bit of home, of the Belfast Hills; the Black Mountain and Cave Hill, that surrounded the city. He knew that's what had drawn him to this part of New York.

He liked to tell people that he had the best view of the lake, even though he knew it wasn't true. The Esperanza Mansion had the best view only because its elevation was higher. He could see its boat, the *Esperanza Rose*, out on the water now, doing the lunch tour, rounding the end of the bluff before it headed back to Branchport with its cargo of tourists.

He rode into the woods and cut a path through the underbrush. Deep in the trees he stopped and picked a random spot. The damp smell of earth devoured the humid air as he began to dig a hole. After a few minutes he removed his shirt. His muscles strained underneath a colorful tattoo, stretching from his chest down to the wrist of his right arm, covering every inch of skin with an Oriental dragon, its body twisted around his own. A mosquito landed on the Gothic cross and banner tattoo that contained the name Frances in script on the inside of his other forearm. He slapped the mosquito, flicked its crushed body from his skin, and rubbed his arm. Another tattoo graced his shoulder, a faded red fist with the words, "Ulster Freedom Fighters," arched above.

Rory continued to dig and slap at mosquitoes. After about fifteen minutes, dripping with sweat, exhausted and thirsty, he stood in a ditch about three feet deep and five feet wide. He rotated his neck from side to side, allowing the vertebrae to pop, then pulled the body from the ATV and dropped it into the hole. Over the sheet he pitched a shovelful of dirt.

"Now look what's become of you." A familiar rage surfaced from deep within him. "Look what you've allowed to happen to yourself!"

When he was finished burying her, he thrust his shovel into the roots of a nearby sapling, cut it from the earth, and planted it on top of her. Then he climbed back on the ATV and rode out of the woods.

The sweet scent of clover filled his nostrils as he crossed the meadow, the dried grasses rocking in the scorching breeze, licking moisture from his skin. He stopped for a moment, panting, to wipe his forehead and noticed a mist of gray clouds on the horizon. A darkness hovered over his shoulder suddenly like a phantom, but he shook it off the way he had taught himself to and instead, revelled wholly in his cocaine high.

Rory spied his buddy's blue vintage Camaro parked on the brick driveway. Simon was crouched down, poking his fingers between the fence links at the pups. He stood, unfolding his wiry frame, when he saw Rory coming. The sun illuminated his vampire-like skin, emphasizing his neck tattoos, and making him look even more like a gang-banger, especially now that he was shaving his head. He always said he hated his curly, red hair, so when Rory began shaving his own head, Simon copied him. He'd probably cut off those prominent ears of his, too, if it would improve his appearance— if improvement was possible for someone as homely as Simon. An image pushed into Rory's mind of them as boys in Belfast, throwing rocks and bricks across the peace line at the Catholics, and later, petrol bombs in the street riots, their lives shaped by the violence that surrounded them.

Rory was a world away from the Troubles now. All the ideals of his people, the violence and the cycle of hatred, the battle against their own politicians, the fight to keep the British Army in Northern Ireland, and Republican ideals at bay almost didn't bear thinking about anymore. He was glad to be away from it all, glad he had managed to escape both prison and death. Now he had a chance at a whole new life in America.

"Hey, buddy," Simon said, with a playful backslap as Rory climbed off the ATV. A grin stretched across Simon's freckled face, exposing a mouthful of yellow teeth.

"Hey, bloody well time you guys showed." Rory snorted and spit, and then placed the dirty shovel against the wall in the garage.

"We been here fifteen minutes already," Simon said, his Belfast accent, like Rory's, still prominent. "Where you been man, planting crops or what? You got a marijuana plantation back there you're not letting on about? Looks like you been hard at it, buddy."

"ATV got stuck in the mud. Had to dig it out." He gave Simon's ear a hard flick with his finger. "You should keep them satellite dishes out of the sun."

"Christ, what's that for?" Simon rubbed his ear and scowled.

Rory threw back his head and unleashed a fierce laugh. He swung an arm around his friend's neck and squeezed him roughly, knocking him off balance. "Awk, don't be such a wee baby."

Mike the Russian, a new guy from Queens, came around from the front of the house, adjusting the fly of his jeans. Rory felt annoyed at the thought of the man pissing on the prized roses that he tended daily with loving care, the dumb bastard. Mike, stocky and muscled, moved across the driveway like a juiced-up pit-bull ready for a kill. Brutality wafted from him like a bad smell. He nodded at Rory, expressionless.

Simon fetched a heavy hockey bag from the Camaro's trunk, and peered around instinctively. They made their way through the garage to the air-conditioned chill of Rory's house.

"Hey man, when you going to buy some bloody furniture for this place?" Simon asked, looking around. He hoisted the bag up on the kitchen's center island.

"Aye, you'd think with all the spare time I have on my hands I'd have it all tricked out like something from *Home and Garden* magazine now, wouldn't you?" Rory guzzled a glass of water then poured himself a whiskey. He offered the bottle to his friends but they shook their heads.

"Don't worry, as soon as everything's finished I'm going to throw a big bash and you guys are at the top of my guest list," Rory said. "For now I got the basics—bed, flat-screen TV. What more does a man need? Maybe a maid."

"Aye, right you are. A French one in a cute, wee frock and high heels."

"Let's take care of business, you guys," Mike said, his face flushed with the afternoon heat. "You got the money all counted out, heads in the right direction this time?"

"Sure I have. Give me a minute, fellas. Have a drink." Rory disappeared into the garage and removed the face of a cinderblock, exposing the two-foot-deep cavity in the wall where he kept his cash. Minus the two hundred thousand he was about to fork over, there was exactly one hundred and eighty thousand left. And of course, there was a small amount in the bank, just to appear legit.

Life was good.

Back in the kitchen, he dropped an armful of money, bound in elastics, on the counter. Mike pushed the hockey bag toward him. Rory unzipped it and reached inside, pulling out one of the tightly packaged kilos of pure Bolivian cocaine. It felt just like Christmas morning.

"Good to go," Mike said.

Rory looked up at him and noticed Mike's eyes were fixed beyond him, out the window. Rory glanced over at Simon and observed that he was backing away, bouncing on his heels. He wasn't making eye contact. And suddenly Rory got a sick feeling; the sensation of weightlessness, like when a plane takes a sudden dip during turbulence. He knew what was about to happen.

They burst through the doors and surrounded him like a swarm of giant hornets, at least a dozen of them, all decked out in bulletproof vests and helmets with face shields.

"Get on the floor! Get down! Keep your hands up!" they barked at him, their guns pointed, ready to plug his body full of bullets if he made the slightest move. Rory swallowed and looked for his friend. Simon—his best friend, his partner, his brother-in-arms, the one he trusted with his very life and would have taken a bullet for—was shuffled out, shielded by his traitor's heart. Rory watched the mob ingest him.

Rory was searched and questioned, his hands bound behind his back, and then hustled outside to a police car in which he was locked and made to wait while they trespassed over his property and his home. From the back seat he spied Deputy Sheriff Gus Linden of the PYPD and two of his cronies standing guard on the road in front of the house. Linden was talking on a cell phone, one foot on the bumper of his SUV, his elbow on his knee. The old bastard was probably gloating. He'd been keeping tabs on Rory for months.

Rory turned to gaze at his house: thirty-six hundred square feet and two stories of refined grandeur, with twelve-foot ceilings, built-in book shelves, a veranda off the master bedroom overlooking the front yard, and a three-car garage, all set on twenty acres of paradise. He looked at the exquisite roses in his gardens. How would they survive if he weren't here to take care of them? And what would become of his dogs?

The hills in the distance were a haze of indigo. They looked dismal and cold through a blur of angry tears. The darkness descended on him and he felt himself buckle inward in defeat as it consumed him whole.

Chapter
TWO

Justine Jameson's heart kicked against her ribs and she let out a gasp. She stopped so abruptly in the center of the kitchen that she stumbled backward, like she'd walked into a glass door she didn't know was closed, and gazed at the specter before her. In the drain board by the sink, in the flatware and utensil holder, a half dozen sharp knives stuck up in a bouquet of stainless steel, their blades glinting under the overhead lights, brutal and deadly. Instantly, the thought sliced through her, *They could hurt the baby!*

The glass of orange juice held forgotten in her hand slipped from her grip and smashed on the tile floor, surrounding her bare feet with shards. She stepped sideways, and then felt a shooting pain up her right leg as one pierced the heel of her foot.

"Jesus! Fuck…Goddamn!"

Awkwardly, she tiptoed out of the circle of broken glass and sticky juice. On one of the kitchen chairs, she sat down hard and inspected her foot, crossing it over her knee and turning it upward. A bead of blood dripped down from the cut on her heel, and she looked around for something to dab it with but there was nothing within reach. She would have to step across the floor again, and try and avoid the glass, to fetch a paper towel from the counter.

A little trilling sound came from the living room where her newborn slept in a playpen. Justine held her breath and waited, but except for that one stray chirp, the apartment remained quiet. The sound of the glass hadn't woken Abigail. Good. She had a hell of a mess to clean up—as if she didn't have enough to do already on any given day.

She sat down again and dabbed at the blood with a paper towel. The bleeding seemed to have stopped, but she couldn't see the end of the shard. It was in too deep. She would need to use some tweezers and dig the stupid thing out. But first she had to get rid of all those dangerous knives and every other sharp instrument she could get her hands on, clean up the glass, and dispose of the entire lot in the incinerator. Fucking hell.

She hobbled out of the kitchen to fetch the broom and dustpan from the closet. With a handful of paper towels, she mopped up the juice and then brushed the floor for every single fragment. She dumped the glass into a Balducci's paper grocery bag, and then went about gathering up the sharp knives. She worked frantically, ignoring the throbbing in her foot, empty-ing the drawers of everything harmful: two pairs of scissors, some steel kabob skewers, corn-on-the-cob holders in the shapes of little grinning pigs, a meat thermometer, even the potato peeler that had a pointy end. Then she eyed the forks in the drawer. Obviously they were too dangerous to keep in the house with a baby. There was no choice; they would have to go, too.

When everything was secured inside the paper bag, she folded the top and realized that her heart was still pounding. Maybe as soon as the bag was out of the apartment she would begin to relax. To feel safe.

She was about to step into the hallway, heading for the incinerator shoot, when she heard a key turn in the lock and the door swung open. Her father, Brett, entered smiling, but then, clearly because of a look on her face of which she was unaware, his smile withered.

"What's wrong?" he said, looking her over.

He was home early; it wasn't even lunchtime. She watched him slowly lower his briefcase to the floor, his eyes fixed on her, his paisley print tie sliding sideways over a crisp white shirt that she'd actually got up and ironed for him that morning—a trade-off for changing a poopy diaper. He ran a hand over his dark hair, which had started to gray above his ears. It was messy, spiked up in that just-got-out-of-bed look, a style that seemed a little too young for someone his age.

"Is the baby okay?" he asked.

She opened her mouth to explain, but no words came out. Tears filled Justine's eyes unexpectedly, and slipped down her cheeks. She could feel her chin quiver as she attempted to control herself and hold it all inside, but the scales had tipped. All the pent-up emotion and fear escaped despite her best efforts, and only succeeded in making her angry with herself.

Her dad reached out and pushed a tendril of golden hair, fallen loose from her ponytail, across her forehead and back behind her ear. She could see his stress in the lines that seemed deeper around his eyes today. He suddenly appeared older than his forty-five years, and she felt sorry that she was falling apart in front of him, that she was being a burden.

If there were ever a convenient moment in one's life to go crazy, then probably now, with the amount of responsibility Justine had, would not be it. As unsuitable as the timing was, though, she could, indeed, feel herself teetering on the edge of sanity. She could feel it bearing down on her like a guillotine, ready to chop off her head, and she didn't know if there was any way at all to stop it from descending. It seemed inevitable.

She reached for him, and he held her as she cried into the shirt collar that smelled of Cool Water and laundry soap. She felt eight years old in his arms, yet she welcomed the sensation in that moment—her father's tenderness and the strength of his embrace. This was so unlike her. What was happening to her? Why couldn't she just be normal like the rest of the world? That's all she wanted. To just be normal.

Her father stepped into the living room to peek at Abigail, sleeping in her playpen. With the paper bag still clutched in her hands, Justine moved beside him and watched the baby make sucking motions in her sleep. Justine smiled sadly, studying the baby's round cheeks and tiny hands with their miniature fingernails that seemed impossibly small and perfect. Although she was told her baby looked just like her, she knew it was a lie that people told to be nice. Abigail looked just like her father, the stupid jerk. It confused her that something imprudent, like dishonesty, could be transformed into a virtuous thing. Wasn't that a contradiction? Lies should be reserved and used only out of necessity, to save yourself or someone else from certain peril, not to be applied offhandedly, without thought, disguised as a compliment. Justine hated casual lies. And she hated her ex even more.

She remembered the first moment she had held Abigail, that intense feeling in the center of her chest like a brilliant light coming to life inside of her. An electric sensation vibrated her entire being as if a mass of angels had swept through her. It was exhilarating. Her whole existence sanctified with the arrival of this tiny being. And now, here she was only a few weeks later, losing it. What the hell was wrong with her?

The last thing she ever wanted was her father and her stepmother's fears about her being a single mother at the age of only seventeen to come true. She didn't just *want* to be normal, she *needed* to be normal. Not only for her own peace of mind, and not only to prove something to her parents, but for her baby most of all. To be a good mother to Abigail. That was more important than anything.

Justine used to be an avid reader of newspapers before Abigail arrived. Each morning, she would sit behind the counter at the music store where she worked, drink her coffee and read *USA Today*. But that changed with the baby's birth. She wasn't able to pick one up anymore. She could no longer watch the news on television, and violent TV shows or movies made her queasy. Motherhood suddenly induced a powerful sensitivity to anything that involved crime, violence, social disorder, bloodshed, tragedies, a child being hurt, a drowning, a fire. Any kind of harm or destruction, whatever the nature or the target—even environmental issues—was now profoundly disturbing. She felt in a constant reactive state. And she would look at her precious child, afraid of all the misery and distress on the planet, afraid of humankind as a whole, and the type of world she had brought her into, wanting to shield her from any unpleasantness that might ever touch her.

There were even moments she felt guilty that she brought her into this world. After all, wasn't parenthood a selfish thing? It was all about fulfilling a narcissistic desire to see yourself reflected in another being, like looking into a mirror. What kind of consideration was given to the quality of the baby's life and its future? Justine didn't have the answer. She didn't even have the answer as to whether these thoughts were rational. Everything inside of her felt as though it had shifted, as though she carried an imbalanced load that might crash at any moment. Her judgment felt damaged.

Frightful images stabbed into her brain, cruel and searing, like a hot knife through a pound of butter. Nightmares tormented her waking moments, colliding into her, knocking her peaceful disposition off kilter. If she could tuck her baby back inside of her stomach like a kangaroo, then she might feel that her daughter was safer in the world. But because Abigail was separate from her, her little body was distinct and complete within itself, Justine worried that she could be easily taken away, stolen in the night, kidnapped at any moment. How would she ever be able to let her daughter out of her sight, even for a second? Isn't that what the parents of missing children always said? *I just turned around for a second and she was gone.* That's all it took. A second.

"What's in the bag?" Her father turned to her.

"I'm afraid something will happen to Abigail."

"The baby's fine; nothing's going to happen to her." He smiled reassuringly. "Now what have you got in the bag, Sweets?"

"I kept thinking about it all day. I kept thinking of all the horrible things that could happen," she said in a quick, high-pitched voice, bordering on panic. "Like what if I tripped as I was carrying her and I dropped her on the floor? She could smash her head on the floor, crack open her skull like a fucking watermelon. It would be that easy. Or when I walked by her earlier when she was asleep in her baby carrier, and I had a bowl of soup, and I thought what if I tripped and spilled the soup on her?"

"Sweetheart, that wouldn't happen."

"And then today, I did the dishes and when I walked into the kitchen later on I caught sight of all the sharp knives sticking up from the drain board and I just stopped in my tracks and I couldn't breathe, Daddy. I just couldn't breathe. I think I had a panic attack or something."

"That's ridiculous.," Brett said. "How could a knife sitting in the kitchen hurt Abigail who's asleep in her playpen? Don't you see how silly that is?"

She watched him laugh. Her vision blurred. And then suddenly she could see the truth, like a light being switched on inside her brain, her fears retreating into the shadows. She understood the truth of how insane those thoughts were, how she had let them take control of her and propel her into a crush of anxiety until she couldn't even think clearly.

"Oh Dad, I needed to hear you say that. I needed you to come home and laugh at me just like you did," she said and let out a breath.

"Good, I'm glad I can help. Everything's going to be fine. There's nothing at all to worry about." He rubbed her back and smiled again.

"I hope that's true, but I don't think this is the end of it."

"Maybe you've got a bit of that postpartum thing they warned us about. You know, the baby blues they call it?"

"I'm not sad. I'm not depressed, either. It's the happiest time of my life; I swear. I'm just feeling so anxious, and today I let it take control of me like a runaway train or something. I'm just so… worried about her. All the time. She's so delicate."

"She needs an exoskeleton, like a turtle," Brett said.

"What a great idea. Do they sell those?"

Brett chuckled, and then said, "She'll be fine, little spark, okay? Don't worry so much. Now are you going to tell me what the bag is for? I know you didn't just go grocery shopping."

She smiled at the nickname he used to call her when she was a girl, when she first came to live with him after her mother's death; a bittersweet time of losing one parent and gaining another she never knew she had. She recalled those tear-filled nights he sat up with her, how he comforted her, reassured her, much like he was doing now. He was surprisingly nurturing, for a man. She remembered how he had decorated her room in anticipation of her arrival—the bubblegum pink carpet and pink walls that still smelled of fresh paint, the canopy bed in the center of the room, piled high with lacy pillows, a giant stuffed panda in the corner.

"Here," she said, pushing the bag toward him. "Can you sort this out? Put the knives back in the kitchen?"

She turned and limped toward the bathroom to take care of her foot, wondering when she would feel like herself again.

"Are you all packed for the weekend?" he asked, peeking inside the bag. A look of concern furrowed his brow. "We've got to get a move on soon. Our real estate agent has five properties confirmed for us to see tomorrow."

"I thought we were heading upstate in the morning."

"Pam thought it would be better if we left this afternoon." He made an adolescent-like roll of his eyes and snorted. He folded the top of the bag and held it absently at his side.

She gave him a sly smile, as if they were in silent collusion against her stepmother.

"I guess she figured we could try and beat the traffic out of the city," he continued. "Although, in order to do that, we should have left this morning. We're spending the night at your grandma's in Watkins Glen so we'll be well rested to look at houses tomorrow. You better get yourself ready."

"Dad, is this really what you want?"

She watched his face slacken, a trace of sadness appear in his eyes, and he turned to look down at the baby. Immediately, she felt guilty for bringing it up.

Maybe it would be okay. Maybe it would all work out, and they would enjoy living in the country, but somehow she doubted this. Something about moving away gave her a bad feeling, like the way you know a storm is coming without even looking at the sky.

Chapter
THREE

"So what's up with the bag of knives and forks, Justine? Are we suppose to eat with plastic spoons? We're pretending we're inmates now?" Brett said, after she returned to find him standing at the dining room cabinet, pouring a glass of scotch.

She looked around for the paper bag containing the knives and broken glass, but didn't see it. He must have ditched the glass while she was in the bathroom tending to her foot, and put the utensils back.

"I was just trying to create a safe environment for my baby, that's all. Any mother would want that," she said, trying to hide her embarrassment.

She turned away to fetch Abigail from the playpen, and listened to the sound the ice made in his glass as he drank. With the baby in her arms, she hobbled over to the recliner to nurse her. She kissed her soft head, breathing in her wholesome baby smell.

"Why are you limping?" he asked, watching her.

"I stepped on a piece of glass. Couldn't get it out."

"Let me take a look."

With the groan people start to make once they hit thirty, Brett sat down cross-legged on the Persian area rug in the living room and lifted her foot.

"Ouch! Careful that hurts." She kicked her leg, trying to nail him with her foot.

"Sorry, just trying to help." He frowned and grabbed her foot firmly.

"Leave it, Dad, I'll get it out later."

"Oh, you're such a baby, Justine."

The window sheers glowed with the sunlight that spilled into the high-ceilinged apartment, across the giant potted palms, the leather furniture, the polished wood tables, and the hardwood floor. Abigail made suckling sounds at her breast, half sleeping and half drinking, lulled by the rocking of the chair and the warmth of her mother. In the next moment, Justine gasped as pain shot up to her knee.

"That fucking hurts!"

"Watch your language around the baby, please."

"Dad, leave it."

"Wait, I've almost got it. Look, it's coming out."

Justine sighed and endured the pain, looking down at her baby and concentrating on the sheer loveliness of her. It was an effort to keep her body calm and relaxed with her foot feeling as if it was being sawed off without the benefit of anesthetic. The shadow of a bird flitted by the window behind the curtains, and she thought how easily their delicate little eggs could roll out of a nest and smash themselves onto sidewalks. How did it feel, looking down at the remains of its babies, like little pieces of its own heart? Such was the treachery of motherhood.

"So you don't want a big new house in the country? You're happy living in this ice-cube tray?" He cocked an eyebrow at her, and one corner of his mouth lifted in what appeared to be a semblance of a smile. "Abigail might have some opinions about where we decide to raise her, you know? Hey Abby girl, you want to live in a big house in the country, or in this tiny box we've got here in the city? I think it's settled; she wants the big house."

"No, she's ignoring you because she finds the idea boring." Justine scowled.

"Boring? Living in the country is boring?"

"It might be, compared to Manhattan. Have you even thought of that?"

"Is that what you think?" he asked.

"I grew up in the city, Dad...ouch!"

"It's peaceful, it's tranquil, but it's not boring. You'll love it, you'll see."

God, he was always so optimistic. It was a trait that she found more annoying than anything else, although she knew he tried hard to inspire her with his attitude. But at this very moment, it just wasn't working.

"I don't know," she said. "There's nothing but good-old-boy types up there, probably a lot of inbreeds too... Ouch! Fucking hell! Stop it now, you're a fucking sadist."

"Got it!" Brett held up a thin piece of glass almost an inch in length, dripping in blood, as if it was a prize. "Talk about a potty mouth, Justine. You're going to have to work on that, now that you're a mother. Stay right there and I'll get a Band-Aid."

He returned with a Band-Aid, a bottle of rubbing alcohol, and some cotton swabs to fix her cut. Justine winced as the alcohol stung in the gash.

Brett stood when he was finished and said, "Give her to me, we need some Grandpa-and-baby bonding time."

He took the baby from her arms, and Abigail strained in a failed effort to hold up her head, like a flower whose tender stalk wasn't strong enough to support the weight of the bloom.

"She needs her diaper changed," Justine said.

"God, how many does she go through in a day, like a hundred?"

"At least." Justine stood up, careful not to put pressure on her injured foot. "Okay, Mr. Mom, I guess I'll go change and get ready."

A relief came over her that her dad was home to take some of the responsibility of Abigail off her shoulders. Despite the fact that she enjoyed being home all day with the baby, when her father got home from the office and took over, there was always a comfort inside like a lessening, an ease of her vigilance. It was at these moments, at least, that she felt grateful to have her parents in her life. She was grateful especially for her father; his love for Abigail was undeniable.

In her bedroom, she changed out of her pajamas into a T-shirt and her most comfortable jeans; a loose-fitting, faded pair of Levi's with holes in both knees that she had bought in a vintage clothing store and had since eighth grade. They were still a little snug at the waist. She had weeks to go before she lost the rest of the weight around her stomach and the backs of her thighs, which were now dimpled. She brushed out her long, wavy hair and tied it into a loose braid. She understood why so many new mothers cut their hair short after giving birth. Who had time for more than basic grooming when you had a baby dominating every minute of your day and night? Good thing she never wore more makeup than lip-gloss. She scanned her willowy body and single-scoop breasts. At least they wouldn't sag as she got older the way big breasts did. She sighed. Thank God for small mercies.

Justine's stepmother, Pamela, arrived home twenty minutes later. She stalked through their condo like a mad pixie in her "shit-kicking" shoes as she liked to call the pointy-toed Jimmy Choo stilettos that she wore on the days she said she needed to rip a strip off a subordinate.

Justine was accustomed to Pamela's catlike presence, the way her muddy kohl-rimmed eyes ignored everyone around her; her bleached, bobbed hair perfect as a wig; her blush like a rash burning her cheeks. But there was something about Pamela, about the adept raise of her eyebrows and the way her gaze slid across your body as if she knew something egregious about you that you didn't know yourself, that always made Justine uncomfortable.

Pamela undressed in the bathroom with the door open. Her casualness about nudity troubled Justine. There was a distasteful and almost confrontational quality in her exhibitionism. It was as if she needed more attention than she could otherwise garner fully clothed. Maybe that's what being only five feet tall did to a woman. Justine wouldn't know. She had never had to wear high-heel shoes in order to be at eye level with the rest of the world, demanding to be noticed.

Or maybe it had to do with pushing forty. Was Pamela trying to demonstrate—for whatever reason Justine couldn't begin to understand—that she could still be considered sexually viable with her thin body, her expensive silicone breasts, and her all-over tan? Regardless of the reason for her incessant display of nudity, it was nearly unbearable.

Pamela showered, changed into a pair of jeans and a cotton blouse, and took half an hour to reapply her makeup. In the dining room, she poured herself some wine. Justine watched her gulp it down—her garish fake nails, sharp and red, making her hands look claw-like; her matching lipstick slick and bright as neon in the night. Justine noticed that her glasses of wine were larger these days. Immediately she poured another one and filled it right to the top. A few minutes later when they all left the apartment, Pamela was in a good mood, laughing and as carefree as a schoolgirl.

"I'm excited," her father said, once the baby was strapped into her car seat in the back of their Lincoln. Justine sat next to her and Pamela was in the front seat. "Can't wait to get out of that ice-cube tray we live in and get out into some open space."

Brett turned to his wife and Justine could see just how hard he was trying to like the decision they had made.

"You sure you can leave the rat race behind?" he asked his wife.

"You're the one who loves the rat race, not me," Pamela said. "I've been wanting to move back home since I was a teenager. And now...well now, it's just become necessary, is all."

"You think you can transfer to the office in Rochester that easily?"

"I've already talked to my boss about it. I told you that. I guess you weren't listening to me again."

Brett tsked and then looked at his daughter in the rearview. "It will be good for Abigail, growing up in the country."

Justine didn't respond. What made him think they would be staying that long? She wasn't planning to live at home forever; this was only temporary. God forbid it would be much longer. While she was indebted to them, the last thing she ever wanted was to move back home with her parents. When she had moved in with Keith she thought she was finally free of them. Now, here she was, looking at new houses with them. How the hell did this ever happen to her?

"Is this even the right time for you guys to be looking at buying a house?" Justine said, "Isn't the country still in an economic slow-down?"

"That makes it the perfect time," Pamela said. "Housing prices are low. It's a buyer's market."

Justine didn't know if the move to the country was such a good idea. Would she be happy in a rural area? It was a big change. But what else could she do? She was dependent on them. At seventeen, almost legally an adult, she was dependent on them for everything once again, as if she'd never grown up, as if she'd never lived on her own before. It was unsettling.

"You don't think Keith will mind us moving so far away?" Pamela asked, as if she wanted to remind Justine of her failures. "He won't get to see Abigail that often."

"He doesn't see her now as it is, so nothing will be different. Abigail will graduate from college before he even notices we're gone." Justine laughed, pretending she didn't care.

"Your grandma will like seeing you and Abigail more," her dad said. "It will be good for her. She needs that now. More than ever. Who knows how long she's got."

"Who knows how long anyone's got," Justine said.

Her father looked at her in the mirror and she knew they were both thinking of, not only her mother, but also Pamela's daughter, Allison. Allison—dead at the age of fourteen.

Pamela ignored them. But the tension was electric, which was exactly the effect Justine was going for.

"Sweet," Justine said in sarcasm, releasing a breath.

She thought of the time she showed up high to her own sixteenth birthday party. She'd shaved her head, except for a fringe of purple bangs across her forehead. She'd donned a tiara and wrapped a green feather boa around her neck. Pamela had made reservations for them at Daniel on East Sixty-fifth. Justine had made sure to show up just slightly late, so that her entrance would be all the more spectacular. She hustled through the restaurant, leaving turned heads and disrupted harmony in her wake as she approached the table where her parents were waiting.

"Hello! I made it! Sorry I'm so late but some pervert accosted me on the subway. Tried humping my leg like a dog. I had to give the guy a good, hard bitch-slapping," Justine announced, her voice an urgent screech. She let rip a cackle she was certain caused everyone's shoulders to stiffen.

The look on Pamela's face was worth the effort she'd gone to. Her jaw dropped and her eyes became the size of dollar coins. After the initial shock, her face reddened.

"Is this some kind of joke? Just what the hell do you think you're doing, Justine? You look like a goddamn clown!"

Her father only looked amused and slightly bewildered by the entire spectacle. It was one of the best birthdays she could remember. But it took the next year and a half for her hair to grow back.

They spent the night at her grandmother's bungalow in Watkins Glen. Her grandmother was Pamela's mother, but Justine always referred to her as Grandma. Justine peered in through the half-closed bedroom door, and watched as Pamela laid childlike, cuddled in bed next to the old lady, embracing her. Sickening, the way she mauled her like that.

Later, after Pamela left her room, Justine took Abigail in to see Grandma. Her bedside lamp was on. The room smelled stale, like the pages inside of an old book. The was odor masked by a now-dissipating floral air freshener and a trace of Pamela's disgusting cologne. She was asleep, her wrinkled face and wispy hair blending with the white of the pillow. Justine was reminded of the shrunken apple faces she had made in art class in school as a kid. It was difficult to see her this way, a woman who'd always seemed so vibrant and full of life, now helpless, nearly blind, and dependent on the private nurses Pamela paid for out of her own pocket. Her last operation had been six months ago. Now they'd said the cancer had come back.

"Who's here?" she whispered, her voice like dried leaves blowing in the wind. She cracked open a frosted eye.

"It's me, Grandma." Justine reached for her bony hand, noticing how much frailer she looked. Her hand felt surprisingly warm.

"Allison?" A smile stretched her dry lips, unveiling gray teeth. She stared up at the ceiling, sightless.

"No, Grandma, it's Justine."

"Justine? Where's Allison? Where's my Allison?"

Justine pressed her lips together and regarded the confusion on her face. She took a deep breath, and tried not to feel the old jealously rise up as she said, "Allison's dead, Grandma. She died four years ago, did you forget?"

"Allison." Her face drew in on itself as she continued. "My little Allison. I miss her. I miss her every day. She was like *my* daughter, you know? Not like Pammy's at all. She called *me* Mama."

"How are you doing, Grandma?"

Justine sat on the edge of the bed. Abigail squirmed on her shoulder and began to cry.

"Who's with you? Is that the new baby? Is that Abigail with you?"

"Yeah, I brought her to see you," Justine said, pleased that she'd remembered about Abigail.

"How lovely. How lovely. I've missed you, dear. I've missed all of you." A low-pitched whine escaped her lips as she sobbed. Justine held her hand. The old lady closed her eyes a moment later and Justine studied her face, realizing she had dozed off. She stood up, shifted Abigail to the other shoulder, and then turned off the lamp and crept out of the room.

Early the next morning, they met Sal, their real estate agent, a sharp-eyed, aging German man with a face like a hawk. Even though Brett butted heads with him as a substitute for conversation, Justine knew that her father respected the man, and that's why they continued with him as their agent.

The first house was a two-story, three-thousand-square-foot Tudor style home set on twenty-five acres in Seneca County.

"It's another foreclosure," Sal said, as he handed the listings he'd printed out to Pamela. "It's a good time to be buying right now. Lots of deals to be had from the economic crisis. So I've got four appointments confirmed for today."

"It's nice," Pamela said, as she gazed up at the house and scanned the property.

"I don't know if this is the right place for you," Sal said, as they got to the front door.

"Why do you say that?" Brett asked.

Abigail was asleep in her baby carrier as Brett carried her up the steps, watching Sal fumble with the lock box.

"You can tell right from the front door sometimes what a place will look like on the inside," Sal said.

Justine studied the chipped paint on the door and the scuff marks around the bottom, trying to see what he was talking about. When the door opened and they stepped inside, she understood what he meant. The foyer was painted a brilliant yellow with a grape trim around the ceiling.

"Fucking ghastly," Justine said.

"How about I charge you a dollar for every time you swear?" Brett said, pushing past her with Abigail in the carrier. "Maybe that would curb your potty mouth, huh?"

Justine pursed her lips and tilted her head. "Yeah, sweet. Can I just give you a twenty now? That way I'll be prepaid for the rest of the day."

Her father snorted in response.

The carpet throughout the main floor smelled of cat urine. It looked like the original carpet from when the house was built twenty years earlier. It was once pink but worn down to a slate gray in all the heavy traffic areas.

"They had cats." Sal made a face. "That's the worst thing to try and sell a house; pets, cigarettes and curry. They'll never sell the house at this price."

The linoleum in the kitchen was cracked and dirty. The kitchen cupboards needed replacement, as did nearly everything else in the house.

"What happened here?" Pamela asked as they entered the master bedroom and looked at the gaping holes in the drywall. "It looks like someone took a sledgehammer to the walls."

"Vandalism," Sal said with a frown. "See it all the time with foreclosures. The owners are pissed they lost the place and end up trashing it out of frustration. I'm surprised the bank didn't have someone come and fix it before they decided to have showings."

"It'll take an arm and leg in renovations just to get this place up to par," Brett said, as they made a hasty exit out the front door.

The second house wasn't at all what they had in mind; a huge clapboard structure with some ramshackle outbuildings set on a narrow lot. The third house was better: a three-thousand-square-foot log cabin, with massive picture windows and beautifully decorated, on a nice piece of property, but they knew it wasn't "the one."

The fourth house was in Bellona in Yates County and looked promising from the curb. The house itself was nice. A two-story brown-brick house with white columns and shutters. The only problem was that it was located on a busy highway, and set too close to the road.

"Want to take a look anyway? We've got an appointment and the people are expecting us," Sal asked, shrugging.

"A quick walk through and that's it," Brett said. "What's this we've looked at anyway? Eight, ten houses in total now?"

"About that," Sal said. "Takes time, my friend. Rome wasn't built in a day, as they say. You've got to be patient."

"Oh, you think I'm not patient, Sal?"

"Maybe you're being too picky."

"Picky? We haven't seen anything close to what we've got in mind. I'm starting to think maybe we should just purchase some acreage and build a custom home."

"That's an option, but you never know when something's going to come on the market. So I'll keep my eyes out this week for some suitable listings and I'll email them to you. Something will come up. You'll see."

"You know what?" Brett said, once they got in the car. "This is starting to get discouraging. This is the third weekend we've come up here looking at houses, and we have yet to see anything suitable. We should look into buying some vacant land."

"What would it cost to build?" Pamela asked.

"I don't know, but it's worth looking into," he said. "At least we'll be able to get what we want. We can hire an architect to design it for us."

"Well, it all depends on if we've got the money for that. If your company wasn't in the toilet—"

Brett sighed and bowed his head. "Let's not do this now please."

"I'm just saying, Brett, I've got enough pressure on me as it is, paying for Mom's nurses and all the other goddamn bills."

Brett rubbed a hand across his face and turned to look out the window, chewing the inside of his cheek. His shoulders were hunched as he started the car and backed out of the driveway. His posture seemed to exude shame, like every decision he'd ever made had been wrong. Justine knew that somehow Pamela recognized this in him and took pleasure in excavating it. She had always viewed their marriage as a tired carnival attraction. Her father was the dumb donkey going in circles on a treadmill, chasing a carrot. Pamela was the monkey on its back that held the stick with the carrot dangling from the end, whipping him for not being able to catch it. Pathetic fucking example of a marriage, they were. Good thing she wasn't that impressionable. Or desperate, the way they behaved.

A moment later, he looked at Justine in the rearview and said, "What do you think if we build a house, Justine?"

She shrugged. "Whatever. It's your cat; skin it the way you want."

"That's a disgusting analogy. Why would you even say such a thing?" Pamela asked.

Justine caught her father's eye again in the rearview and gave him a Mona Lisa smile.

It came as a relief to her, at least a temporary one, that their decision was put off and her parent's unceasing progression toward a façade of perfection was now stalled. In the meantime, she hoped she would be able to figure out how to move out on her own. Her next-best option was throwing a rope over a tree. God! How did her life come to this? The last thing she wanted was to move with these two out to some god-forsaken place in the middle of fucking nowhere.

Chapter
FOUR

Someone was yelling from down the corridor. It was just one voice at first, and then others joined in a chorus of anger, rekindling hostility like a gust of wind on smoldering embers. That emotion never dissipated inside the steel and concrete walls of this place. It only slept and gathered strength.

Rory Madden stepped out into the hallway from his open cell door and found the source of the mayhem in the bullpen. A guy struggled on the floor, kicking his legs, as he attempted to cover his head with his arms. Two men lay a beat-down on him. Something heavy was wrapped inside the pillowcases in their hands. They took turns whacking the guy in the head and torso, anywhere they could get in a shot. Other inmates stood around and egged them on. Guards were on them in seconds. The assailants were separated, subdued on the ground with clubs, then quickly cuffed and carted off. The beaten guy on the floor was left to writhe in pain. A moment later, two other guards came and helped him up.

Everyone was ordered locked in his cell for a head count.

"What up?" Rory asked a blocky Italian guy with Popeye arms nicknamed Flash, an obvious irony meant to jest at his IQ.

"They beat the fuck out of him. He's going to need a whole whack of stitches to close his head. Man them head gashes bleed like a bitch. They had soap tied inside the ends of them pillowcases," Flash said, raising a thick, black eyebrow.

Rory sucked his teeth. "No shit."

"That kid been disrespecting them for days. I tried to tell him, but he's new," Flash said. "What you going to do? Some people got to learn the hard way, you know?"

"What's he in for?"

"Aggravated assault, I think. Caught his girlfriend in bed with another guy and knifed her. She lived. He's waiting on sentencing. Probably give him a deuce. Doesn't have a record."

"Boy's got to get himself into anger management." Rory shook his head.

"Yeah, and get this, his girlfriend, the one he tried to kill? They kissed and made up. She's been coming to see him on visiting days. And the guy just proposed to her. They're getting married as soon as he's out of here." Flash made a can-you-believe-that kind of face.

"Well, that just goes to prove one thing," Rory said.

"What's that?"

"Some marriages truly are a match made in heaven."

Both men cracked up laughing.

After three months, Rory concluded that incarceration was a life of drudgery with a pervasive atmosphere of oppression that likely challenged the most hardened criminals in the system. An inmate never truly becomes comfortable within the confines of these walls; he simply adjusts to the alternate universe he finds himself in, Rory realized. He adapts to the six-by-eight-foot cell and the fishbowl feeling of constantly being watched, the high-powered cameras, the disdainful guards who monitor his every movement, the perverted pleasure they seem to derive from forcing a man to strip if they suspect contraband. The inmate learns to function in an abnormal environment that mimics reality, and to navigate the rules, the code, the pecking order. Then finally he accepts the truth that jail is not a friendly or supportive environment. It's all about punishment.

The one thing Rory had not managed to do in jail was relax. Peace and serenity were something he'd left at the gates when he entered. He worried about how much worse prison was going to be. Mostly he tried not to think about it.

Rory watched the new arrivals at Yates County Jail. They all had that shocked, deer-in-the-headlights expression—a look only time, the one thing they were in abundance of, could alter. Did he have that look in his own eyes when he arrived? Probably.

He went back to his single cell to read. It contained a narrow bed with a thin mattress, a table, a chair, a locker, a few shelves, a toilet, and a small window that overlooked a courtyard. They were let out daily to play basketball, handball, workout, or simply play chess outdoors. They weren't allowed to smoke anywhere in the facility, not even in the courtyard. Along with the rest of the inmates, he was forced to give up cigarettes. The major head counts were at seven and eleven in the morning, and then again in the evening at five and nine. Everyone was expected to stand inside his cell while an officer walked around and counted the inmates.

Rory lay on his bed, trying to escape inside the pages of one of Anne Rice's vampire novels, but a guy in another cell down the block was busy yelling about the toilet paper the guards had withheld, going on for more than a week. Another guy with sinus problems couldn't stop his annoying noises. They echoed down the block and reverberated throughout the entire facility. Noises in here were always too loud.

The insect bites on his legs were itchy. He scratched so hard that one had started to bleed and now looked like it might be infected. His hands were constantly breaking out in a rash. They felt dry and sore and would crack and bleed on occasion. The doctor said it was eczema and gave him an ointment that didn't do anything.

As a boy, he remembered having the same skin condition; the family doctor had said it was related to the stress of his mother being in the hospital for so long. She was on life support, in a coma for two weeks, suffering head injuries and a broken jaw. Rory was only six when he witnessed the beating his stepfather at the time had laid on her. The rash broke out across his hands, in his armpits, and on the backs of his legs. He remembered the scent of calamine lotion on his skin to help stop the itch. He remembered praying that God would take his stepfather away. Eventually, he did go away, and Rory later learned that he'd been mistaken for a Catholic and shot in a raid on a pub by members of the Ulster Defence Association. Some prayers really did get answered. But his mother had just found another heavy-drinking and heavy-fisted man to replace him. And Rory knew that God wasn't going to keep killing them off for him one by one. Eventually, he would have to do something about it himself.

Rory thought of his sister, and her smile pressed into his mind. It caused his chest to constrict the way it sometimes did when he thought too deeply about what had happened to her. Her pale, freckled face with the Dutch coloring of their ancestors on their father's side appeared. Frances was athletic and excellent at gymnastics. She played on the girls volleyball team. As a boy, Rory helped her with her homework, taught her how to ride a two-wheeler, how to kick a football like a boy. She showed him how to do a back flip and walk on his hands. Frances was the only person he knew who could walk up and down stairs on her hands. Her T-shirt would fall down around her ribs, revealing the muscles in her stomach. Her mass of golden hair swept the dirty tiles in the stairwell of their building and Rory would watch her in fascination.

"It's not that hard. You just imagine that there's a pit of crocodiles all around you and if you fall, they will eat you alive. So you have to do it like your life depends on it," she said, sharing her secret with him. And while he did manage to do it for at least a couple of steps, his clumsy twelve-year-old body bumping into the wall and railing, he could never master it as flawlessly as Frances.

Rory thought about Frances all the time. Frances with her wavy hair, soft as a baby's, peach-powder-scented skin. In his mind he could see her lithe body as it flipped and cart-wheeled around the schoolyard. He thought about how she made up cheerleading routines and weaved daisy chains into necklaces. Even after all these years, more than fifteen, almost twice as long as she was in his life, and longer, perhaps, than she might have lived—because there was the possibility that she was dead, a possibility of which he couldn't allow himself to conceive—he still missed her. The darkness tore at his heart like a black hole there were no words to describe, where all the light within him was sucked into, leaving him desolate.

It was difficult, as a boy growing up in Belfast with a besieged mentality, to avoid getting involved in the Troubles. Especially for an angry boy whose childhood heroes were the men in the paramilitary. Channeling his rage into a ready cause was all but impossible to resist, and at seventeen, he found a family in the Ulster Freedom Fighters' C Company, and an outlet for his pain.

Rory and Simon graduated to fighting side by side in the loyalist paramilitaries, where they waged assassinations on IRA members and random Catholics. They were trained how to use a variety of weapons, handguns, AK-47 rifles, Uzi machine guns, and homemade submachine guns. Rory was also educated in commercial plastic explosives and bomb-making techniques. He was schooled in the arts of surveillance, counter-surveillance and intelligence gathering. He was lectured on forensic science, how to avoid leaving incriminating evidence at the scene of a crime, and how to steal cars for use in assassination operations. He was ordered to carry out executions against ordinary Catholics and, eventually, rival loyalist gang members.

He didn't become a gunman immediately. He was required to work his way up, prove himself as a foot soldier. Small tasks were assigned to him at first, being a driver during an attack on an enemy, participating in punishment beatings, selling dope, collecting money, robberies, arson, and "mop-up" duties where he had to dispose of evidence in a murder.

It wasn't that Rory had a lust for murder or enjoyed killing—of course, afterwards there was a feeling of elation, of being high—it was just that as a member of the UFF, he felt an enormous responsibility to the citizens on the Shankill. He saw himself as a soldier, who took the fight to the doorstep of the IRA, and gave back what they had done to the Protestant community for years. And it was an on-going matter of revenge whenever their community was attacked. They were at war.

Still, being in the UFF was a brutal, violent, hate-filled existence. And near the end, there were times Rory questioned why so many people had to die. What did it all amount to? One dead Protestant needed another dead Catholic to avenge him. Back and forth. Year after year. The bodies piled up. The undertakers got rich. When would all the killing stop? And then, when their guns and hate turned on each other, and Rory was no longer fighting the Republicans as much as the UFF's rival Loyalist counterparts, the Ulster Volunteer Force, he knew it was over for him. Everything they believed in and fought for had fallen apart. When the leader of the UFF was ousted by its members and forced into exile, Rory and Simon sided with him and were forced into exile, as well.

After nearly six years of waging war in the paramilitaries, Rory got tired and he got out. Drawn to America, to New York in particular, he bought himself a one-way plane ticket and made his escape. He started a brand new life and moved onto bigger things. But those bigger things had eventually detoured him here, to Yates County Jail.

"What do you mean it's not there?" Rory said.

"Just what I said, it's not there."

"Did you look where I told you?"

"Absolutely. There was nothing there."

"You sure you found the exact location?"

"I looked in the exact spot, third brick from the bottom on the right-hand side. I pulled it out and it was empty, Rory. Like I said, the cops must have found it during their search."

"That's not possible, Blackmore. That ain't fucking possible!"

"Look, they tore the place apart. They were bound to find it."

"No, they couldn't have," Rory said. "There's no fucking way."

"Well, obviously they did."

"I don't believe this. This isn't happening." Rory shook his head. He stood with his back pressed against the cold concrete wall with the phone clenched in his fist. His last remnant of hope had been taken away, and he was left him to drown. Everyone he knew had betrayed him.

"You know how these cops are, Rory, they probably knew you had a stash. Your buddy, the one who ratted you out, might have told them."

"Bullshit! You don't know what you're talking about," Rory said. "You're a liar!"

"Excuse me?"

"You're keeping it for yourself, aren't you? I never should have trusted you, you low-life, knuckle-dragging—"

"I swear—"

"Jesus Christ, you realize the slag I'm getting over this, the position you're putting me in here? The bank is threatening me with foreclosure if I don't start making my mortgage payments. How the hell am I supposed to pay my bills from in here, Blackmore? You tell me that, now. How the hell am I supposed to do that!"

"Hey, buddy, you need to get yourself under control. It's not my fault you didn't make bail. I went to bat for you."

Rory turned to face the wall, and spoke low and fast. "Listen you fucker, you're supposed to be helping me here. That's why I hired you as my fucking lawyer. Now you're trying to pull this shit on me? What the hell do you take me for? Some mutt? You must think I'm as thick as a brick, don't you? You haven't a clue who you're dealing with here, Blackmore, not a fucking clue."

"I'm telling you, there was no money. How dare you accuse me of theft."

"That was all the money I had left!"

"Well, I'm sorry for the position you're in, but it's not my problem. I didn't take your stinking money," Blackmore said. "There wasn't any there to take, and I certainly don't appreciate your accusations and abuse."

"You're going to be one sorry motherfucker when I get out of here, Blackmore, and get my hands on you."

"When? When you get out?" The lawyer laughed and the sound was like the crack of a whip agaisnt Rory's flesh . "Don't you mean if?"

Rory clenched his jaw. He felt something shift inside of him, something powerful that wanted to climb out of his skin. His eyes closed and he pressed his forehead against the wall. In a whisper of a voice he said, "You're a dead man."

"What?"

Carefully, Rory hung up the phone. He moved his head from side to side and popped the vertebrae that released the tension in his shoulders. He drew in a deep breath and allowed a sense of calm to suffuse his muscles.

Chapter
FIVE

Pamela unwound the rosary beads from her fingers, brought the tiny cross to her lips, and kissed it. Then, she dropped it into the cup holder on the console and wiped the tears from the corners of her eyes. She looked out the windshield of her Lexus at the entrance to the New York Palace Hotel as she swung the car up to the front. She parked and checked her makeup in the visor mirror. The incision marks from her eyelift were barely visible now, merely faint lines that could be masked with makeup. She examined the lines on her forehead. Could use another round of Botox. Maybe she'd try that filler for her lips, too. Her mood brightened a bit.

Pamela scanned her text messages again for the right hotel room. She took a deep breath, and resigned herself to what she was about to do. When she emerged from the car and handed the keys to the valet, the cool autumn air caught in her throat, sending a chill coursing through her body. She'd give anything if she could just turn around, climb into the warmth of her car again, and go home. But she'd lost that option a long time ago, nearly twenty years ago when she'd traded off the first small piece of her soul. The rest had gone bit by bit until there was nothing left. It had all been killed off. Annihilated like spiritual suicide.

In the posh lobby she made her way past the front desk to the elevators, walking in her brisk predatory stride, head held high, and her spine stiff as an iron pole. Outside room 1208, she ran fingers through her bleached hair. She stood in the casually provocative pose she had perfected, conforming to her role. She practiced a fake smile and knocked.

"Come in," said a deep voice from behind the door.

"Hello, baby." She entered the room, and looked at the silver-haired man who lay on the bed with pillows propping up his head. She could tell by the overly dramatic moans coming from the television that he had the pornos on. He sat up as she entered and rolled up the sleeves of his white shirt as if he had some hard work to get down to. The tie that accompanied the shirt was discarded; the belt on his slacks undone, and he'd removed his shoes, revealing black socks. She noticed one of his big toes sticking out through a hole. For some bizarre reason, the sight of his naked toe made her feel sick.

"What took you so long? I was going to call someone else," the man said.

"Don't tease me now, Richard. You know there's no other woman who can take care of you the way I do."

"It's true." He grinned and then patted the bed beside him. "Now come here and give Daddy a kiss."

She dropped her handbag on the floor, sauntered over to the bed, and crawled across the sheets. She lay down with her back to him, and allowed him to hold her. His mouth, moist and greedy, like some slimy aquatic creature, moved across her face, and down her neck. A hand groped one of her breasts through her blouse and squeezed. He pulled her to face him, and his rubbery, alcohol-flavored tongue forced itself inside her mouth. She imagined herself biting it off, spitting it out, and watching it flop around on the carpet like a fish torn from water.

"Can you have dinner with me tonight?" he asked, as he slid a chilled hand up her thigh underneath her skirt.

"I don't have time for that, Richard. You know that."

"Well, you have to eat too, don't you?"

"I have a busy day," she said, and looked at that one big toe of his, with its yellow nail and spiky black hairs growing in a swirl pattern. She thought of her husband's toes, how the second and third toes on both feet were the exact same length. They used to joke that it was the sign of a serial killer. She remembered the times she clipped his nails, giving him pedicures and foot massages as they watched television together. That was in the beginning, when things were uncomplicated. It had been years since she had done that for Brett.

She thought about how gradually the changes in her marriage had come, from being in love to being complacent. She couldn't blame Brett entirely for the state of things. She was at fault, too, for not communicating better, for swallowing her emotions and hoping it would all be okay if they just ignored things long enough. But the one thing she had learned in these last few years of marriage was that ESP was not a form of communication. She knew that if she wanted things to improve, they needed to talk. And sometimes she did make an effort, even if she knew it would result in an argument. But most times, she just shut down, drank too much, ignored what needed to be said, and tried her best to pretend they were still happy. It was far easier than facing the truth: that something between them had died. It had happened the same day, four years earlier, when her daughter—her only child—had died.

Pamela closed her eyes as his fingers found the elastic on the edge of her panties and burrowed underneath, stabbing into her. She began to count backwards in her mind, and allowed herself to drift away; *ten...nine...*Inside her head, she could see the sun as it set over the lake. The warm breeze caressed her skin and the smell of the beach filled her nostrils... *eight... seven...*A voice on the wind whispered to her; a force bigger than she pulled her forward. Her bare feet stepped down the sun-warmed rocks sticking up in the path that led to the beach...*six...five...*

His hand slithered over her stomach and fumbled at the buttons on her blouse...*four...*A multitude of birds hovered on the breeze high above the shore, like kites suspended in the sky. As a girl, she could sit and gaze at them for hours, contemplating their simple existence. She yearned to fly with them, free from her body that was too tired to contain her spirit. The sand was soft and hot on her feet, and she sank slightly with each step... *three...*She could see her mother there on the beach in her bathing suit. She sat under an umbrella in her floppy sunhat, the wind whipping strands of her long hair around her shoulders as she watched her children play. She had movie star looks; even after five children, her figure was that of a woman half her age. Pamela's heart ached for her mother, for her home on Seneca Lake, and for the child Pamela had once been, safe in the cocoon of her mother's love...*two...*

"Look at me," he said as her clothes were pulled away.

One... Pamela looked up at his face and saw the blue lake in his eyes. Wandering the shores of her home, she breathed in the essence that flowed through her like wine, trickling into her blood as pure and vital as oxygen. She surrendered herself to it as it consumed her—her heart, starved and broken, claimed by her homeland, drunk on her deliverance.

The sun had begun its descent when she walked back through the hotel's heavy glass doors. The sky was bitter purple behind the soaring spires and sharp angles of St. Patrick's Cathedral across the street. The air had the bone-aching chill of an oncoming New York winter, and she pulled the collar of her coat tight at her throat. She looked up at the towering opulence of the church and felt small in comparison. The windows seemed to gaze upon her in an accusatory way.

A moment later, she sat in her car and counted the fold of bills inside her purse. Richard, as usual, had given her an extra three hundred. He was a good man.

Pamela lit a cigarette and checked her text messages. She was expected at the New Yorker in a few minutes. Nalin, another regular, in town on business from India, was waiting for her. She looked at her watch and calculated the time she would arrive home. She thought of the beef stew she had cooking in the crock pot. She thought of the property taxes on her mother's house that she needed to pay this week, and the checks she had to write to the private nurses. Would she have enough to put in her savings account this week?

On the way home, Pamela phoned the nurse taking care of her mother. "How is she?"

"I've got her sitting up watching her show," the nurse said.

"Watching her show?"

"She listens to it. She's not eating, though. Three days now, and all she's managed to keep down is a couple of spoonfuls of soup," the woman said.

"Well, give her something else besides soup," Pamela said. "Make her some pasta or something."

"She just throws everything right back up. Might need a feeding tube if this goes on much longer."

"Jesus, she doesn't need a feeding tube!" Pamela said. "What the hell's the matter with you? Did you even call her doctor?"

"He's coming to see her in the morning. I'll let you know what he says. Are you still coming up this weekend? 'Cause I have plans to—"

"I know, I know. I'll be there Saturday by noon. Don't worry, I'll have your precious check for you," Pamela said and hung up the phone. She tossed it on the passenger seat, where it bounced and hit the floor. She tossed her cigarette, too, half smoked, out the window, and then broke down in sobs.

It was nearly seven when Pamela arrived at their condo. She unlocked the door, and was immediately aware of Allison's absence, as she always was when she came home, expecting to see her joyful smile, a face that could diminish any lingering sorrow around her heart, instantly, effortlessly. Her absence was like the nonexistence of color that left everything with a grayish tinge.

In the kitchen, she watched her husband and his daughter as they sat at the table and ate the stew. She wondered how, at the age of thirty-six, this was her life. It was like a time warp. Here she was again, supporting her family single-handedly. She'd thought that once she married Brett, that would all change, that never again would she be solely financially responsible for herself or anyone else. How on earth did she get here?

"You're late. We got hungry so we didn't wait for you," Brett said.

"Well, I'm just all broken up over that." She sighed and stepped out her high-heeled boots.

"Ah, there you go again with that rapier wit of yours. Where were you?" Brett eyed her, a controlled look on his face.

After she hung up her coat and turned to look at him, she noticed Justine staring at her with a sparkle in her eyes. It was like the girl could see through her, read her thoughts and all her secrets. Pamela felt a rush of adrenaline spill into her veins. Hopefully, Justine's presence really was just temporary, but that was doubtful. How were they ever going to get rid of this girl now that she had the baby? Immediately, she felt guilty. Her feelings for Justine were so tangled. There were times she loved her deeply, like a daughter, and other times she resented her. It was an ongoing struggle that wore her down, and she didn't know if she'd ever make lasting peace with it.

"I had to stay late at the office and deal with a computer problem," Pamela said.

"Again?"

"Yes, again."

"Isn't that the same excuse you gave me two days ago?"

"Shit happens."

"All the time it seems," Brett said.

"What the hell? I was trying to earn a living. Not that you'd even know what that means these days."

"Can you guys at least wait to have your argument until after dinner, please?" Justine said.

Pamela turned from them to step over to the cabinet in the dining room. She pulled down a bottle of Merlot, poured herself a liberal glass, and took a long, satisfying swallow. Tucked behind another wine bottle was a small prescription pill container with her mother's name on the label. She unscrewed the lid and shook two of the chalky pills into her hand, swallowing them down with another mouthful of wine. It was to ward off a headache, she told herself. Later she'd take a couple of Valium to help her sleep. She looked down at the spot on the floor that pulled at her memory. She could still see Allison's lifeless body laying in that very spot.

Pamela looked into the kitchen and her eyes followed Justine's slender frame as she rose from the table and walked across the floor in her bare feet. She studied that sturdy gait of hers, the spill of golden hair down her back, like some flower child's from the sixties. Even her clothes suggested that nature-loving, peace, love, and groovy era with her faded jeans and the loose-fitted Indian blouse with the needlepoint stitching around the neck. Pamela remembered the day a few years ago that she'd driven down Broadway and laid eyes on a barefoot girl playing guitar on the street. Her guitar case was open to collect coins, her long hair blowing around her in the breeze. She'd watched the girl for a moment, feeling envious of how carefree she appeared. Then suddenly she'd recognized her. It was Justine. The image was engraved in Pamela's memory.

As she looked at Justine, she couldn't help think of Allison and how different the two girls had been. It wasn't fair that Allison was dead. Why Allison? Why did it have to be her? Of all the girls in the world for God to take, why did it have to be her daughter? There were times she wished… she could barely bring herself to even think about it. But there were moments she actually wished…Justine should have been the one. It shouldn't have been Allison!

Pamela griped the wineglass tightly, and willed it to break in her hand. Maybe a shard would sever an artery, with any luck, and put her out of her misery. She gulped the alcohol, swallowing her tears, and felt the edges of her pain begin to blunt. Immediately she poured herself another.

What if she were to die today? What would she have accomplished in her life? The answer that followed shocked her. Nothing. She would have done nothing. Pamela took her glass of wine, the rosary from her purse, and headed upstairs for a bubble bath. She would pray for forgiveness until the water went cold.

Chapter
SIX

"I hope your parents are still looking for a house in the Finger Lakes area, Justine," Sal said over the line. "Because the perfect home just came on the market yesterday, and I know you're all going to love it. I even went out to see it myself, and you know what, Justine? It's perfect for you guys. A brand-new custom home in south Penn Yan with a view of Lake Keuka."

"What's the acreage?" Justine asked.

"Twenty and a half. I don't think it's even been lived in."

Justine sat in the recliner in the living room of their condo, the phone cradled on her shoulder, as she nursed Abigail. The lights on the Christmas tree, left on all night, twinkled in competition with the morning sun that streamed in through the sheers. As she looked at it, she wondered absently how long a tree should stay up once the holidays were over. Christmas had been over two weeks ago. Its presence seemed wrong, like leftovers sitting out to spoil.

"I'll tell my parents to call you back. I'm not sure if they're still into buying up there." God, she hoped not.

"I know if your parents see this place, Justine, they'll want to make an offer right away, and it's going for a good price. It's a foreclosure."

"Okay, I'll have my Dad phone you back."

"Don't wait on this, I'm telling you. It's going to get snapped up quick and I just know it's perfect for you guys."

"Okay, Sal, I'll tell him when he gets out of the shower."

In the bedroom, Justine put the baby on the floor on a blanket with her stuffed animals. She packed the baby bag with diapers, shampoo, lotion, towels, and her bathing suit.

"What are you up to today?" her dad asked. He poked his head into her room as he rubbed a towel on his hair. "Looks like you're going somewhere?"

"Mom and baby swim time starts today. Remember? You said you'd drive us."

"Swimming? In this weather?"

"It's indoors, Daddy." She rolled her eyes.

"The baby's not even eight weeks old. Are you sure they start them this young?"

"It's not actually swimming lessons; it's just getting them used to the water."

"Sounds like a blast." He made a face.

"Sal phoned a minute ago. Says he's found an amazing house for us with a lake view. He wants you to call him. He says it's perfect for us, but it's a long fucking drive to go look at one house, don't you think?"

"Language." He pointed a finger at her. "You know, my friend had to stop using that word when his two-year-old started saying, 'Fox,' every time he got mad at his toys."

"Fox? That's not a swear word."

"Maybe it is to a two-year-old."

"That's funny. So can I say fox instead of fuck?"

"Justine! You just said it again."

They both turned to look at Abigail as she lay on the floor, sucking on a fist. There was a look on her face as if she was listening to them.

"I can't help it," Justine said. "I've been saying that word since I was about two myself."

"Great, that's all we need is Abigail's first word to be 'fuck.'" Brett slapped a hand over his mouth.

"Dad! You said it!"

Brett doubled over laughing and pointed at the baby. "Look she's smiling. Ahh, that's amazing. That's the most amazing thing."

They gazed down at the baby, and Justine turned to look at her Dad, the way his face lit up when he was around Abigail. She wondered how he would handle it when they finally moved out on their own.

In the changing room at the community center, Justine put a new diaper on Abigail and wrapped her in a towel. She set her in her baby carrier on the floor while she dressed herself in a one-piece bathing suit and secured her hair in a bun on top of her head. She tossed another towel over her shoulder, lifted her gurgling baby, and headed into the showers with the other mothers and babies to rinse before they went into the pool. There were about a dozen of them who filed out to the pool area to meet their instructor.

The smell of chlorine wafted in the humid air inside the high-ceilinged room, bringing forth memories of childhood swimming lessons, of lining up soaked and shivering to take turns jumping off the diving board into the deep end.

She was glad it was warm, and hoped the pool water would be a comfortable temperature. The winter sun flooded through the giant picture windows, and she could see cars in the parking lot covered with snow, like vanilla-frosted cakes.

A girl in a red one-piece, whose high pony tail and flat chest made her look about twelve, spoke up and introduced herself as their instructor. There was a whistle on a string around her neck and a clipboard in her hands. Why would someone so young be the instructor for a class of mothers and babies? Could she even swim? The girl proceeded to do a head count and called out names in alphabetical order, checking them off on her clipboard.

Justine turned and gazed out over the still water of the pool. Daylight reflected off its surface like a sheet of glass. Suddenly, a panicky feeling cut through her, sharp as a blade. An image of Abigail sinking to the bottom of the pool burst into her mind. It startled her so much that she drew in a breath, took a step back, and bumped into the woman behind her.

"Oh, I'm sorry," she said.

"No problem," the woman said. A baby boy, about three months old was balanced on her hip.

Justine looked back at the pool and her heart began to thump wildly. What if Abigail slipped from her hands and drowned in the water? Babies could be very slippery. You needed to be careful. But what if Justine fumbled, lost her grip on her and she slid underneath the water? What if her little lungs filled with water and she couldn't be saved? She shuddered at the thought and felt her entire body tremble.

The walls closed in on her. All she could see was the pool, yawning before her like a giant mouth. And it wanted to suck her baby into its depths!

She backed up until the cold tile of the wall pressed into her back. Abigail started to fuss and squirm in her arms.

"Justine Jameson? Justine Jameson? Is she here?"

Justine heard her name and she couldn't speak. She felt like she couldn't breathe. She needed to get away.

"Are you all right?" somebody asked, and touched her shoulder. She jumped and stepped sideways. It was the woman who had been standing behind her. Justine looked up at her, confused. The woman's eyes were strange, frightening, the way they bore into her. Justine looked at the baby in her arms. Something was wrong with him. His face was all bloated and his skin was blotchy and yellow with bluish veins crisscrossing his flesh, like a corpse left floating in a swamp. His mouth, a gaping black hole, hung open as if in a perpetual scream and his eyes were white in their sockets. Her heart pounded in her ears. Her vision narrowed. And then the gray people pushed out from the walls. Their bodies forced from within against the plaster as if it was elastic. They wanted Abigail!

She let out a breath and a little cry escaped, and then she bolted for the door.

She made her way through the showers, passed a girl with eyes like black stones, and continued on without a word. In her baby carrier on the floor, she put the baby down, opened her locker, and yanked her clothes out. She dressed as fast as she could, her hands trembling as her fingers fumbled with the zipper on her jeans. Abigail wailed, her face red with distress.

"It's okay, it's okay," Justine whispered urgently. "It's all right, sweetheart. Don't you worry, baby, don't worry, everything's going to be fine."

"Hello?" She heard a voice and turned to see the instructor with her clipboard, searching for her.

She gathered up the baby bag, slipped into her boots, and lifted the baby carrier. On shaky legs she ran to the safety of the exit.

"I'm taking you to the doctor, Justine," her father said, once they were all belted into the car.

"Dr. Giggles? Please. That madman does more harm than good. I had a panic attack, that's all. It's over now."

"You were screaming on the phone about the baby drowning, for God's sake." His voice was calm. She could see the amount of control he was exerting over himself, as she watched a muscle tense in his jaw.

"I was?"

"You don't remember?"

"I just feel a bit...confused. I think it's the insomnia."

"Insomnia?"

"I haven't been sleeping."

"You didn't tell me that."

"I thought it would pass." What made him think she was supposed to tell him everything? God, was nothing personal?

There was a pause as they stopped at a traffic light and watched a swarm of people cross the street. Brett ran a hand through his hair, turned to look at her and said, "I just about lost it. My heart was in my throat the whole way over here. I'm surprised I didn't have an accident."

"I'm sorry."

"Have you had other...incidents that you haven't told me about?"

Images of people hidden in the walls, brutal, faceless creatures with bodies the color of clay, their claw-like hands reaching out, came to mind.

"A few." She shivered.

"A few? Like what? What happened? Why didn't you tell me?"

"Don't get mad at me, all right?"

"I'm not mad, Justine. I'm just concerned and I don't get why you wouldn't tell me. I thought you were comfortable confiding in me, you know? That we had that kind of trust."

"Because I thought it would pass. I swear, okay?"

"It's all right, Sweets, but I think you need to have the doctor take a look at you." He reached for her hand and squeezed it.

"I told him before that I had concerns, and he just brushed it off, said it was normal with all new mothers and would go away," Justine said.

"Did you tell him about the panic attacks?"

"I told him I was feeling...nervous."

She pulled her hand away from his and shivered again. Her hair was still damp at the back of her neck from the shower.

If she voiced the degree of her paranoia, people would think she was crazy. They would put her in the psychiatric ward for God-knows how long, tie her down with those leather straps, force massive doses of tranquilizers and antidepressants down her throat, and plunge needles into her flesh. She knew all about what they did to you in those places. How they store you in warehouses disguised as hospitals, while well-meaning professionals look at you as a lesser-order human being. How the ones labeled "sick" or "diseased" were actually saner than some of the sadistic, life-hating psychiatrists whose diagnoses savage your life, and whose psych drugs vacuum out your soul. The last thing she was going to do was go back to one of those places. Nobody was going to force her, either. Not ever again.

She turned to look out the passenger-side window and watched a scrawny, homeless man who stood on the street corner a few feet away, mumbling. He stared directly at her with glacial eyes through narrowed slits; filthy hair stuck up stiff from the front of his toque. She stared at the billboard behind him that advertised toothpaste, and displayed a giant smiling face, offering teeth "whiter than white."

"Justine, you need to tell the doctor exactly what's going on with you, because it's not like you. You're generally pretty calm and laid back. You've never had panic attacks before," her father said.

Justine let out a breath and leaned her head back on the seat as the car lurched forward.

"Did you ever discuss your past with the doctor?" he asked.

"My past is nobody's business," she said.

"Maybe there's a connection to your current mental state. I think you should talk about it with him."

"Why would you even mention that, Dad, or try and draw parallels between the two? I thought you understood that I was never crazy back then. I never belonged in that fucking place. It was Pam's fault I wound up there. She's the one who called that stupid hotline and got me locked up."

"Pamela was only trying to do what was best at the time," Brett said. He frowned which revealed all his wrinkles and she caught a glimpse of sadness in his expression. "We were both trying to do what was best."

"Whatever. I needed drug counseling, not a fucking psych ward!" Justine slammed the side of her fist on the door and then pressed her knuckles against her teeth.

"Watch your language please. And you were depressed and having hallucinations. That's why you needed to go in there."

She laughed bitterly. "I was never depressed until I was locked in that fucking hell hole. The drugs they forced down my throat were the bleakest things imaginable, worse than any depression. I swear, it felt like my insides were gutted, like I couldn't feel anything, like my emotions were sucked dry. It was nothing but torture being in there. And all of this in an effort to make me well? Yeah, right."

"And you still blame Pam? After all this time, Justine? It's been nearly two years now. Why can't you just let it go and move on?"

"Has she ever apologized to me, Dad? Has anyone ever apologized to me for how those Frankenstein doctors mistreated me?"

"We didn't know, sweetheart. They told us you were suicidal." He pressed his fingers to the furrows between his eyebrows as if trying to smooth them out. He looked worried, beaten down, but he turned to her and attempted a weak smile.

"They said that about everyone in there so they can keep them locked up and make money off their insurance," Justine said, trying to force calm into her voice and failing. It sounded shrill in her ears. "That's what those private hospitals do. How else are they going to stay open? If Pamela's employer at the time didn't provide such extraordinarily rich insurance coverage for mental illness, I wouldn't have been in there in the first place. Why do you think after a fucking year, when the insurance company decided they would no longer pay, the hospital declared I was cured?"

"Calm down, Justine. You're going to start Abigail crying if you keep yelling."

The traffic clogged. As they stopped, Brett turned to glance back at the baby in her car seat.

Justine took a deep breath, focusing on slowing her heart rate. Angry tears pricked her eyes and she dug her fingernails into her palms. She watched another homeless man sitting in the middle of the sidewalk. He was laughing, or maybe he was sobbing, it was hard to tell. The few teeth he exposed were brown. Perhaps all he needed was the right toothpaste and his life would be splendid, or maybe a little experimental electric shock therapy would fix him up. Four hundred and fifty volts to the brain had a way of changing things. It could make you forget your very name, if you didn't mind the possible side effects of brain damage, epilepsy, cardio-vascular complications, and death. But no matter, the choice would ulti-mately be taken away from you. Inside the psych ward you no longer had to make decisions. The doctors—your new owners—took on that respon-sibility. Justine wondered what type of crazy the man on the sidewalk was. Schizophrenic, perhaps? Had he ever been inside of a psychiatric hospital and had his spirit and mind crushed in a punishment disguised as treat-ment for not being "normal"?

A taxi's horn blared from behind and jarred her out of her trance. When she spoke again, it was in a softer tone.

"You know what, Dad? I blame myself more for what happened to me. It was my own damn fault for reaching out for help in the first place and trusting I would receive it."

"I'm sorry for bringing it up," Brett said. "I'm just trying to be helpful, I just...I care about you. You know I love you...don't you?"

The wait was an hour, but her doctor agreed to see her once her father explained the circumstances.

She sat in a blue paper gown, opened down the back. Dr. Griffin, a beefy man with gunmetal-gray hair and sultry, puffy lips that would have better suited a girl, listened to her heart through his stethoscope and asked her questions. His bowtie was on today, reinforcing her idea that he looked just like that creepy Dr. Giggles from the horror movie. She wondered if the similarities were intentional.

"Do you have feelings of anxiety?" he asked.

Yeah, right now as a matter of fact, you fat bastard, Justine thought. "Yes. Anxiety and panic attacks. I've had a few of those. My heart races, I can't breathe. It's like the walls are closing in on me."

The band tightened around her bicep as the doctor pumped air into it from the little ball in his hand. Sweat dripped from her armpits and ran uncomfortably down her sides. She watched his face for a reaction to what she'd said, hoping he didn't have plans to call people who would come and take her away. What if her dad was out there right now, signing consent papers to have her committed? They wouldn't let her see Abigail. She would be taken away. For sure, something would happen to her baby then. Anything could happen to her at any moment. She was so little and helpless. What would she do without her mother?

"Have you had hallucinations? Do you hear voices telling you to do things?" he asked.

"No, nothing like that."

The last thing she was going to do was tell anybody she was hearing voices. That was a one-way ticket to the loony bin, and there was no way in hell she was going to help them lock her up, not when she had a baby who needed her mother. You were supposed to be able to tell your doctor anything and it would be kept confidential. But even though Dr. Griffin's bedside manner was gentle enough, she didn't trust him. He was Pamela's doctor, and Justine only started seeing him out of necessity once she became pregnant. Still, she didn't like all the prodding and poking with cold instruments and hands, and all the questions. There was something creepy and unnatural about it. The entire thing was always an ordeal.

But it was true; she had seen something that day that could only be described as a hallucination. And there was that issue of the gray people living in the walls, whispering to her all night. But mostly, it was disturbing thoughts, like images coming into her brain that she couldn't seem to control. Sometimes it felt like she was going insane. It's as if there were two parts to her brain, one trying to reason with the other, to reassure her that everything was all right. And the other part arguing back, telling her that, no, she *was* losing her mind. The two sides continually argued back and forth. It was dragging her downward in a spiral of terror.

"How about insomnia?" he asked, as he unfastened the band from her arm.

"I don't sleep well at all, and if I do, it only seems like a half hour at a time."

"Depression? Feelings of sadness or hopelessness?"

"Nothing like that; it's not the baby blues," she said.

"Delusions?"

"Just what I've described, and just irrational sort of feelings and thoughts…of my baby being hurt."

Oh God, she'd revealed it! Why had she done that? Maybe she really was crazy and a part of her was on a mission of self-destruction. Why else would she tell this prick doctor anything he could use against her? He was the enemy. Now they would take her away for sure!

"When did these thoughts start?" He looked into her ear with a little flashlight.

She sat rigid, annoyed at the poking. She had an overwhelming desire to punch him in the face, watch the blood spurt from his nose, then run out of the room.

"A few weeks ago. Shortly after Abigail was born, maybe two weeks. But it's nothing. It's not like I'm worried about it. It's really nothing, I swear. Just nerves."

"You did the right thing by coming in, Justine."

Great, now she'd done it. Now they would strap her down in a five-point restraint and Dr. Giggles would dig her heart out of her chest. Goddamn, why didn't she just keep her mouth shut? Justine shifted her legs, trying to unstick her damp skin from the paper-covered table crinkling underneath her. The gown rustled in the suffocatingly warm air, thick with the odor of her own perspiration. Blood pounded in her ears as the doctor wrote something in her chart. She scanned the room for something to hit him with.

"No reason to suffer in silence," he said, not looking at her. "But unfortunately, not many new mothers seek the help they need. They're too afraid. So I'm giving you a prescription for Halodol. It's a low dose for now. See how you react. What you've described to me, these symptoms you're having, sound like a mild form of postpartum psychosis. It's a rare occurrence in new mothers, usually triggered within a few weeks or months of childbirth, and it can be successfully treated with medication. Psychiatric counseling is also recommended, and I'll give you a list of psychiatrists."

That was it? He was just going to give her a prescription and let her walk out of here? She wouldn't have to kill him after all? This must be his lucky day.

"So, it will just go away, then?" she asked.

"It's a very effective medication and you should start to feel better within a week or two," he said, scribbling on his perscription pad.

Halodol. Sweet. Just what she never wanted to experience again in her life.

"Will this condition I have ever go away completely and allow me to feel like myself again?"

"It's believed to be triggered by hormones from childbirth," he said, and turned to give her his full attention. "So yes, it can diminish in time. Fortunately, it sounds like a mild form, as I say, but I want you to monitor how you're feeling on this medication and contact our office immediately if you feel worse or if you have thoughts of suicide or any other dangerous thoughts or feelings. I want you to check back with me in about a month and let me know how you're functioning on the drugs."

"Okay," Justine said. "What about breast-feeding?"

"It's not a problem. Just take note if your baby seems unusually lethargic or shows any other behavior that concerns you. But generally, it's safe for breast-feeding."

"Okay, if this is what I have to do, then fine."

"Take care." He nodded, twitched his sexy-girl lips, and closed the door to let her get dressed.

Justine sighed. She would be okay, she told herself. She wasn't going back to the psych hospital no matter what, even if that meant it was necessary to take the stupid Halodol. As long as she didn't have to go back, she would be okay. She hoped that she would be okay. Normal. Like everyone else.

"Oh, my God!" Justine drew in a breath as they followed Sal's vintage Mercedes from East Lake Road onto Welker Road and she caught sight of the house through the trees. "Is this it?"

"Holy cow," Brett said. "It's amazing."

"It's beautiful, Brett. Oh my God, look at the view of the lake from the back. How much does this place cost? Can we afford this?" Pamela said.

"What's the asking price on the listing?"

Pamela flipped the pages in her lap. "Five twenty. Seems a bit low for something like this, doesn't it?"

"Well, it's within our price range. That's all I care about."

Justine got out of the car and gazed up at the two-story home with the veranda above the entrance and the cedar shingle roof, all partially hidden by tall trees. She looked beyond it at the land that gently sloped in the distance, and made way for a breath-taking view of the frozen lake. She knew even before she entered the house that she wanted to live here. A feeling of joy surfaced inside of her, and the idea that maybe this could actually work for her and Abigail. Maybe her parent's ideals weren't so far-fetched. Maybe she could actually allow herself to believe they could all get along, move past the resentment and be happy. Seeing the house gave her a new sense of hope.

It was the perfect country dream home. It already felt like home, and they had yet to even step inside.

Chapter
SEVEN

"Madden, you got a visitor," a guard announced.

After waiting for the door to buzz open, Rory was led down a long hall to the visiting area and let into the locked room where he found his new lawyer sitting on the edge of a table. Hugh Henderson was wearing a grin. His eyes looked excited, as if he was high, and Rory wondered if the man ever slept. Where the hell did he get his energy? He never tired, and always looked as fresh as nine a.m. with his clean-shaven face and spruced hair the color of steel. But maybe that's what was required to do the type of work he did. Maybe you needed to have a hyperactive, obsessive, type-A personality in order to be successful as a criminal defense attorney. Or perhaps it was the paycheck that made him look so perky. Pocketing all of Rory's money must be exhilarating.

"You might want to sit down for this," Henderson said.

"What is it?" Rory took a seat at the table.

"I've got good news for you," he said and his grin widened even more. His dentures looked like they were actually sparkling.

"Well? What are you waiting for? Bring it on, Henderson."

The lawyer nodded and pressed his lips together, still smiling, as if savoring an inside joke. His stalling only angered Rory.

Finally, Hederson made the announcement. "Your case has been tossed out."

"What?" Rory said, certain he'd heard him wrong.

"They've dropped the charges Rory. You're getting out of here."

"You're kidding me? Really? How? What happened?" Rory leaned forward in his chair.

"What those stupid cops did was they searched your house without a warrant and then went to get a search warrant to conduct the search they had already done." Henderson punctuated his words by hammering his finger on the desk. "That's state cops for you, famous for their prowess in catching speeders and directing traffic, but can't remember basic protocol. And that's what's saved your ass, Rory my boy, when the judge granted suppression motions. This whole thing was botched right from the very beginning."

Rory rubbed his hands over his face and looked up at the ceiling. Then he folded his arms and slouched in the chair. He gave the lawyer a deadpan stare.

"You're absolutely sure about this, Henderson?'

"Basically, someone fucked up, and in your favor," Henderson said. "A ten-month investigative operation down the tubes on a technicality. They ought to be ashamed of themselves."

"So, I'm getting out of here? For real?"

"You're a free man, Rory."

"Am I getting deported back to Ireland?"

"No, they're not deporting you. It was a clear violation of your Fourth Amendment rights, and the state did the right thing by abandoning the prosecution," Henderson said, and stood up, his lanky body in his expensive suit unfolding. He put his hands in the pockets of his pants, posed in a wide stance that demonstrated his massive self-confidence, and continued talking eagerly. "Basically, what I'm saying, Rory, is that you got lucky. You got very, very lucky. Without the suppression of this evidence, you would be doing a minimum mandatory prison sentence. And I'm talking twenty years, here. You must have horseshoes up your ass, my friend."

Almost a half-year of sitting in pre-trial custody and all the charges against Rory were finally dropped. Maybe Henderson wasn't such an ignorant country lawyer after all, as Rory was beginning to think of him.

If he had found this lawyer first, instead of that other bastard, Blackmore, things might have been different. Henderson might not have ripped him off the way that first crooked lawyer did. Now everything was so much worse because of it. He'd lost it all because of that one greedy son of a bitch whom he didn't have any choice but to trust. Getting his money and getting even were the first things on Rory's agenda when he was released.

"What about my property? My house, my vehicles? When do I get them back?"

"Not so easy, I'm afraid." Henderson pursed his lips, the happy grin of victory now gone. His exuberant eyes showed signs of genuine worry.

"It's my understanding the bank sold your house after foreclosure proceedings."

"That's bullshit," Rory said. "I got ripped off. I told you what my first lawyer did to me."

"Bullshit or not, your luck just might have run out there. Didn't they deposit a check in your bank for the difference between what you owed and what it sold for?"

"Aye. The bastards were trying to appease me."

"How much was the check for?"

"One hundred and ten thousand."

"Not a bad start. The best advice I can give you is to talk to a civil attorney and see what rights you have if you really want to fight the foreclosure," Henderson said, knodding. "Call my office tomorrow and my assistant can get you the number of somebody who might be willing to help."

Rory was released from jail that same day with the clothing he wore in, his wallet with a lone ten-dollar bill the police didn't confiscate, his Zippo, his Movado watch and not much else. They did not return the key chain with the keys to his house, his Cadillac SUV, his custom Harley, his ATV, and his snowmobile. They took it all and left him with next to nothing. Even his tools were gone. Probably directly into the hands of those crooked cops. He still had his Challenger, which he'd paid for outright, and a few boxes of belongings. The police had impounded it and were waiting for him to pay the storage fee. He found his long, black leather coat with the red-fox fur collar, stuffed in a bag in the trunk. He shook the wrinkles out and put it on, feeling good that he got some of his possessions back.

The first thing he planned to do was to get himself an eight ball, a bottle of whiskey, and get higher than the clouds. Next, he would visit that thieving lawyer and get his money back. Then he would hire a lawyer and get back all his property those fuckers seized. Rory wasn't just going to stand by and allow those bastards to take away everything he'd worked for. There was nothing for him to lose now. They had taken it all. So, if it meant he was forced to do whatever it took to get his property back, he was prepared. They were not going to get away with stealing from him.

Later that day, Rory breathed in the scent of freedom as he gassed up his Challenger, staring at the snow-covered hills of Yates County, and thinking that they looked just like the Black Mountain and Cave Hill back in Ireland. He paid for the gas with his debit card, surprised that it actually still worked, and bought himself a pack of Just Black chocolate-flavored cigars and a pack of Marlboro Lights.

He washed his car, vacuumed the inside, cleaning and polishing it until it was spotless. Then he went to the bank and withdrew a thousand dollars in cash. He drove out to the house of a guy he knew near Dresden and bought four guns—a .357 Magnum, two Colt .45 semi-automatics, and a Remington twelve-gauge pump-action shotgun.

As Frances taught him when she was just a girl of eight; *"You have to do it like your life depends on it."*

Chapter
EIGHT

"We've got just one box left to unpack in the kitchen and I think that's it. At least for the main floor. I've still got a few boxes in my room to go through," Justine said, wandering toward the massive living room windows that looked out over the frozen lake in the distance. Pamela stood bathed in the weak afternoon sunlight, holding Abigail.

"It's massive isn't it? Compared to our condo," Pamela said, as she gazed out at the expanse of the property.

"This is such an awesome view. What way does it face? South?" Justine asked, as she peered out at the hills. A fog surrounded them and softened them against the February sky.

"It's southwest looking this way, so we'll see the sun setting over the lake."

"God, it's so sweet," Justine said. "It's like a resort here."

"It's got that feeling, doesn't it?"

"I heard it's wine country up here."

"Yeah," Pamela said. "You know, outside of California, Yates County is the largest wine-grape growing county in the U.S?"

"Awesome. We should go on some of those wine tasting tours." Justine thought about all the empty wine bottles that went into their recycling bin every week. It used to be six or seven bottles, but then Pamela started buying the large bottles, so now it was three or four a week. Justine wondered if she should be encouraging her to go on wine tours when the women went on her own tour every night once she was home from work.

"Sure, that will be fun." Pamela touched her arm affectionately. "As long as they don't ask you for I.D."

The sensation was so unfamiliar that it actually startled Justine. Perhaps Pamela's good mood was just due to the move and their new house and the fact that she was now closer to her mother. She watched the way Pamela looked down at Abigail with a smile, a softness in her normally stony eyes, knowing that tomorrow it could all change. Tomorrow the internal battle within Pamela could be triggered and the old resentments would overpower that look of love she now displayed, and cause her to turn away from Abigail. Nothing was ever simple or established with Pamela. She was as volatile as the weather. If only Justine could have been more like her stepsister Allison, then her relationship with Pamela would have been better; she might even have been loved, at least. But being anything like Allison or her stepmother was never something Justine aspired to.

She remembered the awkward, frizzy-haired little girl with the chalky complexion and perpetually skinned knees that she once was. A few weeks ago, while packing for their move, she came across a photograph of herself at the age of eight. It was in a box of old photographs, letters and papers that she kept in her closet. The snapshot took her right back to that moment in her life, and the helpless anxiety that was the total sum of her childhood. And the despair. So much despair from her mother's death. Looking at the picture of herself, she felt like she'd been punched in the stomach.

In the photo she was sitting on the grass in her grandmother's front yard in Watkins Glen, kneeling between Allison and Pamela. In Pamela's lap was a gray and white kitten lying on its back, and she and Allison were looking down at it and smiling. Justine was staring straight at the camera, faking a happy smile. In the background, piled up beside their car, was Allison's luggage. She was saying good-bye to her grandmother and coming to live with them in Manhattan with the new kitten. There was a scab on Justine's chin from some random scuffle with a neighborhood kid, and her unruly hair was a mass of tangles. Her cheeks were red with jealousy.

When Allison died eventually, Justine felt sorrow, naturally; but also a sense of relief.

"We've got a sweet deck out there, too." Justine pointed out the window.

"Brett wants to put in a hot tub so we can take in the view. He says we can watch the hills roll," Pamala said and then snorted. It was a sound that Justine wasn't sure was a lighthearted laugh or an expression of reproach. She could never tell with Pamela.

"Sweet. Why did the previous owner end up selling? Didn't Sal say it was a foreclosure?"

"I guess they didn't make their mortgage payments or something. Must have been heartbreaking to lose a beautiful place like this," Pamela said. "I can't imagine owning this chunk of paradise and then watch it being taken away. They probably lost their life savings."

"You know, Pam, I didn't realize you guys were doing this well financially."

"We're not." An exasperated look crossed her face briefly and then was gone. "Your father's company has actually lost a couple of major contracts in the last year, to tell you the truth. Doesn't look like it's going to survive, not in this economy. He's going to have to fold. It's become a money pit. He hasn't had a pay check in five months."

"I had no idea."

"Not to worry," Pamela said, "Our investments have done well in spite of the economy, and I'm making good money these days. We had a good chunk of equity in the condo, so that helped a lot with the down payment on this place. We've been very lucky in that respect. So many people have lost their savings and their jobs."

"What's Dad going to do for work if he closes the business?"

"I have no idea," Pamela said and let out a heavy sigh. "Look for a job I guess."

Pamela's cheek dimpled as she smiled down at the baby. She lifted a hand and touched the baby's face with the backs of her fingers, the sun glinting in the miniature rhinestones fixed in the ends of her acrylic nails. Her subtle gesture was comforting to watch, as if her love was never tenuous, could never be withheld or taken away for bad behavior, and could never be used as a weapon. At least, maybe not with Abigail. Justine knew the darker side of Pamela's love, if it could even be called love; a brittleness, a coldness in her heart, a resentment for not living up to her expectations. For thriving while her own daughter lay dead. Sure, she provided the basic necessities—food, clothing and a roof—but that's all. Anything else—time, affection, encouragement, acceptance—were either in short supply or non-existent.

Justine marveled at the way Pamela interacted with Abigail in that moment. She studied Pamela's profile as she looked out the window, and regarded the sharp angle of her dainty nose, the pout of her glossy lips, the way her eyeliner arched upwards at the corner of her eye, and thought of her own mother. She imagined her mother there in Pamela's place, with Abigail in her arms. Some days she couldn't remember her mother's face and she had to look at photographs.

"This is a nice, big fireplace isn't it? We'll roast lots of marshmallows in there now won't we Abigail?" Pamela said.

"Can I ask you something, Pam?" Justine smiled, and found that she wanted to open up to her stepmother. She wanted to tell her about the frightful thoughts that plagued her after the birth of her daughter. The medication seemed to have lessened it to a certain degree. But it made her feel strange sometimes—foggy. Her head felt like it was full of sand, reminiscent of the nightmare of her early teenage years, although far less severe. She hoped she would be able to get off the drugs soon and feel sane, the way she was before she had the baby. That's all she wanted: just to feel like herself again; to feel okay.

"Did you ever worry about Allison when she was a baby?"

"Worry? Well, of course. Every mother worries about her babies. Comes with the territory, Justine."

"I guess I'll just have to get used to it." She looked out at the forest of bare trees. It was obvious Pamela didn't understand what she meant by "worry". She probably never went through it, wouldn't know what she meant if Justine told her about the horrible images she harbored in her mind, or the gray people who plagued her like a nightmare, waking her from sleep, whispering in her ear. She would just have to learn to cope. What else could she do? The drugs helped, but it didn't make them go away completely.

Pamela said, "You never stop worrying about them. That's a mother's love. But you've just got to trust, that's all you've got to do. Trust in love, trust in God, in the universe, in your guardian angels, in spite of everything, no matter what happens."

Pamela's eyes betrayed a glimpse of something familiar—a brief look of despair—and she knew Pamela was thinking about what happened to Allison. Of course Pamela would know all about a mother's anguish and pain. So much pain.

"I've got a few extra guardian angels that I've sent to watch over Abigail." She smiled at the baby who reached up her little hand to pat her grandmother's face. "They were just hanging around, not doing much of anything, so I thought I'd put them to good use."

Impulsively, Justine reached for Pamela and embraced her as tightly as she could without squishing the baby. It was the first time she could remember ever embracing her. It felt awkward, their bones colliding. She breathed in her powdery Channel perfume and the scent of tobacco. Was it possible they could put all their mutual resentment behind them? Her Dad was right; she needed to let the anger go and move on.

"You're a good mother, Justine," Pamela rubbed her arm. "I can see it in you. Abigail is lucky to have you."

Trust. It was good advice; the only advice of Pamela's that Justine actually thought was valuable. She would have to remember to do this. Maybe that would help her to feel like she was normal.

Later that afternoon, Justine watched her father's Lincoln through the trees as it turned onto the road, heading in the direction of New York City. It was a beautiful winter's day, crisp and cold. She studied an osprey as it flew above the treetops, hovering on the breeze.

She went back to bed with the baby, her breasts sore and full. She looked down at Abigail, stroking her warm head, and recognized a trace of the baby's father in the shape of her nose and the arch of her brows. An image of the first time she met Keith came to her.

She couldn't have known then, as much as she was struck by his smile and his dark eyes, as they walked out of the coffee shop together and then stood talking impulsively on the sidewalk with their paper cups in hand, how her existence would change so dramatically. The rain had just started. Yet they stood there like children, not caring, and smiled at each other as they got soaked. He was tall, good looking, in his early twenties, with a fledgling management company and recording studio. He seemed perfect for her, like it was meant to be. But like so many things that appear one way but in reality are another, she was wrong about Keith.

Within three months of meeting that day in the coffee shop, she was pregnant. Her Dad wanted to have him charged. But she moved in with him anyway. They separated only four months later. She had felt it from even before she'd moved in, somewhere in the depths of her heart; a lingering sensation of deficiency that she glossed over with hopefulness. But then all illusions were lost once they began living together in his small fifth-floor apartment on West Sixty-Seventh Street. Keith still behaved as if he was single. He was gone out all night with friends; sometimes he would be gone for days. And his promise of recording a new CD and shopping her demo to record companies never materialized.

She tolerated his bad habits: his indiscreet nose picking, the flecks of toothpaste he left on the bathroom mirror, the dirty socks draped over the back of the sofa as if they could somehow be considered decorative, and his sports obsession. But the one thing that finally did in their short relationship was the issue of his bowel movements. It never failed when they were out somewhere Keith would inevitably have to go to the bathroom.

"I have to poo," he would announce to her across the dinner table in a restaurant, proud as a two-year-old.

A bowel movement, for Keith, was no small affair. He could be in there for forty-five minutes. It was ridiculous. Who had time for that? And why his internal clock timed those instances for when they were out in public somewhere was beyond her. For herself, she was able to take care of that bodily function efficiently and quickly in the mornings. Didn't most people do the same?

The very last time they were ever out together having dinner, Keith announced the arrival of his bowel movement to her as if they were about to have a visit from the Messiah, himself. She told him to hold it until they got home. He insisted that it couldn't wait. Justine knew right then it was over between them. She wasn't going to spend the rest of her life waiting at tables by herself while he labored in public restrooms. Getting involved with him in the first place had been a complete mistake.

She tossed her napkin on the table and told him she'd see him around. She left him calling her name as she stormed out of the restaurant and hailed a cab on the street. The next day, she packed her bags and moved back with her father and Pamela.

Pamela yelled out a hasty good-bye as she headed out the door for work. Justine changed the baby and watched her car through the nursery window as it retreated down the driveway and turned onto the road. The silence of the house bore down on her. She wondered, as she looked out at the distant hills, why she ever let her parents bring her out here. There must be some other options. This couldn't be all there was for her; a grown woman, raising a child, dependent on her parents for support. There must be something more for her than this.

What became of her dreams? Where did they go?

When she came down the stairs with Abigail, Justine spied Pamela's cell phone on the dining room table, and realized she'd forgotten it. Maybe she would figure it out in another moment and turn back. The screen lit up as a text message came in. Justine picked it up, and read the message. It was from some man named Russ. There was an address and room number for a hotel in Rochester with the message, "Looking forward to seeing you, sexy lady."

Justine was confused. Who the hell was Russ?

Chapter

NINE

"You know what the worst day of my life was?" Rory said, his face tomb-stone cold. "When my sister didn't come home from school. She was eight years old. We put posters with her picture up all over town. Search parties combed every inch of our neighborhood for weeks. The police came out with dogs. Days turned into weeks, months, and years, and there was no sign of her. She just vanished. Every now and then we'd get a call about a sighting, but it never lead anywhere. One day the police called our house because they had a Jane Doe down at the morgue, and my mother had to go to see if it was Frances, but turned out to be someone else's little girl. It's been fifteen years and I'm still looking for her."

"I'm sorry." The man looked away uncomfortably, his fleshy booze-face reddening even more than it already was naturally—or unnaturally, if not for the obvious alcohol problem. Tiny droplets of sweat formed on the man's upper lip.

Rory snorted and nodded his head in a superior manner. "*You're* sorry? Why? Did you abduct her?"

"No, of course not. I—I just mean I'm sorry you had to—to experience that."

"Frances was only eight. She was just a wee girl, a happy, wee girl, who thought the world was a friendly place and only bad things happened in storybooks or in films, you see? But when she didn't come home from school and nobody knew where she was, well, we knew something had happened." Rory sucked his teeth, nodded his head slowly, reflectively. He lifted the collar of his leather coat, brushing his cheek next to the soft fur in some vague comforting gesture as he continued. "They questioned every sex offender in the neighborhood. They dredged the bottom of a creek near our house. They searched our entire building and the yard with cadaver dogs, and they even questioned my mother's boyfriend about her disappear-ance. He later abandoned my mother but that's okay, he was just another bloody maggot. But they never solved the case. A body has ever been found and nobody's ever been charged. It was just forgotten, just like Frances. Everyone just forgot about her; even my mother couldn't bare the mention of her name. My mother, she just drank herself into oblivion. That was her way of coping, I suppose—or not coping, depending on which way you look at it."

"That's...that's a terrible story."

"It's not a story. It happened. It was real!"

"Yeah, no, I just meant that—"

"You know what the second worst day of my life was?"

The man shook his head and pressed his lips together, as if bracing himself for more bad news. He stared at Rory with watery eyes, the overhead lights gleaming on his bald scalp.

"When those fucking bastards took away my house, and my lawyer I made the grave mistake of trusting because I basically had no other choice, goes and robs me. When I'm at the most vulnerable moment, confined to a jail cell, my home and my possessions all hanging in the balance, and I turn to the only person I can, what does he do? He helps himself to my money. What kind of lawyer, can I ask you, Mr. Blackmore, does that to a client?"

The man didn't reply. He just gazed at Rory with a frightened look, like a video screen on pause, capturing and freezing a face in some bizarre half expression.

"What kind, Mr. Blackmore, huh?"

"Please...please put the gun away, Rory."

"Aye, I told you you'd regret this, didn't I? I told you I'd come for you."

"Rory, please I have a family, three kids and my first grand baby on the way and—"

"Shut the fuck up." Rory was so calm that it surprised him. He thought for sure he would lose control of himself when he laid eyes on this scumbag lawyer again. Up until that very moment, he felt certain he wouldn't be able to hold himself back. Perhaps all that time in jail had conditioned him to being more patient. Or maybe it was the feeling of the twelve gauge in his hands that allowed him control of his emotions. His long coat had been perfect for concealing it when he walked into the office. Maybe it was the blow he snorted in his car in the parking lot—he'd wasted no time finding the drug sources in town—before he came into the building. Possibly it was a combination of all these things. Yet he knew it was only a matter of time before he killed this man, and he marveled at how things sometimes worked out, how the tables could turn. How easily power could be gained and lost.

Rory leaned back comfortably in the chair, his right leg crossed over the other with the shotgun resting on his knee, pointed at the lawyer's fat face. He watched the man loosen the collar of his shirt, as if it was a ligature choking him. The lawyer sat stiff behind his desk in his big green leather chair in his swanky office. Rory sat across from him in another, smaller, leather chair, designed to telegraph the difference between the lawyer and his clients, so there was no doubt about who held the power in the room. Although now, the irony of this was blatantly clear. All illusions had been stripped away.

It was a masculine-looking office—slick, dark wood and sparse furnishings—but lacking in character, much like its owner. The secretary had left minutes earlier, having poked her head inside the room to say a friendly good-bye and ask one last time if Rory was sure she couldn't get him a coffee or something.

How about his hundred and eighty thousand dollars? Could she get that for him?

"I didn't take your money," Blackmore said. "There was no money. There was nothing there. I swear, there...there—"

"Now you want to add liar to the list of things that you are? Don't try and deny it," Rory said. "Of course you bloody well took it. There is absolutely no doubt you did. It was so well hidden the police could never have found it unless they knew where to look."

Blackmore swallowed audibly, and shook his head, his cheeks quivering. "Maybe a police dog sniffed it out."

"There were no dogs with them. Besides, they're trained to sniff drugs, not money," Rory said.

"Money always has traces of cocaine on it," Blackmore said. "There was a study—"

"Sorry, pal, I'm not that daft. You were the only one I told where my money was. You were the only person who had that knowledge."

Moments ticked by as neither of them spoke, only gazed at each other. Dust motes drifted silently in the afternoon sunlight streaming through the slats of the wooden blinds.

The lawyer swallowed and attempted to clear his throat. "I swear to you—"

"Shut your dirty mouth. I've got no patience for liars and thieves. I'm on the edge here, and anything at this point could set me off. I'm a man with nothing left to lose, Blackmore, and I'm not afraid to end your miserable life. I just don't care about you at all. All I care about is that you get me my money."

The man drew in a shaky breath and let it out slowly, a look of pain on his face. He cleared his throat again and let his eyes dart around the room. "All right, okay. I don't have all of it. I've got about half at the moment. I can get you the rest in a day or two."

"You fucker, I want it now. All of it! Otherwise, I'm going to blow a big fucking hole through you."

"Listen, I've got it. I've got it. Please calm down, Rory"

"Where is it?"

"I've got it, but I just can't get it all to you right now. I've got about eighty thousand in my safe. The rest I can get to you once I transfer some money from my savings account. It usually takes a day or two. But I'll do it, I swear. I just need a bit of time."

"Where's your safe?"

"In the cupboard." He pointed to a large, wood cabinet across the room. "Open it."

Blackmore rose from the desk awkwardly and ambled over to the cabinet. His heavy footsteps shook the floor as he moved.

Rory shadowed him, watching him closely in case the fucker had a weapon hidden somewhere and tried to pull it on him. He stood over him; the gun pointed at Blackmore's head as he crouched down, knees popping, and breathed as if he'd just run up three flights of stairs. He opened a door to reveal a small, fireproof safe with a dial on the front. Rory watched the man turn the dial, not interested in the combination, and kept an eye on his movements.

"Here, Rory. Here's your money." Blackmore pulled out four bundles of bills, secured with paper sleeves.

"Get me a bag to put it in. I'll count it later and it better be eighty thousand."

"It's around eighty thousand. It might be a few hundred shy. Just let me know and I'll make sure you get all of it back."

"Aye, you're bloody right you will."

The lawyer stood up and closed the door of the cabinet, and then looked around for a bag. He found a paper shopping bag behind his desk that contained an unopened box of chocolates, obviously a gift for someone or from someone, and dumped it on the desk. He dropped the money inside and handed the bag to Rory.

"Give me two days, Rory, and I'll have the rest of it."

"Two-thirty-two East Main Street. That's your address right, Blackmore?"

"How do you know my address?"

"If you fuck me over, I'll burn your house down in the middle of the night with your family inside. Do you understand?"

"I get the message loud and clear."

"Don't fuck with me."

"Rory, I apologize for all this."

Rory gave him an icy stare. With the gun flanked at the side of his leg under his coat, he made his way out of the lawyer's office and let the door bang behind him.

Rory stuffed the bag of money and the gun under the seat of his car and went down to O'Leary's on Elm Street.

Chapter
TEN

Rory sat up at the bar and sucked back Jim Beam on ice, trying to submerge the deep sense of despair he had picked up somewhere like an objectionable hitchhiker. *Johnny, I Hardly Knew Ya* wailed from the speakers above, a tougher sounding remake of the old Irish song by The Dropkick Murphys. The song pulled at his memory like a darkness passing through him, calling him forth, praying to him from the shadows of his spirit, and dragged him back to his days in the UFF. The violence he was born of was still in his bones and in his blood. His heart was a cold stone.

> *"Where are your legs that used to run, hurroo, hurroo*
> *Where are your legs that used to run, hurroo, hurroo*
> *Where are your legs that used to run*
> *When you went for to carry a gun*
> *Indeed your dancing days are done*
> *Oh Johnny, I hardly knew ye."*

Memories surfaced inside of him, rising up, twisting around him like smoke, and he remembered himself at seventeen. He remembered his first kill. It sat in his mind, immovable as a warm bullet deep in his flesh. He was ordered to assassinate a Catholic taxi driver in County Derry. Armed with handguns, three of them wearing balaclavas ascended on their victim in the night. Rory's heart pounded throughout his entire body. His finger shook on the trigger of his gun as they forced the man's car off the road and ordered him out. Rory grabbed him by his sweater and tried to drag him out through the open window. The man opened the door and fell to the ground.

"Don't shoot. Please don't shoot!" he pleaded and attempted to raise his hands as he lay face down.

They robbed him. They beat him. Rory put a bullet in his head as he lay on the ground bleeding, sobbing. He didn't die right away though. It took pumping three more into his back to kill him. After, they went home, burned their clothes, washed, and scrubbed any traces of gunpowder from under their nails, and even swabbed their ears. Then they went to celebrate at a party that lasted two days. It was there that Rory had his first taste of cocaine, and it was just like falling in love.

His next hit was a on a member of Sinn Fein outside their office on the Falls Road. He rode up on the back of a stolen Suzuki motorcycle and hopped off. He shot the man in broad daylight, three times in the back of the head as he was about to get into his car. They sped away, and another member of the group disposed of the bike. Again, they burned their clothes, washed up, and spent the night partying.

A few weeks later, he planted a bomb on the Belfast-Dublin train, killing two people and injuring six more when it exploded upon arrival at Connolly Station. He was involved in breaking down the front doors of people's homes and shooting men in front of their families. He participated in tortures, savage beatings, and the killing of innocent Catholics just for being Catholics.

On one occasion, when they sledge-hammered their way into a house and murdered a man as he ate supper with his family around the table, the man's wife came at them with a kitchen knife. She wailed like a demon, her bare feet bloodied on the glass from their break-in. Her children watched from the top of the stairs.

"You dirty, murdering bastards! I'll kill youse myself, I will! You bloody orange scum! Rot in hell!" She jumped on the back of one of Rory's men, brandishing the knife. He struggled with her as he stumbled out the door.

Rory raised his gun to her head and fired. From behind his mask, he watched her drop to the ground and fall on her back, the knife clutched uselessly in her hand. He looked inside the house and spied her small children, huddled at the top of the stairs in a cluster, like kittens just out of the womb. Their round eyes staring at him.

"They're rolling out the guns again, hurroo, hurroo
They're rolling out the guns again, hurroo, hurroo
They're rolling out the guns again
But they never will take our sons again
No they never will take our sons again
Johnny I'm swearing to ye."

"Hey, Rory, long time no see, buddy. You just get out or what?"

Rory turned and looked sideways through blurry eyes at a young, gaunt-faced man. A dark curl lay across the man's forehead, fallen loose from a slicked-back pompadour, looking just like he'd walked off the set of Grease.

"Hey, Douggy." Rory smiled and greeted his old friend, towering over him, the ghosts in his head dissipating. "How's it going, man?"

"Good, man. So when did you get out? It's good to see you. I thought you'd be going away for a long time, buddy."

The man put out a skeletal hand for a shake and Rory took it, letting him slap his palm, knock his knuckles in that street salutation that was meant to show somehow that you were cool.

"Got out three days ago," Rory said. "My charges got dropped."

"No way, you are one lucky dude." Douggy laughed, that old familiar hyena cackle of his. Rory hadn't realized he'd missed his laugh until that very moment.

"Aye. That's me, lucky as a leprechaun," he said, and laughed himself.

"Hey, this calls for a celebration, my friend. Can we get another round?" Douggy hollered to the girl behind the bar.

Rory pulled out another chocolate-flavored cigar from the pack of Just Blacks. He felt happy to see his old friend again. Douggy and his father had put up some of the drywall at his house last summer. He worked as a private investigator and had helped in the past with Rory's search for his sister. Douggy gave him a small fortune, buying eight balls from him every weekend. They had spent many nights partying together right here at O'Leary's. Rory missed those weekends when "Ballbreaker," an AC/DC cover band, came to town and the place would be packed. When the bar closed, they would line up inside of Cam's New York Pizzeria to get a slice. You could always see a Penn Yan police car parked nearby. After routinely getting called to break up fights between intoxicated customers in the pizzeria, the cops started waiting outside until the bar closed so they could just step out of the patrol car when the action started.

Douggy swallowed a mouthful of beer from his glass. He lit the end of Rory's thin cigar, and then leaned in close to Rory with his forearms on the bar. He spoke in a low voice as he gave him a level stare, his eyes dark and shining.

"You back in business now, or what?" he asked.

"Me? No man, cops are going to be watching my every move. I'm sure they're pissed about me walking." He puffed on the end of the cigar. "No man, I got to lay low for a while. Once I get my house back, we'll see about getting back in the action, but for now I got to behave."

"So, hey man, sorry to hear about your house. I heard the bank took it back."

"Aye, but I'll get it back. No worries. I'm going to get a good lawyer and sue the pants off those fuckers who took it."

"That's a sweet property Rory, and the house you built? Fucking awesome. I'd hate to lose a place like that. I really feel for you, man."

"I'll get my house back, I'm not worried."

They both looked over at two girls playing pool, and watched as one of them, who didn't look old enough to be drinking, leaned over in a short denim skirt. She held the pool cue in a way that showed she didn't have a clue about what she was doing. She hit a striped ball, and then sewered. Predictable.

"Did you know this place used to be a bowling alley in the sixties?" Douggy said. The lights above glinted in a silver ring piercing one eyebrow.

"You're a regular encyclopedia. Is there anything you don't know, Douggy?"

"Middle name is Google." Douggy made a clicking sound with his tongue and winked. "My dad used to come here all the time. They had ball boys who manually reset the pins after each shot."

"Is that what they called them, ball boys?"

"Yeah, bet they had a gay old time, too. As in happy I mean, when gay still meant happy."

Douggy and Rory broke into a fit of laughter.

"So, where you living now?" Douggy asked after a pause.

"In my car. Got my Challenger back from impound, but I had to pay the fuckers a huge storage bill first. It's the only thing I owned outright that didn't get confiscated. Thieving fucking bastards."

"Your car? That sucks, Rory. Why don't you get an apartment or something? In fact, I know of a place over on Main Street for rent. Nice place, too. My brother-in-law owns the building. Hey, why don't I call him and see if we can go over and take a look at it?"

Rory shrugged. "I guess, sure. My car's not so bad, though, more comfortable than a bloody jail cell. Got lots of room but it ain't got a shower and there's nowhere to put a flat-screen TV. So, sure, I'm up for checking out a flat."

"Cool, let me give him a call and see," he said, and flipped open his cell phone.

Rory swiveled around on the barstool, stood up and stretched his arms. The girl in the denim skirt smiled at him. She was pretty, with a sweet face and perky breasts, maybe too much makeup because she wasn't old enough to know how to apply it properly. She looked like the kind of girl who would make him date her at least three times before parting her legs. Most girls he knew gave it up pretty quick. Her friend was a dog though, had a doughy figure and hair that looked as if she'd last washed it in a previous life.

Rory thought of Connie, buried on his property. Just as he knew, nobody had even reported her missing, at least that he'd heard of. The life of a dancer, traveling from town to small town across the country, living hand to mouth. She had no family—not any who gave a shit about her. She was society's cast-off, homeless, worthless, forgettable. Rory wondered how far the decomposition would be at this stage. She was probably looking pretty nasty. What a shame.

He cast a seductive look at the girl with the pool cue, letting her know he was interested. His gaze slid down the girl's legs, under that short skirt. Likely she came from a strict family with a mean old man; had a ten o'clock curfew, midnight on the weekends if she pleaded. She looked like a good girl and he would probably have to tell her that he loved her. Oh, well, whatever it took. He was in dire need of some sex.

In the men's room, he stood over a urinal and dipped a miniature spoon into a glass vial. He scooped out a small heap of the powder and snorted it up one nostril and then scooped out another mound for his other nostril. The drugs exploded through his brain. He sniffed and craned his neck from side to side so the vertebrae popped. He felt more in control, not so sloppy drunk.

His eyes in the mirror were red, the pupils dilated. His skin looked pale. He ran a hand over his stubbly hair and thought that he needed to get back to working out and taking care of himself. He'd lost serious muscle mass since the arrest. Once this shit was all over with and he got his house back, he'd start working out again and give up the tobacco and the drugs. He would pull himself together.

The door of the men's room creaked as it opened and someone hesitated in the doorway. Rory turned just in time to recognize the red hair and those ears before they vanished.

Simon.

"Hey, you fuck!" Rory yanked on the door handle. He bounded down the hall after him and spotted Simon as he retreated out the back door of the bar. Rory chased him.

"Simon!"

Simon didn't stop. He ran like he'd seen the devil, and disappeared around the corner of the building. By the time Rory made it to the front parking lot, he'd lost sight of him. Rory scanned the area, but there was no sign of him. Then a car's engine fired up and he watched Simon's vintage Camaro peel out of a space. The tires squealed as the car fishtailed on the tarmac and sped up the road.

Rory stood and watched his retreat, panting from the exertion. It was plain to see that Simon somehow had managed to keep all he had earned from their years of drug sales. He probably still had that nice house in town, his forty-two-foot luxury yacht and his custom Harley. Not bad for a guy who was busted with ten kilos. Wonder if he even spent a night in jail? The life of a rat was good. No matter. He'd catch up with him. The pain of the betrayal was now crystallized into a rage so immense it was an effort to contain. Rory snorted, spit on the ground and then turned to go back inside O'Leary's.

That afternoon, Douggy took him over to see the apartment his brother-in-law had for rent. It was a good-sized one-bedroom above a Chinese restaurant on Main Street; one of the original nineteenth-century buildings in Penn Yan, with high ceilings and creaky wood floors. He agreed to take the place and move in right away, telling himself it was just temporary until he got his house back. That same evening, Douggy backed up a van in the parking lot out back. Together, they hauled out a mattress and box spring, lamps, end tables, a small TV, a floral print armchair and a box of dishes— all from his grandmother's house.

"My mom's been storing this shit since my granny died," Douggy said. "She was planning on getting rid of this stuff in a yard sale in the spring, but then when I told her you just got out of jail she said you should take it."

"Hey, that's really nice of her," Rory said. "What a sweet lady. How much she want for all this?"

"No, no she wouldn't take money from you. You know how she is. She always liked you, Rory. You always were good with the ladies. Must be that bad-boy charm of yours."

"Hey, I respect your mother, Douggy. You're parents are good people. You're right lucky, you know that?"

"Yeah, I know," he said as they maneuvered the chair through the doorway. "We got a kitchen table, too, if you want it. I can bring it by tomorrow."

"That's fantastic," Rory said. "I appreciate it."

They set the chair down by the window and Rory sat down, checking it out.

"This place looks just like my granny's," Douggy laughed.

He produced a bottle of Jim Beam and a tightly rolled joint.

"Let's celebrate your release, buddy."

Douggy cracked the seal on the bottle and sat down on the end table, his long denim-clad legs sticking out awkwardly. He poured shots into china teacups from in the box. After a moment, he said, "Hey, whatever happened to that broad you were seeing before you got popped? Connie? I haven't seen her around. She wait for you or what?"

"Got rid of the bitch. Too much trouble." Rory took a whiff of the whiskey in his cup and then gulped it down. He let out an exaggerated gasp and then asked, "and what about that crazy one you were seeing last? Amy? She still around?"

"No, thank fuck. Ditched that psycho bitch from hell," Douggy said, tossing back the shot in his teacup and smacking it down on the end table. He let out a burp, tapping his chest with his fist, and said, "she was a fate worse than death, I tell ya. But we stayed friends, for my own personal safety. I subscribe to the philosophy of keeping your friends close and your enemies closer. That way, I always know exactly where she is at any given time. And I know that she's not hiding underneath my bed with a knife, trying to kill me."

Rory threw back his head and laughed.

"Yeah, she's completely nuts," Douggy said. "You know when you get in a huge fight with your woman and it's at the point where you've got to leave the room before you do something you might regret? I'd just go take a walk and try to cool off and here she is running after me on the street yelling how she's not done with me yet. Can you believe that shit? Crazy fucking broad."

"Aye. You know, Robert Plant had it right when he said the soul of a woman was created below." Rory laughed and swallowed a mouthful of whiskey, then said. "So, tell me what my old chum, Simon's, been up to?"

Douggy smirked. "He's living high on the hog. Pays to be a police informant. I'm surprised the cocksucker has the balls to show his face around town. Everyone knows not to trust him now. He's still got that house out on Lincoln Avenue, still got his cars, that boat of his. He's not all squeaky clean, though. Hear he's running some check-cashing scam, credit cards, too. Making himself a shit load of money. Him and his in-laws. Got the whole goddamn family in on it."

"Awk, so many douche bags, so few sledgehammers."

"You got that look in your eyes," Douggy said. "I can see the wheels turning."

Rory grinned, leaned forward, and lit the end of the joint in Douggy's lips with his Zippo. "You think you know me so well."

"That I do, my friend."

"The fucker owes me big time."

"He really fucked you over, man."

Rory took the joint from him, inhaled a deep drag and held it in his lungs. He leaned back in the chair, blew out a long stream of smoke at the ceiling, and said, "And I'm going to catch up with the wee fag and give him a knee-capping."

Chapter
ELEVEN

The remnants of snow on the ground began to soften, and the ice was melting on Keuka Lake, ending the ice-fishing season. Gone were the groups of little blue huts that dotted the lake. Soon they would buy patio furniture, trade their boots for sandals, and barbecue on the deck. Justine was looking forward to doing some gardening, although the sheer magnitude of the property and the amount of gardening it would entail felt a bit overwhelming. There were a number of rose bushes in the gardens at the front of the house. Their dry, brown stalks stuck up from the frozen ground, and it seemed impossible they could actually regenerate themselves in the spring and come to life.

Gardening was not Justine's forte. She had lived in apartments and condos all of her life. This was entirely new to her. She would need to pick up some books and magazines to figure out what to plant. What did one put in a garden? It's not like Pamela would even know, or care. Roses, lilies, sunflowers, those little black-eyed Susans? She didn't know many other flowers. Forget-me-nots, weren't those some sort of flower? Although she didn't remember what they looked like—so much for not forgetting.

"I'm going to take Abigail for a walk around the property," Justine called to her father, who was down in the basement mudding the drywall he put up the other day. Likely, he would be at it for the rest of the morning and emerge around lunch, dusty and hungry. "I'll be back in a few, okay?"

"All right. Leave a trail of bread crumbs so you don't get lost out there in the woods," he called up the stairs. "And watch out for wolves dressed as grandmothers."

"Thanks for the tip, Dad. I'll be sure to plant my corn early, too," she said, laughing to herself.

She wandered into the living room and smiled at her daughter, who lay on her back in her playpen, her little feet pedaling in the air.

"Let's go for a walk, baby." Justine picked her up and set about dressing her in her snowsuit, hat and mittens. She put on her own ski jacket, boots, mitts and a pair of fuzzy earmuffs, her long hair hanging down her back. From the garage, she retrieved the baby's sled, put a fluffy blanket and a little pillow inside, and tucked Abigail in. The sled was one of those old-fashioned wooden ones, varnished maple with red trim, and three wood slats bending around the back to hold little ones inside. Justine had had one just like it when she was a little girl. There was a vague memory of her mother pulling her along the snow-covered sidewalks in their neighborhood in Brooklyn. They'd lived in a small apartment with a gray parrot named Ramses, just down the street from the hair salon her mom had owned. Justine spent years hanging around the salon after school, sitting behind the desk coloring, or playing on the computer. Even today, the smell of hair color and perm lotion could stir up her emotions.

Abigail made happy gurgling sounds as Justine pulled her over the slopes and hills. Their breath emerged in clouds of steam in the crisp air. The sun shone brilliantly on the lake, streaming though dark tree branches, glimmering over the melting ice and making it look like a bed of smashed glass. She imagined Abigail's sled careening out of control down the hill. It would crash through the ice into the freezing cold water. What if she lost her grip on the sled and that happened?

The pain in her chest was like an icicle stab to the heart, and Justine crumpled inwardly. When was the last time she took her medication? She had run out over a week ago. But she had been feeling okay. She could handle things just fine without being drugged. The pills didn't do much anyway, just made her feel weird. All she wanted was to feel like herself again.

She realized she was holding her breath and she knew she needed to get a grip on herself. Trust. She had to trust, that was all. She didn't need any fucking pills. There was nothing to be afraid of. Abigail was safe and so was she. Nothing was going to happen to them. Everything was fine. They would be okay. She took deep breaths, willing her heart to stop pounding.

The sun hurt her eyes, and the melting snow sucked at her boots. Patches of yellow grass revealed themselves, wet and soggy. A little face peeked at her from behind a shrub. A kitten.

"Hey, kitty, come here. Psss, pssss, pssss."

The animal looked at her with terrified eyes, and then leapt into the woods. How the hell did it end up out here all alone? Must have been dumped at the roadside. Poor thing. What would become of it out here by itself? Another animal, a coyote maybe, would get a hold of it. Justine shivered. She would leave some food out for it, a can of tuna and some milk, and try to rescue it.

She sang to her baby as they wandered around the property. But her thoughts were consumed with the kitten, wondering where it slept and what it did when it rained.

"The wheels on the bus go round and round, round and round..."

Maybe she would go out later and look for the kitten. It needed a home, someone to look after it. A darkness settled over her, and she thought of the friends she'd left behind in Manhattan. Maybe once spring came she would feel better about their move to the country. March felt like it was dragging on, as if winter would never end, and perhaps that accounted for her moodiness. She would have loved to take a vacation somewhere down south, but she had no money for that. A vacation was a luxury that would have to wait until she got herself a job. Once the warmer weather was here and she could get out and plant some flowers, she would feel better. God, would she have to be here that long?

Justine felt exhausted and decided to go back inside, hoping the baby would have a nap and allow her one, too. That's all she needed, just a little sleep. Thirty goddamn minutes. Was that asking too much? It was one thing to want it, but it was another for sleep to actually come. Even if she could get the time for a power nap, it didn't guarantee her mind would shut down long enough to allow her to slip away into the numbing silence of slumber. More than likely, she'd just lie there, begging desperately to be put out of the misery of her insomnia.

She rounded the corner of the garage and immediately caught sight of somebody at the end of their driveway peering into the mailbox. It couldn't be the mail delivery person. He came by in a little van. This person looked as though he was on foot. She couldn't see a car. She watched him stoop over at the waist, pull out the mail, and then stand there and shuffle through the envelopes. It was a man, definitely. He wore a long, black coat, with a cap pulled down low that hid his face. Justine waited to see what he was going to do. And then he looked up at the house and caught sight of her watching him.

"Hey!" she called out and headed toward him.

He stood still and waited as she approached. She looked back at the sled to see that Abigail had fallen asleep. As quickly as she could go without overturning the sled, she sprinted down the driveway toward the man.

When she was only about ten yards away, he tossed the envelopes back in the mailbox, turned and walked off.

"Hey, wait!"

He looked back at her and stopped. It was odd, she thought, to see someone who looked like him out here in the middle of nowhere. He seemed more like someone she would see shopping on Fifth Avenue with all the other young, rich sophisticates dressed in that long, leather coat with a fox-trim collar, rather than out here in the sticks. Still, he could pass for one of the mink-and-manure crowd with that air of refinement.

"Hello, can I help you with anything?" she asked, as she stepped up to him, thinking she sounded just like a Macy's sales clerk.

He smoked a thin cigar and stared at her without responding. She noticed, as she looked up at his face, that his eyes were the palest blue, with pupils the size of pinheads. He rubbed a finger over a small patch of a beard shaved into a line on his chin and broke into a smile that Justine found disarming.

"I'm sorry, I was looking to see if I had any mail." He spoke with an accent she couldn't place. British or Irish perhaps?

"Mail? Why would you—oh, you must be the previous owner."

Justine looked back at her baby asleep in the sled, and considered the fact that he lost the house to the bank. She didn't know what else to say to him and she felt embarrassed to be here, living in the house he had lost.

"I hope I didn't frighten you," he said.

"Not at all, I was just surprised to see somebody looking in our mailbox. What's your name?"

"Rory. Rory Madden."

"We did get some mail for you, but my stepmom sent it back."

He extended a hand. "And your name?"

"Justine Jameson." His hand was firm and he seemed to want to continue holding hers. She withdrew it after a moment and looked away.

"Justine." He repeated her name slowly and gave his head a shake as if she were somebody he had known once and was trying to place. He puffed on his cigar and stared at her.

"Are you still living in the area?" she asked.

"Aye. Well, unofficially. I'm just trying to get myself sorted out at the moment. I see you have a wee angel. She's lovely."

"Thank you."

"Can I ask you where you're from?"

"Manhattan," Justine said.

"Where did you grow up?" He smiled and she noticed that one of his incisors was crooked. It was one of those unique little flaws that people sometimes have that become an interesting attribute, like a celebrity who turns a quirky feature into a trademark. She thought of Barbra Streisand.

"I grew up in New York City," she said.

"My father lived there," he said, and paused. He studied her face so closely with those intense pale eyes that it made her self-conscious. Or maybe it was the fact that he was absolutely hot.

"You ever been to Ireland?" he asked. "That's where I'm from."

"Ireland. Well, you're a long way from home."

"You ever been?"

Justine shook her head.

"You look exactly like somebody I know...Frances."

She looked at the trees in the distance, stark and bare among the patches of melting snow. She looked back at the house to see if Pam was watching from the window. There was an expression on his face when she turned back to him, as if he expected something from her. Like he'd just asked a question and she missed it. She felt a peculiar energy emanating from him, something strong, powerful, and yet she couldn't determine the mood of it, if it was friendly or menacing. It seemed to be a mixture.

"All those roses should have been cut back in the fall." He motioned with his cigar to the gardens at the front of the house.

She looked out across the property at the thorny stalks sticking up from the earth. "There's quite a lot of them. Did you plant them yourself?"

"Aye, I did."

"Well, you must have a green thumb. Not many men are into gardening, at least not the ones I've known."

"You've got a big job ahead of you, making sure they survive. Do you know anything about caring for roses?"

"Can't say that I do."

His eyes narrowed at the gardens. He didn't speak.

"What color are they?" she asked.

"You'll just have to wait and see for yourself now, won't you? If you're here that long, girl."

She pondered that statement for a moment. Just what did he mean? She wasn't sure she wanted to ask him. He broke into another smile, exposing his crooked incisor.

"You sure you're not from Ireland?" he asked.

"New York. Born and bred."

"Well, if you get any mail for me, can you put it aside and perhaps I can come by and pick it up sometime?"

"Sure, whatever. Or if you want, you can leave me a phone number—"

"I haven't got my phone hooked up just yet."

"Okay well, I could—"

"If it's all the same, I'll just stop by again sometime," he said.

"Okay. Well, nice to meet you."

"And you, as well. Hope you're enjoying my house. Just don't get too comfortable."

She glanced back at him after she turned away, confused by his words, and noticed that his smile had faded. His eyes seemed to darken as he stared beyond her at the house.

Rory Madden's heart raced as he hurried along the trail that cut through the clearing at the edge of the property. He felt as if all the air had been sucked out of him, and he wondered if he would always do this. If he would always see traces of her everywhere—a face in a crowd that looked like hers, a glimpse of her golden hair, the sound of her laugh.

One time, about a year after her disappearance, Rory ran down a street in Belfast, chasing a girl with the same wavy hair, certain it was Frances, only to be heartbroken when he caught up to her and laid eyes on an unfamiliar face. Another time, when he was in a movie theater, he caught sight of a girl a few rows ahead that looked like Frances, cuddled next to some guy. Unable to concentrate on the movie, he interrupted the couple to ask her name. He was promptly told to go fuck himself.

One other time, he was going up an escalator in a New York shopping mall and spied a girl going down the opposite escalator who looked like she could be Frances all grown up. He ran after her, and knocked a kid to the ground in the process. But he lost her in the crowd. He searched the stores for the next hour before finally giving up.

When he was a kid, he used to pretend she was living in Hawaii. That she had run away and was dancing on the beach in one of those grass skirts with flowers in her hair, her skin golden brown from the sun. He still liked to imagine that sometimes.

After all this time, he just couldn't get the idea out of his head that one day he would find her. He wanted to see her again, to hold her again, to hear her little ringing laugh again. He wanted to save his sister. And now, here he was after all these years, still doing the same thing, thinking he would find her. Would he ever just accept that she was probably dead, and move on? The guilt was like a shard of glass that had lodged in his heart.

He had stood there dumbfounded in the driveway as the girl and her baby approached him. She was pretty, with a head of thick wavy hair, a little darker than Frances's had been. He could have sworn it was his sister, although she looked a little young. But she appeared how Frances might look in her twenties. Frances all grown up and living in his house. Could it be? It seemed impossible. It was too much of a coincidence to be real. He must be going mad. But as she neared and he studied her features more closely, the exaggerated lips, the deep-set eyes and broad forehead, he felt every hair on his body prickle. With every ounce of his being, every fiber of his flesh, he ached for her to be Frances.

She was probably dead. It was fifteen years, after all. They would have heard something by now if she were still alive.

Frances! It was all his fault!

The darkness tore at his heart. He needed to do another line. It's the only thing that seemed to keep him going.

Justine. She could have just changed her name, and she might have lost her Irish accent by now. Maybe she didn't want to be found. That, of course, was another possibility; that she was living a new life and she just didn't want to be found. It was a long shot, but he needed to know the truth. He needed to find out what happened to his sister. Even if it took the rest of his life.

Chapter
TWELVE

The next morning, Rory sat on a stool at the counter in the Penn Yan Diner on Elm Street, feeling his head pound with the beginnings of a hangover, waiting for his breakfast to be served.

"Haven't seen you around much." The geriatric woman behind the counter gave him a gummy smile as she set the plate in front of him. The smell of bacon and eggs over easy rose up and assaulted his senses. "What's wrong, you don't like my cooking anymore?"

What was her name again? Maggie? Yes, that was it: Maggie. She was the cook and sometimes the waitress, and probably the janitor and the bookkeeper too; also known as the owner. She'd gotten thicker around the waist since he'd last been in here. She placed a bottle of ketchup beside his plate, the harsh sound of glass connecting with Formica too loud in his ears, and then showed off her gleaming gums again. Any other day, he wouldn't have had a problem with her, but this morning with his tender stomach debating whether it could even handle the gelatinous globs on his plate and his head feeling as if the whole River Dance troupe were using his skull as a rehearsal hall, he just wasn't coping well.

"I love your cooking, darling," Rory managed, forcing the words out. "You make the best damn breakfast in all of New York State. I missed your cooking more than I missed my mum's."

It hurt to smile, but he did anyway. He winked at the woman and that hurt, too.

"Ahh, you say the sweetest things."

"Only 'cause it's true."

"More coffee for you, Love?"

"Aye, I think I'm still down a pint."

"Well, it's good to see our old customers coming back."

"Good to be back." He raised his coffee cup in a toast when she'd finished pouring.

Once he'd succeeded in getting the eggs into his stomach, he actually felt better. The headache had subsided, the nausea was gone, and the caffeine woke him up. He'd always enjoyed coming here for that "down home cooking," as Americans liked to call it. But minutes later, as he was driving down the road with the charcoal sky rising above the hills in the distance, a dreary mood surfaced inside of him.

Rory stood in a vacant parking lot off Highway 54A, at the edge of Keuka Park. Blackened trees like dead sticks, and straw that was once green grass stitched the roadside, the discarded shell of last year's living, breathing summer. He hated this time of year, just after the winter thaw, before the spring, when everything was barren and desolate. He turned his attention to the afternoon sun that shimmered over the water, sparkling on the choppy surface. It shined on the lawyer's bald dome and reflected in his sunglasses.

"Got the rest of my money?" Rory said.

Blackmore held up a plastic shopping bag as he closed the door of his Cadillac, stretching an arm toward him without saying a word. He was shaking visibly, the plastic of the bag rustling in his leather-gloved hand. Blackmore looked as if he might piss himself.

Rory took the bag from him and looked the fat man up and down, thinking how he resembled an undertaker in his black suit and long coat. Rory looked inside the bag, heavy with the bundles of cash secured in paper bands, but didn't feel a sense of relief or justice the way he had expected. He felt only anger. This man was the reason he was living in a drafty, one-bedroom apartment above a Chinese restaurant, the stench of fried food and the noise of late-night drunken idiots leaching up into his living room. He was the cause of all the shit in Rory's life.

"If you'd been an honest lawyer in the first place, you wouldn't be in this mess, would you now? And I'd be back living in my house," Rory said, moving aside his leather coat, which he wore like a cape, and exposing the shotgun he held beside his leg.

Blackmore put his hands in the air. "Please, Rory. I've given you your money."

"How about you get me back my house?" He lifted the gun and pointed it at the lawyer's chest.

"I...I would if I could. God, I'm so sorry. I'm so sorry about everything. I thought you were getting deported to Ireland, Rory. I thought they would take your house anyway under civil forfeiture laws once you were convicted. I never thought you—"

"So, you figured I never had a snow ball's chance in hell of getting off at all, did you?"

"You didn't have a defense, you—"

"Maybe if you were a better lawyer you would have checked out the date on that search warrant."

"You're right, I should have checked. I'm so sorry."

"So, as it turns out, it was a good thing I had to get a new lawyer, wasn't it? Someone who knew what the fuck they were doing."

Blackmore started to cry, high-pitched sobs like a little girl. Rory smirked and sucked his teeth.

"You're fucking pathetic. You think you can just say you're sorry and everything will be fine?"

"Please, please, just let me go. I've got a family who needs me. I know I screwed you over, Rory. I'm truly sorry, I—"

"You're sorry, is that right? The only reason you're sorry is because I caught up with you, you dumb fuck. That's what you're really sorry about, now isn't that right? Didn't I tell you you were a dead man? Didn't I fucking tell you?"

"I can get you more money. Is that what you want, Rory? D...do you—"

"Fuck you, Blackmore."

Rory pumped one round into the man's chest. He watched him drop to his knees in the gravel, hands still raised stiff in the air. He released another little sob as blood appeared on his white shirt. He fell face first into the dirt. Rory rotated his neck, letting it pop on each side, as he watched the man. He walked back to his car, got in, gave the man one last look, and peeled out onto the highway. He was late for an appointment.

"You can certainly sue the lender. Anyone can sue anyone," Verna Hargrave said as she wiped a spot of sauce that had dripped on her silk blouse with a tissue. "What you've got to prove is why you have a legitimate case against them. Generally, even if the lender did make some mistakes, it's difficult to overturn a foreclosure, especially after the appeal period. In the court's eyes, you've had your chance."

Rory stared at her from where he sat on the other side of her desk, still waiting for the good news he was certain she was about to give him. He watched her bare her stained teeth and sink them into the hamburger again, trying not to get lipstick on the bun, an impossible task, from his point of view. He heard once that women consumed, on average, six pounds of lipstick in their lifetimes. That was about the weight of his twelve gauge. People also consumed, on average, the equivalent of one entire Styrofoam cup over the course of about three years from the leaching of chemicals into their coffee, or so he had heard. Rory pondered this as he watched her jaw working on the food in her mouth.

"What if I wasn't told about the foreclosure by the bank?" he said.

"They didn't send you a mortgage foreclosure notice?"

"I received something about my mortgage when I was in jail, but what could I do? I was in jail."

"If you don't file an appearance or answer by the date specified, the court can enter a default judgment against you and then they automatically foreclose. Did you make any mortgage payments at all during that time?"

"I couldn't. Like I said, I was in jail."

"And you weren't in contact with the bank?"

Rory sighed, frustrated. He adjusted his body in the chair. "I didn't think I was even getting out. I thought I was looking at a long prison sentence, so at the time with the charges on me, keeping my house didn't seem likely."

"That's a problem," she said. "It would be one thing if we could prove they didn't notify you of their plans to foreclose, then you can argue that they failed to give you the opportunity to make payments. But the fact that you didn't even call the lender puts you in a very bad spot. It doesn't look like you have much of a case here."

"There's got to be some recourse. It's not like I didn't want to keep paying on my house. I got ripped off. My lawyer, my first lawyer, stole money from me. I had some cash that I kept in the house and I told him where it was and he stole it."

"Can you prove it?"

"Can I prove it? Why do I have to prove it?"

"Maybe you can sue him." She shrugged, dropped the squashed burger into the Styrofoam container and sipped from a straw stuck in a cup of soda. The ice made a dull churning sound as it hit the sides.

"Whatever." Rory waved a dismissive hand at her. "I got my money back. He gave it back."

"He gave it back? So, he admitted to stealing it?"

Rory nodded, feeling suddenly that all the hope in him had been sucked out. He felt like shit. Sure, he had a bit of money, but what did that mean? He wanted his property back. He'd worked so hard for so long and now he was stuck living in some stupid apartment. That's all he wanted, was just to get his house back.

"So, sue the guy," she said.

"Will it get me my house back?"

"I don't think so, but maybe you'll get a judgment against him and you can buy another one."

"I built that house myself. I designed it, hired an architect to create the plans. I was there working alongside the crew, swinging a hammer for more than a year. It's my bloody house and I want it back."

"Doesn't look like that's going to happen." Verna shook her sable curls, her mouth turned down in a frown, making her jowls more pronounced. She seemed smug, the way she leaned back in her chair and rudely picked food from her teeth with her thumbnail, like she didn't even give a shit, like she was already thinking of some other case she was working on. Rory felt like reaching across her desk and choking the life out of this crude little woman.

"So, what you're saying is you're not going to help me?"

"You don't have a case," she said. "You didn't make your mortgage payments. How on earth is that the bank's fault? What exactly do you think I can do about that? I'm just a lawyer, not a magician."

"They stole my house from me!" He pointed his finger uselessly in the air, trying to maintain his calm.

"Listen sweetheart, the best advice I can give you," Verna began in a tone that was unmistakably patronizing. "Is cut your losses and move on. To be very frank with you, you've got as much a chance of winning this case as a one-legged man in an ass-kicking contest."

Rory stared at the woman, stone faced. If he hadn't been so angry he would have laughed.

"Aye, it's going to happen. I'll get my house back, one way or the other. With or without your fucking help." Rory stood up, pushed back his chair with unnecessary force, and walked out the door of Verna Hargrave's sterile office.

Chapter
THIRTEEN

"You look tired. Do you really have to go away this weekend? Can't you call in sick?" Brett asked.

"Call in sick? Call myself and tell myself I'm not feeling well?" Pamela laughed. "Who's going to take my place?"

"There must be somebody who can pick up the slack."

"I'm the regional manager," she said. "There's nobody above me but the CEO and I'm sure she would be just thrilled if I left a roomful of new trainees with no training."

"Pamela, you work too hard. You need to relax. I can see how stressed you are. We could both stay home this weekend and just take it easy. Maybe we can paint the bedrooms together and then we can go out for dinner."

"Somebody's got to pay the bills around here, now don't they? God knows you can't," she scoffed. "What are you going to do, Brett, go down with the ship? When are you going to wake up? When are you going to cut your losses and close the damn business?"

Justine lay in bed, her window still darkened, as she listened to her parents in their room across the hall, and wondered why they didn't try to keep their voices down. Did they forget she was living back home? She realized that she should have closed her bedroom door last night before going to sleep. What time was it? She checked the clock radio. Seven-thirty in the morning. Abigail was still asleep, lying on her back in her cradle beside the bed. She watched her little chest rise and fall in the shadows, reassured. Justine turned over on her side and shut her eyes.

"Stop it. Don't," Pamela was saying, her angry words drifting out from their room.

"Come on, stop punishing me, Pamela," Brett said. "This isn't fair."

"Don't!"

"Why do you always do that?"

"I'm not in the fucking mood, all right?"

"I can't remember last time you were."

"I've got a lot of pressure on me."

"You think I don't?"

Justine got up to close the door, tiptoeing across the carpet so they wouldn't know she'd overheard anything.

"What the hell is wrong this time?" His voice was angry.

"I don't have time for this, Brett. I've got meetings today that I can't be late for. We've still got to consider traffic, as well."

Justine closed her door and got back under the covers. She wondered if their feelings for each other were, in fact, genuine. A quiet animosity had been born between them years earlier and still festered at everything unspoken. There was coolness between them that was obvious to anyone in their presence, especially to Justine.

Minutes later, unable to sleep anymore, she left Abigail asleep in her cradle. She took the baby monitor with her and wandered downstairs in her pajamas for a glass of juice and a Tylenol. She found her father making coffee in the kitchen.

"Morning, Sweets, how did you sleep last night?" He turned to her smiling, his hair spikier than usual this morning. He was dressed in a crisp white shirt she'd ironed for him yesterday and a pink tie.

Justine shrugged in response. His cologne made her head pound even harder. She felt like she had been dragged behind a pickup truck in a burlap sack for ten miles. Every part of her body ached with fatigue.

"You should be wearing your slippers." Brett motioned with his chin at her bare feet.

When the hell were her parents going to realize she was an adult?

"I don't own slippers. I always walk around in my bare feet. I have since I was a child, which I'm not anymore in case you haven't noticed."

"Did you get any sleep last night?" He looked at her sidelong as he emptied a little packet of sweetener into his cup.

"Maybe an hour this morning." She yawned. "So, you're driving to Manhattan again?"

"Yeah, I'll be back tomorrow night, though."

She gave him a look as she opened the fridge door.

"What?"

"Pam's going with you, too?"

"She's got a couple of appointments in the city, and then we'll both be back tomorrow night... Are you okay?"

"Fine."

"You don't seem fine."

"I'm fine."

"What's wrong? Tell me."

"I don't want to talk about it."

"Justine?"

"I said I don't want to talk about it!"

She poured herself a glass of orange juice, opened the bottle of Tylenol, shook two into her palm, and popped them in her mouth.

"I thought you were going to trust me, Justine."

She sighed, and gazed out through the window at the dead grass. She watched a robin swoop down and land on the soft ground; tilt its head, listening. She thought about the little kitten in the woods, wondering if it had eaten any of the tuna she'd left for it. The dish she placed outside at the garage was empty every day, but she didn't know if it was the kitten or something else feasting.

"I feel so isolated out here, Dad."

"It is quite a change."

She stared at the bird, felt tears well up.

"You'll get used to it," he said. "Give it a bit of time."

"There's nothing out here."

"Well, why don't you go into town, take a look around, do some shopping."

"I'm not the shopping type, Dad."

"You've got your music you can work on. This is the perfect place for creativity, isn't that what you said before? That the peace will help your creativity?"

"I know, but..."

"Have you even picked up your guitar since we moved here?"

She shook her head, watched the robin take flight and disappear.

"Why not?"

She shrugged.

"What is it?"

It was only five weeks since they moved in and suddenly she was questioning if she made the right decision coming out here. While she loved the solitude, the beauty of the property and the house, sometimes, usually at night, she felt unnerved. And knowing she was going to be here all day and night alone, with just her baby, set her on edge.

This wasn't like her. She was fearless, independent, and able to take care of herself. She'd overcome so much in the last few years. She was so profoundly schooled by bitter experience that all the hardships only served to make her stronger. She was a New Yorker, she reminded herself. We are a resilient lot, having lived through the trauma of 9/11. Nothing can keep us down. But then again, she had never lived on a twenty-acre property out in the middle of nowhere, surrounded by deep, dark woods that seemed creepy and foreboding. Especially on moonless nights. The woods could transmit strange and eerie sounds.

"I just feel... isolated. It's lonely here," she said, not telling him that she was afraid. She didn't want to give into those feelings, and voicing them would only make them seem so much more real.

"Well...why don't you take the baby and go visit your grandma? She'd like that."

"Maybe." She swallowed back the tears.

"She might not have that much time left, you know?"

"I'm aware of that, Dad."

"You know, I think it's just going to take a little while to settle in out here. There's always a period of adjustment following any major change, and this really is a major change, moving out here. For all of us. Just give it a bit of time, Sweets. It will feel like home soon enough, you'll see."

"Sure, whatever." Justine sipped her orange juice as the sensation of being submerged under water, fighting for breath, engulfed her.

"You could always come to the city with us. See some of your friends."

"Maybe next time." She shrugged, thinking it might just make her feel worse.

She thought about her mother and how if she hadn't died, then Justine wouldn't have had to move in with her father. She would never have gone to the psych hospital and she would never have met Keith and gotten herself knocked up. And she would never have had to move out here in the middle of fucking nowhere and lose her marbles the way she knew she was doing.

She often thought of pivotal points in her life and how everyone's decisions, as simple or as personal as they might seem, could alter the direction of other people's lives so profoundly. It was easy to trace it all back through the years and see, for instance, how her mother's decision to dump Brett had allowed him to meet Pamela. If Pamela hadn't married Brett, then she might not have moved to New York City and brought Allison with her. Allison might still be alive today, living with Pamela, or off somewhere preparing to start college—if Justine's mother had never made the choice to break up with Brett.

Justine remembered the text message on Pamela's phone the other day. "Hey Dad? Do you and Pam know a guy named Russ?"

"Russ? Not sure. What's his last name?"

"I don't know."

"So why do you ask?"

"No reason. I just happened to see Pam's phone the other day when she forgot it here. It's not like I was snooping or anything like that, I just happened to notice when the screen lit up with a text message and so I read it and it was from somebody named Russ."

"Oh…well what did it say?" Brett crossed his eyebrows, fixing his eyes on her.

"I don't know. Something about how they were meeting that day. It sounded like they were well acquainted, I guess you could say. So, since I've never heard of him before, I was just wondering who he was."

"Sounds to me like you're concerned about it, Justine. What exactly did this message say?"

"Look, Dad, I'm sure it's nothing. I don't mean to be making a big deal out of it."

"What did it say?"

"Just like…'Can't wait to see you,' and he referred to her as 'sexy lady.'"

Brett took a sip of his coffee and made a face as if he'd just tasted something disgusting. He turned toward the counter, and poured another half package of sweetener into his cup.

"Well, I guess I'll have to ask her about it," he said, twirling a spoon inside his coffee.

"I'm sure it's just somebody from her office goofing around or something like that. Don't say I was the one who told you, Dad."

"I won't. Thanks for telling me. Hey?"

"What?"

"I love you," he said.

There was something in his eyes that caused her to pause. Something unfamiliar and more than a little disturbing. He seemed like a stranger suddenly. What was happening to her? A moment later, she forced a smile.

Chapter
FOURTEEN

Rory slowed in front of the house on Welker Road. There was no car in the driveway today. They must be at work. He parked the Challenger about two hundred feet down the road. He tucked his handgun into the waistband of his jeans and walked back toward the house. The temperature had risen considerably in the last couple of days, and melted the last traces of snow. The earth possessed that warm smell of spring getting ready to come to life. He could feel it now, just on the edge. It was beautiful here in the summer. He wanted to be back here before then. He *would* be back here before then.

He stood on the road at the bottom of the driveway, and gazed through the trees at his house, thinking how magnificent it was. He had enough cash to start over, get his renovation business going again, and make a living without selling drugs—at least for now. If something promising came down the pipeline in the future, he might want to make some extra money. For now, he needed to lay low. Appear legit.

He wandered up the driveway to the front door and peered in the window. He could see straight through the house and out the windows to the deck. He looked for the young woman, Justine. He wanted to see if she wore the locket. Then, for sure, he would know the truth.

He stepped around to the back of the house and then heard a door close. It was the front door. From his position behind an old, dying oak tree that had been gouged by lightening last summer, Rory caught sight of Justine, and it struck him like a blow. All he could think of was Frances and the idea, the irresolute hope, that he'd found her. He watched her walk down the driveway, pulling her baby in a wagon. He watched as they retreated up the road and disappeared. Then he went back around the side of the house and stepped up to the deck. He turned the handle on the back door. Locked, just like he figured it would be. He went around to the other side and checked the basement window. Unlocked. Stroke of luck. With a gentle kick, the screen pushed in and fell to the floor with a clatter of aluminum on concrete. He got down on his stomach on the damp earth, and shimmied feet first through the opening. He closed the window, but left it unlocked.

Rory chuckled to himself as he brushed dirt from his shirt and looked around. There were a few cardboard boxes down here, but nothing else. He looked at the partially finished walls; drywall and insulation that he had erected—noticing that it recently had been worked on—and all his plans to finish the basement rushed back to him. He wanted to make this a party room with a wet bar, a pool table, a jukebox and a vintage pinball machine or two. He still would, he reminded himself. Heading up the staircase, he opened the basement door, walked down the hallway, and wandered into the kitchen. There was a table and chairs sitting in front of the kitchen window with a basket of yellow apples in the center. On the counter by the sink sat a clay pot of herbs. Dishtowels with roosters on the front graced the wrought-iron railing at the side of the counter. On the stove was a pan with some drying scrambled eggs. Dirty dishes filled the sink. He stood peering around, thinking how odd it was to see other people's stuff here in his house.

From the fridge he got himself a bottle of water and gulped it down, still feeling dehydrated from his night of drinking. He lifted an apple from the table, took a huge bite, and then wandered into the living room. It was decorated with a cinnamon-colored leather sofa and chairs. There were two animal-print area rugs on the wood floors. He ran a hand over the mantle of the fireplace, admiring the brickwork he had watched being constructed, and thought what a beautiful job the masons had done. It was the focal point of the entire room. He sat in one of the leather chairs, feeling the hard metal of his gun press into the small of his back, and put his feet on the coffee table. With the remote, he turned on the television, flipped the channels, and stopped it on Oprah. He ate his apple, enjoying being in his house.

A moment later, his apple chewed, he turned off the television, and set the apple core on the edge of the coffee table. He looked at the spot on the floor by the back door and an image of Connie's lifeless body appeared in his mind. He could see her lying there like a broken doll, the blood pool widening around her skull. He could see those beautiful, long legs of hers underneath the cotton summer dress that fell around the tops of her thighs. It's not that he had wanted to kill her. He certainly hadn't planned it. He hadn't taken pleasure in it. She just pushed him over the edge and he simply snapped.

"You've got to do the right thing here, Rory, and marry me. It's your responsibility, too. You did this to me, Rory." Connie's words echoed in his head.

She had looked at him that morning with those pleading eyes of hers, like some half-starved dog wanting to follow him home. They were deep into another argument, and he stopped yelling for a moment to study her damaged face; the purple circles underneath her eyes, the blood congealed in her split bottom lip, the bruises on her arms and legs from days earlier, now yellow at the edges, and he realized she looked exactly like his mother. It was as if he was looking at a ghost from his past come back to haunt him. The revelation hit him like a bomb. His mother; her face like some retired boxer's, deadening herself with alcohol and pills, a waste of skin, a parasite living on the dole, a pathetic excuse for a parent. Looking at Connie, seeing this history in his life repeat itself, he felt sick. As if he wanted that stupid bitch to be the mother of his kid. She couldn't even look after herself. She would make a rotten parent, just like his mother. He wanted nothing more than to be rid of her, toss her away like the human garbage she was, purge every trace of her and his mother from himself. Vomit them both back up.

He didn't regret killing Connie. He hadn't loved her, hadn't wanted her in his life. His regret was that he was forced into a position in which he became so enraged that he killed her. His regret also, was that there were countless women in the world just like her. No one to care about them, no one to love them, least of all the women, themselves.

He stood up, stretched his arms in the air, and moved over to the acoustic guitar propped on a stand in front of the window. He plucked a string with his thumbnail and listened as a solitary note rose up and slowly died in the still air around him. He walked up the curved staircase with the fancy twisted wrought-iron railing he had selected himself.

Outside the master bedroom, he stood in the doorway looking at the furniture. He wondered where they kept the family photo albums. If he were able to see pictures of this woman as a girl, he would know for certain if it was Frances. He looked under the bed, and searched for photo albums or perhaps a shoebox of loose photographs, but found only dust balls. He searched the shelves of the closet. He looked in a couple of cardboard boxes that were yet to be unpacked.

He went into the room across the hall. This must be Justine's room. He opened and closed the drawers of the dresser, stopping to run his fingers over the lacy bras and panties he found. There was a jewelry box on the dresser—a lacquered, rectangular box with an Oriental design on the lid.

His mother had had a similar one with white cranes on top. She had bought it on a trip to New York City, which is where she met his father. He came to Ireland, where they married and bought a house on the slopes of the Cave Hill in Belfast. And then, once Rory and Frances were born, he tired of their domestic existence and left for the States, abandoning all of them.

A tune played as he lifted the lid and looked inside. He poked around the chains and earrings, looking for the locket. It had been a birthday present to Frances from their grandmother. Frances had pressed a little photo of the old woman inside the locket. She'd kept little secret notes inside, too.

The music stopped as he closed the lid on the jewelry box. There was another ceramic container with a lid in the shape of a star embedded with blue rhinestones. Maybe that was where she kept the locket. He fingered the collection of earrings, not finding it. Maybe he was grasping at straws to think this woman could actually be Frances. Yet he couldn't get the idea out of his head, even if it was farfetched.

In a drawer in the night table, he found a flat floral-print box. He pulled it out, sat on the edge of the bed, and opened it up. It was a baby book full of pictures. He knew as he looked at them that they were all photos of Justine's baby. Cute, but no cigar. He closed it up and replaced it in the drawer.

Out of the room he wandered and opened the door down the hall. It was the baby's room. The air was scented with powder. He smiled as he looked around at the stuffed animals; the soft color of the walls; the bedding inside the white crib; the framed painted pictures of zoo animals, zebras, tigers, giraffes. Such innocence.

"Awk, how lovely," he said and closed the door again.

Downstairs, he peeked through one of the narrow windows at the side of the front door to see if he could catch sight of the woman and her baby returning. There was no sign of them. In the living room, he spied a glass-framed picture on an end table and lifted it. It was Justine. He turned the frame over, opened up the back, and removed her picture. He set the frame back on the table and stared down at the photo in his hand. She was beautiful, with her big blue eyes, and that charming smile. Frances had blue eyes.

Rory tucked the picture in his shirt pocket. He should leave now. There were things to do.

Back at his apartment, Rory sat in the floral-print armchair. He peered out the window at the sun as it set in a gray sky. He lifted the receiver of the new phone that had just been hooked up and called Douggy.

"Hey buddy, how's it going?" Douggy asked.

"Put on your Dick Tracy hat," Rory said. "I got something for you to check out, man."

"Cool. What's up? Is it related to the Frances Madden case?"

"Aye, it might very well be. There's a woman by the name of Justine Jameson living in my house. Her parent's names are Brett and Pamela, according to their mail. They're from Manhattan. Anyway, I'd like to find out everything I can on Justine and her parents. Any dirt on them, any questionable move they make I want to know. I want to know everything I can about these people."

"I'm on it, buddy. Can you spell the last name for me?"

Rory spelled out the last name.

"All right, give me a day or two. I'll find out everything I can. Just leave it in my capable hands."

Rory replaced the receiver, stood up and moved over to the window. He struggled to lift the heavy window, stiff in its old, wood frame, and cracked it a few inches, letting in the noise of traffic and barking dogs. The scent of last season's dead leaves and the earth waking up to a new spring drifted in on a cool wind, and saturated the air. He watched the clouds rise above the rooftops in the distance.

Then he remembered Frances, and a wave of anger moved through him.

Chapter
FIFTEEN

"Let's make an appointment with the doctor, Justine. Maybe you need to increase the dosage on your meds, or maybe he can prescribe something else," Brett said over the phone.

"Prescribe something? Like what? There's a pill for someone breaking into your house?"

"I mean like Paxil or something, or a tranquilizer."

"I'm not crazy, Daddy. And I'm not depressed, either. I don't need medication. Maybe I need you to come home," she said, as she paced the living room floor with the phone pressed to her ear.

"Okay, look. I'll try and cut things short around here if I can, and get home in the morning. But I'll have to talk to Pamela. I know she's got some meetings in the afternoon."

"You don't believe me, do you?"

"Believe you?"

"You don't believe someone broke into our house."

"Justine, it's not that I don't believe what you're telling me. I just think there's another explanation. You said nothing was taken, just the front door was left unlocked."

"I locked that fucking door! I know I locked it!"

Brett sighed over the line. "Aside from the door being unlocked, what else happened? You said you found an apple core, right?"

"There was an apple core sitting on the coffee table. I didn't put it there, Dad, and unless you or Pam did, there's no way Abigail did, so how do you explain that?"

"Maybe you ate the apple and forgot, I don't know."

"I told you I didn't! I didn't put it there!"

"Okay, maybe it was Pam, then."

"I just called her and asked and she said it wasn't her. She told me to call you." Justine felt suddenly cold. Her body was shaking. She felt out of control, on the edge of panic.

"Aside from the apple and the front door being unlocked, is there anything else that's been disturbed or taken?"

"I don't know. Nothing that I can see."

"Okay, well, perhaps I ate the apple this morning myself and forgot, I don't know. It's possible. I mean why would somebody break into our house just to eat an apple? Who would do that?"

"I don't know."

"Well, why would he just come in and not take anything?"

"I don't know, Dad."

"How would he get in if the doors are locked?"

"I don't fucking know! Why are you asking me these questions? Why don't you come home and try and figure it out for yourself?"

"I see you've had some time here to work yourself up about this. Have you been taking your medication every day, Justine?"

"You know what? Just fucking stay in Manhattan. I don't give a shit." She slammed the phone down. When she turned around her gaze landed on the glass picture frame on the end table. Her photograph was gone. Why was the picture of herself not there?

Abigail, having heard her mother's angry voice, started to cry. Justine looked at the baby in her playpen and sighed, rubbing a hand across her face. And then she cried herself.

The sensation of being lost, suspended in some other dimension, trapped between reality and insanity, gripped her in that moment. She realized then that her father would never completely trust her. The stint in the psych ward had doomed her forever to being unreliable. Being labeled as a lunatic was to have your very humanity stripped from you. And Justine knew the stigma was a key element that could make psychiatric diagnosis a self-fulfilling prophecy.

After wiping her tears, she took a deep breath and picked up her crying baby.

"It's okay, baby. It's okay. Mama's here now," she sang, patting her back and walking with a gentle, swaying motion.

She breathed in Abigail's warm scent, pressing her lips next to her downy hair, as images of Fair Oaks Psychiatric Hospital floated into her thoughts like phantoms hovering over her shoulder. Being inside the psych ward had been completely surreal. The people working there were power-ful, soulless, and angry. She felt patronized and disempowered by her psy-chiatrists. The nurses were cynical and frightening, too busy to talk to the patients. She was only fourteen when she went into the psych hospital in New Jersey, where they diagnosed her as having "borderline personality dis-order," a catchall label psychiatrists slap on people who don't fit more a spe-cific diagnostic category. The one thing Justine had found so unusual about Fair Oaks was that they locked up her dental floss and her hair straightener, yet allowed her to keep her sneakers in her room. Couldn't sneaker laces have inflicted just as much damage? Perhaps it was just an oversight on the part of the staff, but she always thought that was odd.

Every day, there was two group sessions that were more like lectures dis-guised as therapy. There was recreation every afternoon, when the patients were allowed to play ping-pong, watch television, or glue macaroni to pie plates. She chose the macaroni. Every morning, the patients were awakened at six and made to stand in line for their medication. Justine was so heav-ily dosed on a cocktail of Halodol, Luvox, Risperdal, and a couple of other drugs that there were some mornings she couldn't walk, let alone stand in a line. There was a two-week period she actually blacked out and couldn't see—other than hallucinations—or speak. On one occasion, overmedica-tion left her groveling on the floor like an injured animal, unable to stand up or even form words. When she refused the medications, they strapped her down to the bed and gave her an IV of Halodol.

Abigail had stopped crying. Justine continued to walk and sway with her, feeling soothed, herself, by the motion, humming softly. She glanced at her guitar in its stand against the window. When was the last time she'd picked it up? She couldn't remember. Something about it felt painful, like visiting an old lover who'd broken your heart and it still hadn't mended. What had happened to her plans to get back to writing music? She felt scattered living out here, so far from civilization. How was it possible to feel happy and optimistic one moment and then simply downhearted in the next?

She had the sensation of sinking. It was as if her mind was splitting down the middle. Had someone really been in the house, or had she imag-ined it? Was it possible she simply left the door unlocked? Perhaps she should call the police. She didn't feel the least bit safe out here in the middle of nowhere. Justine put the baby back into her playpen and stuck the soother in her mouth. Then, in the kitchen she took a sharp knife from the block on the counter, comforted by the feel of it in her hand. At that moment, she heard a strange noise. It came from out back, a high-pitched wailing.

She crossed the room with the knife in her hand and tried to peer out the windows but it was dark; she couldn't see a thing except the reflection of herself in the glass. She wrenched open the back door, her heart pounding, and stood looking into the woods, ready to take on whoever was out there. The frigid air rushed over her body.

There! Something moved in the darkness!

She waited for it to appear again, and then sucked in a breath as the gray people emerged from behind the trees. They moved in unison, at least a dozen of them, as if they were one, and stood staring at her with their hollow eyes; bizarre clay creatures with elongated limbs, sexless, faceless, with nothing more than black holes in their faces, like bowling balls. Justine slammed the door and backed up. Her heart pulsated wildly throughout her entire body, pounding in her ears like angry marching feet. She felt her legs weaken. What the hell did they want from her? Who the hell were they? God!

Her body stiffened as she heard them in the walls all around her. They began to scratch, their voices rising up in loud whispers like a rush of wind seeming to come from a great distance. They cried out to her. *They're coming for you, Justine. They're coming for you and the baby. Save yourself, Justine! Save yourself! Save yourself!*

The voices stopped. Her vision came into sharp focus all at once, allowing her to see the truth before her. What the hell just happened? It was as if she had slipped through a door inside her mind; a place that was cut off from reality, suspended in time and space. Some alternate existence. She felt confused.

What was happening to her? Was she losing her mind?

Chapter
SIXTEEN

Pamela flipped her cell phone closed and looked out at the darkenss through the passenger window.

"How's your mother?" Brett asked, gazing at the broken line in the middle of the blacktop, reflecting in his headlights. "She asking you to come see her?"

"Do you even have to ask? Who else has she got? Those two nurses are nothing but functionaries."

"Why don't you try calling your sister or your brothers—"

"Please, as if they care," Pamela said. "I'm handling it fine myself."

"I just don't see why you always have to be the one responsible for everything—"

"It's just the way it is, Brett. You have to rely on yourself when it comes right down to it. People always say they'll come through for you, but in the end, it's only yourself you can really trust to take care of you," she said, searching through her handbag. She yanked out items and dumped them on her lap, looking annoyed. "Nobody else can truly be relied upon, not completely. The one thing people can be relied upon to do is disappoint. Believe me I know, I've been depending on just myself all my life."

Brett was silent, allowing her words to seep inside of him, knowing they were directed at him. He watched as she upended her handbag and dumped its contents at her feet. She let out a growl and then reached down to scoop up her pack of cigarettes. She pulled one out, lit it, took a long drag, and then leaned back on the seat, leaving the stuff on the floor that her purse had barfed up.

After a moment, he cleared his throat and then cracked her window a half inch. "There's no reason you can't ask them to pitch in financially," he said.

"That's not going to happen," she said. "Between them all, they've never pitched in a dime before, so why should they start now? I guess they're just used to me taking care of everything, like I've always done. They figure that's just my role. Suppose it is."

The puppy whimpered in the pet carrier in the back seat as Brett and Pamela headed north on Highway 81 through Pennsylvania. He turned the radio to the Sinatra station and cranked the volume on a Tony Bennett song, allowing his smooth voice to fill the car, hoping it would calm the pup.

They drove in silence for a few minutes. He knew Pamela was still angry at having to head home early and cancel her next day's appointments.

He took in a deep breath and let it out slowly, thinking of his daughter, worrying about what the future held for her. Maybe if she got back into her music, she would have some sort of direction. But for now it was best that she was living at home with them. After all, she was only seventeen, turning eighteen in another week. There was plenty of time for her to think of her future and a career. For now, being a mother to her child was what was important. Everything had its season.

Brett thought of Justine's independent nature, knowing that living at home with them was tough for her. He admired his daughter's rebellious heart and creative soul. She possessed the kind of qualities, even at a young age, that he wanted to emulate—her courage, her confidence, her self-awareness, and her fiery determination. And yet she was also complex, containing characteristics that seemed in complete opposition. She was a sensitive soul who felt things deeply, worried sometimes over trivial things, over analyzed, and fretted about issues that often didn't concern her. Likely she had inherited these qualities from him. But this measure of fragility in her, so paradoxical, left him bewildered. Perhaps it had evolved from enduring so much trauma as a child.

Sometimes he wondered if it would have been easier for Justine to lose her mother if he had been in her life from the beginning, if her mother had not made the decision to give birth to her and raise her in secrecy. It actually came as no surprise to Brett when Jenny called him up one day and confessed the truth, that he had a daughter. Brett had been twenty-six when he met Jenn. She was ten years older. During their short, tumultuous relationship, she talked constantly about her wish to have a baby, even saying she would have one on her own.

Brett gazed at the painted lines of the road, listening absently as a Frank Sinatra song came on, and filled the air aorund them. He glanced at Pamela. "I'm worried about Justine," he said. "I'm really concerned about her mental state. I think she needs to be back on her meds."

"She needs more than meds. And just so you know, I'm not cleaning up after that animal you got her."

"Nobody's asking you to, Pam." Brett said, "Sometimes I wonder if we made the right decision bringing her out there. You know, Justine's a city girl. We should have expected she would feel this way. I guess I was just hoping she'd come to like it."

Was buying that house a good decision? He wasn't sure. Especially with the economy the way it was. His business had suffered more losses than he ever anticipated in recent years. Global warming was to blame. People just weren't buying boots for subzero temperatures as much as they used to, and losing two major contracts, one with the U.S Army, forced a dozen layoffs at his plant. And then with the economic crisis, his business took a wallop. They were now relying completely on Pam's income. It was inevitable that he would have to close down. But he just wasn't ready to let it go. That would mean admitting defeat. Where would that leave him?

"I don't know why you feel you owe her, Brett. She's a grown woman now, she should be supporting herself. I've supported myself since I was sixteen. And my mother and all my brothers and sisters, too. Sixteen years old. Nobody helped me out." Pamela took a drag on her cigarette, inhaled sharply, and continued. "And even at the age of thirteen, I was contributing to the household income. Did you know that? I gave all my babysitting money to my mother to pay for groceries."

There was an edge in her voice that made it sound like she was talking to a disobedient child, as if she blamed Brett for the situation. Of course she blamed him. He was a convenient punching bag.

"She's my daughter, for God's sake," Brett said. "I'm not going to turn her and the baby out on the street. Is that what you want, Pam?"

"She shouldn't have left Keith. Jesus, what's wrong with people these days? Doesn't commitment mean anything anymore? I mean they weren't officially married, but they were, for all intents and purposes," Pam said. "Where's the loyalty?"

She was a fine one to talk about marriage that way, Brett thought bitterly. Talk about a hypocrite! Could she forget their history so easily? How was it she could put it all behind her that way, when it was always playing in the back of his mind, those times that had nearly severed their marriage. And yet he didn't want to resent her; tried hard not to blame her. Mostly he blamed himself, for not being the kind of man his wife wanted in a husband. He knew it was true; she didn't need to voice it. But the disappointment was mutual.

A memory came to him with an agonizing clairity. Him standing outside of a hotel room in Niagara Falls, banging on the door. What was that, five or six years ago now? It was just before Allison's death. Pam had made the mistake of not logging out of her email account on their home computer, and he found all the incriminating evidence of what he'd thought was an affair. She had told him she was going on a business trip for the weekend. As it turned out, it was business—just not the kind he had assumed.

Like an idiot, Brett had stood at the hotel room door and pleaded with the man who answered it, blubbering about how Pamela was all he had, and how he needed her, and how they had two little girls who needed their mother. Brett had rushed into the room when he saw her inside, sitting on the bed with a sheet wrapped around her. Like some fool in a melodramatic romance movie, he broke down in tears and begged her not to throw it all away. He pleaded with her to come home with him, telling her how much he needed her.

The man who'd answered the door started to complain and looked indignant. Brett couldn't help feeling that he should be the one who was angry, but the pain was so overwhelming that all he could do was cry. Pamela told the man to go down to the hotel bar and have a drink while she sorted things out.

After the man reluctantly left, she slipped her arms into her dress in silence, a grave look on her face, as she did up the buttons. She moved over to the mirrored dresser and ran her long nails through her hair. Then she told him the truth. The man was paying her.

Brett had felt like such a fool standing there as the humiliation welled up in him. Without saying another word, he turned and stormed out the door.

He tried hard to understand. He knew Pamela had issues about money. Likely from being raised in poverty and being the eldest child, feeling it was her responsibility to help. He knew she had been supporting her mother and her daughter for years, from the age of sixteen when she gave birth to Allison. And he knew she had worked as a call girl back then to bring in money. Was he so foolish as to assume she would give it up once they were married? He must have been naïve, at any rate.

He was a good man, Brett reasoned. He was a good father and he was a good husband to Pamela, even if their marriage was void of romance these days. But in spite of his disappointments, he did not walk out on his family. Even through his wife's stints in prostitution, going back into the business she swore she would give up, he hung in there, forgave her, and tried to forget as best as he could.

Brett never left when things got tough, never gave up or abandoned them. Wasn't that what a good man was supposed to do? He stayed through all the hard times, through Allison's death—something for which he felt personally responsible and for which, he knew, Pamela blamed him also. He had stayed in spite of his discontentment, supporting his wife and family, and he hadn't even asked her about this Russ person who'd sent her the suggestive text message that his daughter seemed so concerned about. Didn't he deserve a reward for that? Didn't he deserve a little something for himself once in a while for all that he did, all that he endured and sacrificed?

An image of Lorena pushed into his thoughts. He could almost smell her perfume; taste the heat of her skin. Brett glanced at his wife, slumped in the passenger seat with her eyes closed. Nine years with a woman who had never completely respected or appreciated him. Certainly he deserved some compensation. At the same time, he felt enormous guilt for what he was doing. It was wrong. He knew that now that they had left Manhattan and he inevitably would have to close his business, things with Lorena would end, as well. It was for the best. The entire affair left him feeling ashamed and dirty. It's not the way he was raised. It shocked him that he had allowed it to happen in the first place.

He was a good man. He had done everything he was supposed to. All his life. Since he was a child. He listened to his parents, played by the rules, helped around the house, studied hard, and got good grades in school. He never smoked or drank or did drugs. He worked hard and saved his money. He respected women as his father had taught him. He kept his nose in his textbooks at college and graduated with a degree in finance, and then he got a loan and opened his own business. How was it he had done everything right—everything that was expected of him, never cheated people or hurt anyone—and still he wound up with a failing business, facing financial ruin, and in a marriage that felt like a one-way street? Of course, he knew the answer. There were no guarantees in life. Things didn't magically fall into place just because you were a good person and worked hard. There was no reward for that. Life wasn't designed to be fair or just. No matter what you did, you would still get burned eventually, in one way or another. That was just the nature of life. There were no guarantees. End of story.

Still, sometimes he couldn't accept that. He couldn't accept that everything he'd grown up believing in was just his own idealism. He thought of himself as a good man, that was the bottom line, and that had to mean something. With every fiber of his being, he knew this had to mean something.

"Happy birthday!" Brett said as he came through the front door hours later.

Justine turned with the baby in her arms to see the little bundle of brown fur her father was holding.

"Oh, Daddy! A chocolate lab? How did you know? He's adorable!"

"You've been telling me for years that you've always wanted a chocolate lab."

Pamela emerged behind him, carrying their bags, an annoyed look etched in the lines of her face. She didn't say a word, just headed toward the dining room cabinet and poured herself a glass of wine.

"He's just ten weeks old." Brett smiled and held the puppy out to her. It licked at her face, his little whip of a tail slapping back and forth. Abigail watched him in fascination, her blue eyes wide with wonder. She reached a hand toward him, and let out a delighted squeal when the dog licked her cheek.

"He likes you Abby-girl," Brett said. "Here, trade me babies."

He took Abigail from her arms. Justine lifted the puppy and hoisted him in the air to look at him.

"Is it a boy?"

"It's a boy."

"What should we call him?"

"I was thinking he looks like a Duke. But it's your birthday, so you can name him anything you like."

"I like that. Duke." She grinned. "I don't suppose the little bugger's house broken is he?"

"Not likely, but labs are pretty smart. He should catch on fast. Just in case we, should probably let him out now. He might need to go."

They let the pup out on the deck and stood looking through the glass door as he hopped around clumsily, ears flopping like he might take flight. Then he squatted down to do his business and came right back to the door.

"Maybe we should train him to go on the grass," Brett said.

"What a good boy," she said, opening the door to let him in. "Pam seems upset. Is she mad about the dog?"

"Don't worry about her." He waved a hand. "She'll get used to it."

"Well, it's a good thing we have hardwood floors."

"Listen, sweetheart, I made an appointment for you with a doctor who comes very highly recommended. He's in Manhattan, so I thought you and the baby could come in with me. It's in two weeks, and that's just luck because he's booked months ahead, so I thought—"

"A doctor? What kind of doctor are we talking about?" She looked up, eyeing him suspiciously.

"He's a psychiatrist, and he's not cheap, either, so—"

"You think I'm crazy, don't you?" It was more of an accusation than a question, her words laced with anger. She stood up and folded her arms, and it was then she noticed the way he was looking at her. There was a shadow in his eyes, a menacing look, as if he wanted to devour her. She turned away, afraid of what it meant.

"I don't think that at all, Sweets. But I do think you've had a lot of stress lately with the baby and separating from Keith and—"

"So, what do I need a shrink for if I'm not crazy?"

"Just...to talk. Help you sort things out."

"Help me sort things out? What things Dad, do I need sorting out?"

"Look, don't get upset, all right? I'm just trying to help."

He touched her shoulder and it felt like an electric shock. She jumped back.

"Justine?"

She watched the figure of her stepmother ascend the stairs like a silent apparition, a glass full of wine in her hand, her unspoken hostility wielded like a weapon, visible in the stiffness of her movements. It was her! She was behind this, Justine knew it! Her body trembled. Her teeth began to chatter.

"I don't need any fucking help. I'm not crazy," she glared at him as she lifted Abigail from his arms. "Somebody was in our house. I don't care if you and Pam believe me or not, but somebody was here, and that doesn't make me crazy, all right?"

"You're misunderstanding, Sweets."

"I understand perfectly. Next you'll be trying to convince me to sign myself into a psych ward. Is that what you want? Have you and Pam discussed this behind my back?"

"Oh, for God's sake."

"Well, have you?"

"Of course not."

"Bull shit!"

"I'm not arguing with you about this," Brett said. "I'm going to bed, I'm beat. We'll discuss it in the morning." He threw up his hands in a gesture of surrender and walked away shaking his head, leaving Justine to stare after him.

Crouching down, she scooped up the little dog and nuzzled him against her face, trying to absorb his warmth. He had that new-puppy smell. She looked at a reflection of the baby, the puppy, and herself in the blackened window, shocked to see how vulnerable they all appeared. Would her parents ever try to have her committed again if they thought she was nuts? She felt the shackles of their power around her limbs, holding her down. Maybe she should be more careful of what she said around them, and how she behaved. They couldn't be trusted.

Just before going up to bed, Justine took another sharp knife from the block on the kitchen counter. She carried it upstairs and hid it underneath her pillow.

Chapter
SEVENTEEN

A faint glow of morning sunlight crested the horizon through his living room window. Rory hadn't slept yet. Maybe it was all the blow he had done that night, or the thought of his house being taken away that kept him up, or it could be the force within him pushing him into action. It could also be the thwarted hope that Justine was actually Frances. Likely, it was a combination of all of those things that tormented his heart and mind. He had drunk half a bottle of whiskey and watched two episodes of *Law and Order* and then found an old episode of *The Three Stooges*. For an hour, he sat roaring with laughter. He hadn't watched them in years, and they were funnier than he remembered.

Rory lit a cigarette and switched off the television. He struggled to pull on his boots with the cigarette clenched between his teeth, and then staggered out of the apartment.

He took a drive down East Lake Road. He knew that if he was pulled over, he'd get arrested for drunk driving, but what were the chances of that happening this time of day? He probably just looked like any other working stiff, heading out before sunrise to his lousy, low-paying job.

A few yards ahead, he spied two deer at the side of the road looking in his direction. He slowed down, anticipating their sudden dart across the road. They stood watching his car and Rory flashed the headlights at them. He'd heard from someone that the headlights transfix them and flashing them would get the animals moving. He eased his foot onto the brake until the speedometer ground down to twenty-five. There was no shortage of road kill around these parts and he'd hit a couple of animals himself, traveling in the dark. Last summer, the leopard frogs had reproduced in record numbers, and whenever it rained, they'd come hopping out onto the roads and get flattened. Rory kept his eye on the deer. When he got within two yards, they bolted in front of the car, just as he thought they would. Rory hit the brakes and stopped in time for them to make their way across.

Stupid deer. Well, he couldn't be that intoxicated if he was able to stop for suicidal wildlife.

He turned onto Welker Road, and when he approached his house, instead of sitting out front and staring at it the way he usually did, he drove the Challenger right into the driveway and pulled up behind the Lincoln. Rory put it in park and sat staring at the car in his driveway, gripping the steering wheel until his fingers were numb. He opened the door, climbed out, and stumbled, falling to the ground. Rory laughed out loud. He rolled over and lifted himself to his knees, struggling to his feet, and swaying as he walked. It was unseasonably warm outside. The wind whipped across his face, forcing tears from his eyes. The sun was cresting the bare treetops of the distant hills around the lake. He could see the clouds of morning mist receding with the shadows, devoured by the sun. Bleary-eyed, he gazed at the view of the lake, and watched a great blue heron take flight. He recalled the first time he'd seen this piece of property, how he'd stood in front of this very view and imagined the house he would build. He'd wanted big windows facing the lake and a huge deck where he could spend his evenings watching the sun set on his new life here in America, all the death, grief, and bloodshed left behind him in Belfast. Or so he'd thought.

Rory turned to look at the Lincoln in the driveway. A rage so immense burned in his veins that it overpowered him. Before he even realized what he was doing, he picked up a rock from the garden at the front of the house and with both hands, smashed it down on the windshield of the car. It made a loud, satisfying crack, and a starburst exploded across the glass. He smashed it again and again until the glass gave way and a gaping hole appeared. Then, Rory hurled the rock across the lawn with a grunt.

He got back in his car and backed out of his driveway, his heart racing, his eyes seeing double, reveling in the first small flames of revenge leaping from his soul. And yet, as he drove off he realized how pathetic that was; smashing a window in the early morning hours. What the hell was the matter with him? This seemed like such a trivial thing, such a schoolyard antic, given where he had come from. He wanted to feel satisfaction, like he had accomplished something. But this was not a victory that he could enjoy; it was only a lesson in frustration. He knew it required a greater show of force if he wanted anything to change. He never imagined he could feel so desperate.

Rory ate breakfast again at the Penn Yan Diner, smoked two cigarettes, drank four cups of coffee, and read *USA Today* cover to cover. There was no mention of Larry Blackmore's death, but in the Chronicle Express, it made the front page. A smiling picture of the man, which looked at least ten years younger and thirty pounds lighter, defaced the paper. The police, in an effort to find the killer, were appealing to the public for information. Rory felt nothing as he looked at Blackmore's picture, not even a vague twinge of any emotion. The only thing that mattered was that he got his money back, and he'd gotten even.

When he was done eating, he headed out to Dresden to see his buddy. Rory purchased five pounds of C-4 plastic explosive. He felt it rising up on those phoenix wings, a power surging from him, bigger than anything trying to destroy him. He *would* be victorious. He *would* smash his enemies into dust. Nothing could hold him back. He was at war.

"Do it like your life depends on it."

Chapter
EIGHTEEN

"Don't open the door!" Justine said, rushing toward her father and giving him a body check.

"Why? What's wrong?"

"There's a bird's nest above the door with three eggs inside."

"Let me see."

"No! Don't open it! The mother's all freaked out already!"

"Justine, we have to be able to use the front door. What kind of stupid bird builds a nest above a door?"

Brett yanked on the knob and swung the door open. Immediately a bird swooped down from above, circled around and then came back to hover in the air in front of them chirping madly.

"You see? You can't disturb her, Dad. Close the door. Close the fucking door!"

Brett stepped outside and turned to look at the nest made of grass and mud pasted in the corner of the door's enclave.

"Get away from it!"

"Oh Justine, stop."

"No, get away from it! Get back in the house! Leave them alone! Just leave them alone!"

"Okay, okay. I'm leaving them alone. Geez," Brett said, and then broke into laughter. "Come on, we'll use the garage door, then. Don't cry, Sweets, I'm not going to touch the baby birds."

Justine felt her entire body vibrate as she followed Pam and her dad out through the garage.

Brett stopped short as they opened the garage and Justine nearly collided with him. "What the hell?" he said.

"What's wrong?" Pamela asked and then drew in a breath when she saw the Lincoln's windshield.

Brett looked over at her with an expression of anger and confusion, his hands raised in the air.

"How the hell did that happened?" Justine said, moving beside her dad, laying eyes on the damage.

"That's what I'd like to know," he said.

He looked around at the trees, down the brick driveway, and out into the field in the distance across the dirt road. He opened the driver's door. A shard of glass fell away from the edge of the hole in the windshield and onto the seat.

"How could your window get smashed like that, Brett?" Pamela said. She held Abigail in her arms. "I mean, we're out in the middle of nowhere. It's not like somebody could have just walked by and done that."

He was quiet as he looked around on the ground, not responding, searching underneath the car.

Justine could tell he was angry. She looked over at her daughter in Pamela's arms, feeling nervous. She didn't like Pamela looking at her baby, let alone touching her. Still, she didn't want Pamela to know she was on to her. That she knew Pam wanted to send her away and take the baby. Better to play it cool while keeping her eyes on her.

"There's nothing here that could have done it," Brett said. "There's no rock, no tree branch, no nothing."

"What about a bird?" Justine said.

Her father cocked his head, put his hands on his hips, and issued an angry laugh. "A bird? Are you kidding me?"

"A bird couldn't do damage like this." Pamela's shook her head.

"Maybe it was a big bird," Justine said.

"You think this is funny or something, Justine?" Her dad took a step toward her.

"I'm not trying to be funny."

She thought a bird made sense. There were hawks, osprey, and cranes in the area. She wouldn't be surprised if there were eagles here, too. Okay, granted, it was a lot of damage for a bird to do, even a big one. So it was a dumb suggestion. Whatever.

Abigail started to fuss in her grandmother's arms. She was drooling furiously on a frozen teething ring, looking out of sorts. Justine caught a look of collusion that passed between her parents. A look that substantiated her fear that they thought she was crazy.

"Maybe it was the guy who broke into our house," Justine said. "Maybe now you'll believe me?"

Neither of them responded, other than giving her silent pathetic looks as if they felt sorry for her.

They all stood there in the driveway, confused and annoyed. Justine couldn't stop thinking about the break-in. They still didn't believe her. After the hallucinations she'd experienced in the past, how could she really blame them? But at the same time, she was frustrated and still angry with them. She knew that break-in had been real. That much, at least, she knew was true.

"It would have to be hit with quite a force to break like that. It's not easy to break a car windshield," Brett said, looking out at the back of their property, the forest of trees with their new spring leaves.

"Maybe it was my psychosis that did it?" Justine smirked, feeling a smug satisfaction. "Do you suppose your big shot New York City shrink can fix that?"

"That's not funny, Justine." He shot her an angry look.

"Really? I thought it was. I'm cracking up over it. Literally."

"Justine, what's the matter with you?" Pamela said.

"You know, that would never have occurred to me to think that, but you know what? Now you've got me wondering," Brett said, and gave her a level stare.

"Oh, please, you think I would actually break your fucking windshield? What are you nuts?"

"Not me, I'm not the crazy one."

Justine glared at him as the realization sank in that he was being serious. She felt her body go rigid.

"Fuck you!" She spat and turned to march back inside the house.

"Justine. Justine!" Pamela called after her.

Her parents came back into the house. Brett phoned the nearest dealership. After a few more phone calls, a windshield was located. He arranged to have the car towed.

"We need to call the police, and report this," Pamela said.

Justine watched as Pamela put Abigail in her playpen with a few of her soft toys. The baby looked up at her grandmother with her bright blue eyes and smiled her happy little grin. And she felt a twinge of concern that her stepmother was trying to take over her role. Justine looked over at her baby with tired eyes, feeling suddenly exhausted. When was the last time she actually slept an entire night?

Brett put a hand on her shoulder and said, "I'm sorry about what I said, Sweets."

She shook his hand away. "Whatever."

"Justine, please don't be like that."

"Why don't you give it a rest? Just call the cops and deal with your stupid car." She marched up the stairs, leaving her parents to stare after her.

More than an hour later, a Yates County Deputy Sheriff showed up at their door. Justine had a minor panic attack, knowing the mother bird was going to be disturbed again.

"Gus Linden," the cop said, chomping enthusiastically on a piece of gum as he lumbered through the door; a tall, solid man who looked as if he'd played college football in his youth, but now appeared days away from retirement. He stuck out his hand and gave Brett's a firm shake, a neat moustache stretching with his smile.

Justine ignored him, angry that nobody was taking the safety of the bird's nest seriously. She sat on the living room sofa, watching an old Bette Davis movie on the television. *Whatever Happened To Baby Jane?* She imagined herself in Joan Crawford's role, trapped in her house, dependent on her crazy sister for everything. She could feel that raw look of panic and distress in Joan's eyes right down to her soul.

"I apologize for the length of time in getting out here. Police force has got its hands full with the shooting out by the lake," Linden said.

"Somebody was shot?" Brett asked.

"A local man. He was a lawyer in town. Body was discovered last night, just a few miles from here."

"Oh, my God," Pamela said.

Justine looked over at them, interested, now, in what they were discussing.

"Yeah, pretty tragic. I knew the guy myself, and his family. Went to school with his older brother, in fact. We've both lived in Penn Yan all our lives. Quite a shock is what it is."

"Did you catch the guy who shot him?" Pamela asked.

"State police have taken over now. Hopefully, they'll solve it quickly."

"I thought we were getting away from big-city crime moving out here," she said.

"Well, people are people no matter where you go." The cop shook his head. "But Yates County is generally a safe place to live. Haven't had a murder around here in—gosh about ten years, as I can recall. An old man was found stabbed to death on his sofa out in Himrod. His woman left him alive on the sofa just before heading off to church in Dundee, and when she came home a few hours later, he was dead. It remains unsolved, too."

"You never caught who did it?" Brett spoke up.

"Nope. We were pretty sure who did it, but they lawyered up right away and we never had enough evidence to charge, so they walked. And before that, the only other homicide as I can recall was about twenty or twenty-five years ago. Man put his wife's body out on the railway tracks near Dundee after he strangled her to death. Train ran her over and decapitated her. But since there was an absence of blood at the scene, it was obvious she was dead before she got on those tracks. If she was alive when the train stuck her there would have been blood everywhere."

"Jesus. So was that murder solved?" Brett asked.

"The husband pled guilty to manslaughter. Says he didn't intend to kill her when he wrapped his hands around her neck and squeezed." He cocked a hairy eyebrow, his wrinkled eyelid sagging under the effort, and hooked his thumbs into the front of his leather belt. He nodded at the door. "That your car out in the driveway you called in about?"

"Yeah, did you get a look at the windshield?" Brett said.

"Sure did. Somebody did a number on it. Did you see anything? Any idea when it might have occurred?"

"Probably sometime during the night while we slept. We didn't see anything. I'm surprised we wouldn't have heard it."

"Well, it's a big property you've got here. Any idea who might have done it?"

Brett shook his head. "We just moved here in February so it's not like we know anybody yet. We haven't had time to make enemies."

"You had any trouble with the former owner of this place?"

"The former owner?"

"Guy just got out of jail not long ago. I heard he was looking to get this place back. Was talking to a lawyer about it."

"You're kidding," Pamela said.

"Small town. Word travels fast around these parts. He's sketchy, at any rate. Did some time in jail on drug charges, but they got dropped. That's when he lost this place, when he went to jail. I know he was real mad about it being taken back by the bank. Rory Madden's his name."

"My daughter thinks somebody might have broken into the house a few days ago," Brett said.

"You don't say? Anything taken?" The cop looked over at Justine, who was stunned that her father mentioned this to the police when the entire time he'd been acting like he didn't believe her. What was that all about? He only believed her if it suited him? She felt indignant. How did she ever manage to be born into a family with people who behaved this way?

"Nothing, except for her photograph." Brett crossed his arms and pursed his lips.

"That's odd, isn't it? Just a photograph, nothing else?" The cop spoke directly to Justine, chewing his gum slowly now, as if contemplating this information more seriously.

"That was it," Justine said. "Guess he was overcome with my beauty."

"You have an alarm system?"

"That's hardly necessary out here," Brett said.

"You might be surprised how many break-ins go on in this area," Linden said. "My advice would be to have one installed. You might want to consider surveillance cameras, as well."

"Well, suppose it's this Rory guy, what can we do? Can we have him charged?"

"At this point, unless you actually saw him on your property and can identify him as Rory Madden, there's not much you can do. Suspecting someone isn't enough. We've got to be able to prove he did something in order to charge him with an offense."

"Is this guy living in the area?" Brett asked.

"He's got himself an apartment in town. Above Chen's Chinese restaurant."

"So, what can we do?" Pamela said.

"Well, from a legal perspective there's not a whole helluva lot we can do just now. At any rate, I'm gonna pass on by Mr. Madden's place and pay him a visit," Linden said. "Let him know he should stay clear of this place and not be bothering you good folk. And if he knows what's good for him, he'll heed my advice."

"That would be great. We'd appreciate that," Brett said.

"I'd advise you, though, to get yourself an alarm and surveillance system if you can afford it. That's the best advice I can offer. That way if it's him coming around your place, you can get it on tape and then we can arrest him. Maybe some watch dogs, too. You're kind of secluded out here."

Secluded wasn't the word. They were more like sitting ducks. Justine turned away and wandered over to the living room windows and looked out at the horizon. How did she ever manage to get here? Is this really what she wanted? Pinned inside of a nightmare like Joan Crawford while Crazy Jane pranced around in her little girl ringlets and bows like some hideous four-year-old with the face of a grandmother.

How had her own life become this ordeal? All grown up but trapped here, living with her parents, immersed in their marital disharmony. Her life was one big disappointment. Certainly not her daughter, but for sure the rest of it. This truly was all there was for her. She was completely trapped here.

Gus Linden said good-bye, shook both Brett and Pamela's hands, and handed them a business card. "Be sure to let me know if there's ever anything I can do for you folks. Penn Yan is a great place to live, so don't let this experience taint it for you," he said. "You be sure to stop on by the sheriff's department when you're in town next and say hello. I'd be more than happy to show you around, if you like. I'm also an avid fisherman. Got a boat down by the marina, if you ever think you might want to spend the day on the lake. Just look me up."

"Thanks for coming by," Brett said, opening the door for him.

"Give the PYPD a call if you ever see anyone suspicious hanging around. Any time day or night, we're open twenty-four seven."

Justine sank through layers of slumber, shreds of memories strung together in the realm between wakefulness and delirium, haunting her as she appealed for the mercy of sleep. She peered with one tender eye at the clock on her bedside table. It was three-thirty in the morning. Sleep was not going to come. She drifted down the stairs in her bare feet with the baby monitor in the pocket of her bathrobe. She felt like a zombie, like she was sleepwalking. Her mind was in a fog. She stood in the living room looking out at the darkness. Light from a half moon cast lacy tree-branch shadows across the deck, spilling into the house and across the hardwood floor. The furnace hummed and then shut off. The house was perfectly still. Gazing out at the trees, she waited to see if the gray people were out there. They didn't appear to be. But then she heard them. They were inside. Their voices whispered to her in the darkness from behind the walls, coming to her from far off, sounding as though they were carried on a breeze.

"They're coming for you, Justine. They're coming for your baby. Save yourself. Save yourself…"

Over and over, the gray people chanted in their whispering voices. Over and over, they scratch, scratch, scratched inside the walls. And she would argue back, telling them to stop, telling them to be quiet, to leave her alone. They might be silent for a few minutes and then before she realized it, they would start back up again, torturing her. Scratch, scratch, scratch.

"They're going to send you back, Justine. They're going to kill the baby and send you back. Save yourself. It's not too late. Save yourself, save yourself, save yourself…

And she knew whom they meant. She knew it was her parents they were warning her about. Somehow, she had to break free from them. She had to protect herself and Abigail at any cost.

She wandered into the kitchen, withdrew a knife from the block on the counter. She touched the edge of the knife to her cheek. The cold of the stainless steel seeped into her skin. It felt good. Soothing. And a thought occurred to her that could take away all her pain. With the knife in her hand, she went back upstairs.

Chapter
NINETEEN

Behind a Verizon work truck on Lincoln Avenue, Rory parked his car. He gazed through the windshield across the street at the vintage, 1979 electric-blue Camaro in the driveway of a house three doors up. There was a U-haul truck parked in front of the house. Was Simon moving? Simon had known Rory all his life and was smart enough to know that Rory was going to kill him. Only a bonehead would not pack up the very day they saw each other at O'Leary's and high-tail it out of town. Now, his tardiness was going to cost him his life—the dumb fuck.

Rory slouched in his seat and waited. It was growing dark, the sun sinking in a coral sky on the horizon. The wind picked up with a sudden force and blew trash and the remains of last fall's leaves across the road. The rain had started again. He could hear its soft patter on the roof of his car and on the sidewalk through the window he had cracked open an inch.

He thought of his house. It was April now. He wanted to be back there by summer, at the latest. June. Somehow he would get those people out, one way or the other. A few minutes later, the front door of the house opened and a flabby-bellied kid with a bald head emerged, carrying the end of a mattress. Simon was on the other end. There was no mistaking those ears of his. Rory watched as they hoisted it up into the truck that already appeared to be pretty full. Stupid idiots, not putting the big stuff in first. Rory laughed as he watched them standing there scratching their heads like a couple of comedians, trying to figure out how to get it in with all the other crap packed in tight.

Simon jumped up into the back and rearranged a few things, removing a couple of boxes and handing them to the fat boy at the curb. One of the boxes crashed to the ground and Rory could hear Simon swearing at the kid. Rory threw back his head and unleashed a stream of laughter. This was better than the *Three Stooges*. With some difficulty, they forced the mattress inside the back of the truck. They stood talking for a moment on the street, and then Simon pulled down the roll-up door of the truck and latched it. The fat kid left in a car that had been parked across the street, and Simon went back inside the house.

Rory lit himself a cigar and waited, trying to formulate a plan. A few minutes later, the front door opened and Simon emerged. He got into his Camaro and pulled out of the driveway. Rory started his own car and followed. He kept a safe distance behind him as they drove through Penn Yan. The Camaro made a turn onto Liberty Street and pulled into the parking lot of Walgreen's. Rory sped up fast behind the car as it pulled into a parking space, and took the spot immediately beside it, parking so close Simon wouldn't be able to open his door. Killing the engine, Rory jumped out of his car. He rounded the Camaro just as Simon was opening his door trying to get out. Rory jumped into the passenger seat. He pulled the handgun from his waistband.

"Close the fucking door!" he said, pointing the gun at Simon's head and cocking it.

Simon put his hands up slowly and sat back down. He looked over at Rory with a mixture of fear and anger.

"Fuck," he said.

"You got any weapons on you?"

"No."

"Bull shit. Put your hands on the steering wheel. Show me your pant legs."

"Awk, come on."

"Show me, you fucker!" Rory knew Simon used to keep a blade strapped in a sheath to his ankle.

Simon lifted his legs while Rory reached down, keeping the gun pointed at his stomach and quickly frisked him.

"Lean forward," he said and looked at the back of his pants.

"I'm clean. No guns, no drugs. I got nothing."

"You got nothing. That's right funny now. Aye, you got nothing. You've got a cheek now haven't you? Seems you've kept everything. I was the one to lose it all, now wasn't I? Cause of you, you fuck."

"Rory, look it's not like that man, I didn't turn on you like you're thinking."

"Drive."

Simon started the engine, a contrite look on his face, and pulled out of the parking space.

"Where are we going?" His Irish accent was still as thick as the day they'd left together for America seven years ago.

"Head out to the interstate."

"What the hell for?"

"Shut up. Don't ask me any fucking questions." He lowered the gun, pointing it at the man's ribs.

"It wasn't me. I wasn't the one who rolled over on you. It was the fucking Russian."

"You expect me to believe that? Why wasn't you next to me in jail then?"

"They cut me a deal," Simon said.

"A deal if you put the finger on me, isn't that right, *Brother?*" Rory nudged his ribs with the gun.

"No, not on you, on our up-line in Canada. That's who they were really after. We were small time, compared to them. We were just the weak link in the chain."

"That still makes you a rat doesn't it? You're a fucking, lying, wee fanny, no better than the Taigs we put in their graves back in Ireland."

"I never ratted on you. Not on you, man. I would never. We're brothers, Rory."

"Correction: We were brothers," Rory said. "We stopped being brothers the day you betrayed me."

"You've got it all wrong. I would never do that to you, I swear—"

"I don't believe a word. Not one word."

Simon checked his mirrors as if searching for a way out of his predicament. "So what, you're going to kill me now? Is that it? Is that going to make you feel better?"

"Aye, it just might."

They headed north on the interstate. The sun was a remnant of crimson in the sky. After a few minutes, Rory ordered him off on a side road that bisected a forest and the remains of a vineyard. The car rocked and swayed over the potholes in the dirt road as they drove alongside the blackened grape vines tied to wires, like miniature trees in the haunted forest of a child's nightmare.

"Stop here."

"Now what?"

Rory reached over, turned off the engine, and pocketed the keys. He opened his door, stepped out, and took off his jacket so as not to get any traces of gunpowder on it. He kept his eye on Simon as he tossed the jacket on the hood of the car and got back inside, closing the door. With his gun pointed at Simon, he looked at the UFF tattoo peeking out from under Simon's shirt sleeve, on the inside of his forearm. He remembered the time they stood facing three men armed with tire irons and bats, ready to beat the daylights out of them, and Simon had turned and run. He had run down the alleyway, rather than stand and fight. He had abandoned Rory.

Lighting the petrol bomb behind his back, Rory had dropped to the ground and hurled it at the men. The explosion singed the hair on Rory's arms, but he got away. They were only seventeen at the time. It was one of several key moments when Simon showed his true colors. Rory knew his mate was always a bit of a mama's boy, too eager to be a man but lacking the backbone to succeed. Why had Rory always forgiven him? Was it some misguided protective quality that Simon brought out in him? Why didn't he see the moment coming when Simon would betray him? It was as if Simon was his Achilles' heel. Hadn't Rory always known this, deep inside? Of course he had. He had nobody and nothing to blame but his own stupidity. The knowledge shamed him.

"Look, I'm sorry you lost your house and all. I'm sorry about all the slag you got over this, but Rory, we're brothers, man. No matter what. I wouldn't turn on you," Simon said in a fast, high-pitched voice. Sweat glistened on his forehead and he rubbed at it with a trembling hand.

Rory stared at him in the gloomy light and it occured to him how ugly Simon actually was. It wasn't just the big ears that stuck out from the sides of his head, it was the shape of his face. His eyes that sagged at the corners as if his skin was slidding off his skull. And the puffiness of his cheeks, that protruding bottom lip. He had a sloppy face.

Simon stared straight out the windshield, panting suddenly, avoiding Rory's eyes. "We fought the war together, remember?" Simon continued. "Even right to the end, we never wavered in our loyalties when all that shite was going down with the UVF and we had to choose sides. We kept our heads about us. We never lost focus. We weren't the ones who stopped buying the ammo and started taking holidays with our drug money like them other inbred fucks. Remember Rory? We were solid through and through. The sons of Ulster, never backing down from the scum, child-murdering IRA. British blood in our veins till the day we die. The sons of conquerors. No surrender is our battle cry. Remember? UFF forever. Remember, Rory? Remember?"

"Aye, I remember. But there's just one problem."

"What's that?" Simon turned to look at him with terrified eyes, his breathing coming hard and fast.

"We're not in Belfast anymore."

He put the gun under Simon's chin, forcing his head back on the seat. Simon's Adams apple snapped up and down. Beads of sweat turned into rivulets on his forehead and upper lip. A part of Rory had hoped that Simon would run after they saw each other at O'Leary's; that he would go so far away Rory would never find him. He regretted the position this left him in.

Rory pulled the trigger and fired a bullet through Simon's jaw and into his brain.

Carefully, he wiped his prints from the gun. He pressed Simon's hands firmly around the gun and then rubbed the back of his own hand across the back of Simon's to transfer gunpowder residue. He left the gun in Simon's lap. A trail of blood thick as molasses ran down the side of his neck from his ear. His head lolled on his shoulder and he rested his cheek on the window of the door as his body slumped over.

Rory wiped clean the car keys and put them back in the ignition. He wiped his prints from inside the car. He went around outside and wiped the door handle. He would go back to his apartment, burn his clothes in the parking lot out back and have a shower.

He took a deep breath of the cool night air as he put his jacket on and walked back along the highway into town, knowing that life was a balance between pain and ecstasy, between madness and understanding, between life and death. It was a choice we made—in every moment of every day—to decide who we are, a choice meant to destroy us and restore us.

Between the clouds, a half full moon suspended in the darkening sky followed him, illuminating his path, watching him as he wandered down the side of the highway. Its presence was comforting, as a cold wind tore at his jacket. He walked, entangled in the gloom of his soul from so long ago, screaming inside of him. Shaped from the fire that burnt him to ashes, his spirit unfolded as a great bird, a yearning calling him forth, all the while knowing there was no escape from the wasteland of his heart.

Gravel crunched underneath his boots. *Where have I been?*

Chapter
TWENTY

Justine glanced out the bedroom window and spied someone standing at the end of the driveway, looking up at the house. The late afternoon sun reflected in the smooth leather of his jacket. It wasn't the elaborate fox-trimmed one she'd seen him in before, but a short biker jacket he wore today. Duke was in his arms.

She collected Abigail from her crib and hurried down the stairs. She settled the baby on a blanket on the living room floor with her toys, then she cracked opened the front door so as not to startle the mother bird in her nest. Slowly she peeked out and turned her gaze upward. The mother bird wasn't there. Must be out gathering food. The nest was silent. They probably still had weeks to go before the babies hatched.

She stood with folded arms inside the door, watching the man walk up the driveway carrying Duke.

He stepped up the porch and said, "He was on the road."

"Thank you." She took the puppy from him and shooed it into the house.

"How are you?" he asked, smiling.

"What can I do for you, Mr. Madden, isn't it?"

"You can call me Rory." He paused to stare at her for a moment, and then said. "I thought I would drop by and see if you have any mail for me."

"Why don't you put in an address-change at the Post Office, and then you wouldn't have to drop by like this?"

"Maybe I want to drop by." He grinned exposing that one crooked incisor. He took a step up as if he was just going to walk into the house, then paused to lean inside the doorframe casually, smiling at her in that beguiling way, as he had the last time.

The baby let out a high-pitched wail like an ambulance siren that made Justine's muscles go rigid.

"Abigail!" She crossed the room in seconds. Duke was fighting her for her soother again. Justine let out a breath and wrestled the soother away from the dog and scooped up her baby.

"It's okay, Sweetie. Don't worry, Mamma will wash it for you."

She looked up, startled to see Rory step inside the house, closing the door behind him.

"Is she all right? That must have given you a scare. I know it did me." He chuckled. There was a warm look in his pale eyes as if he thought of himself as an old friend.

"Oh, the dog is always trying to steal her toys. He's a little bugger. And then she'll get a hold of one of his toys,." Justine said, with a nervous laugh.

"Well, you've got your hands full with two babies, now haven't you?"

Abigail looked over at him and immediately stopped crying. Tears smeared her fat cheeks. She stared at him with eyes the size of nickels.

"Are your parents off to work, then?"

"Yeah, they're both out of town for a while on business."

Instantly she realized her mistake. Why did she go and tell him that, she wondered? It didn't seem like information that just anyone should have; the fact that she was here alone.

"The windshield on my dad's car got smashed in our driveway." She changed the subject. "Looks like it might have been vandalism, which is kind of strange way out here."

She searched him for a reaction but he was smiling at the baby as if he hadn't heard her. It occurred to her that he might be the one who broke into their house, too.

"You've got a three-car garage. Why doesn't your old man park his car in there?"

"He's finishing the basement and he's got all his tools and stuff set up there for now. Then there's my stepmother's car in one space and my car's in the other space. Not that I ever use it much."

Rory looked at the baby. "She's lovely. What's her name?"

"Abigail."

"Well, Miss Abigail, is it? All the angels in heaven must surely be jealous of those beautiful eyes you've got."

Abigail's face broke into a lopsided smile. Rory threw back his head and unleashed a hearty laugh.

"I think she liked that." Justine laughed.

"Awk, she's grand," Rory said and reached up to pinch her cheek, an innocent gesture, and yet Justine found something a little unsettling about it. She didn't know this man. He was a stranger in her house.

"Do you mind if I use your phone? I just got one of those iPhones," he said, pulling it out of a pocket and handing it to her as if she would know what to do. "But I forgot to charge it last night and now the battery's died. Have you seen the new one? It's pretty cool."

"I've got a Blackberry."

"Is your phone in the kitchen?" he asked, moving down the hall like he still lived there.

The fact that he knew his way around her house was perplexing. Justine put the baby in her swing and followed him into the kitchen, keeping a safe distance, and yet she found herself curious about him. He removed his coat and tossed it over the back of a kitchen chair. She studied the way he walked, the way the gray dress shirt draped over the muscles of his upper back. The shirt fit him perfectly. She could tell that he was in good shape. He wore comfortable-fit faded jeans and a gold watch. He hadn't offered to remove his shoes. In spite of the fact that they often walked around the hardwood floors in their shoes, most people would automatically remove their shoes out of politeness.

She rinsed Abigail's soother in the kitchen sink and studied the smooth skin on his face, the planes of his cheeks, how a muscle in his neck tensed, how his eyes looked her up and down as he stood there so comfortable in her home with the phone pressed to his ear.

"Where do you keep your phone book?" he asked, opening and closing a cupboard. She could see one forearm was completely tattooed in turquoise pigment, and she wondered if it covered his entire arm.

"We don't have one."

"You don't have a phone book?" He put the phone down.

"There wasn't one here when we moved in."

"How about a cup of coffee, then? Do you have that?" He took a step toward her and stood just slightly too close, looking down at her, his gaze sliding over her face. She found it surprising that he was a complete stranger, who may have even vandalized her father's car, and yet she couldn't help being struck by how incredibly hot he was, in a bad-guy kind of way. There was something powerful and dangerous about him that she realized appealed to her.

A smile tugged at the corners of her lips as she looked up at him. She hesitated for a moment, handing back his iPhone, and then said, "All right. How do you take it?"

"Black with one sugar."

He leaned on the counter staring at her as she abandoned the soother and proceeded to fill the coffee maker with water. There was a peculiar feeling inside of her, equal parts uncomfortable and exhilarating.

"Must be strange for you, living way out here. It's a far cry from the city," he said.

"Yeah. It takes getting used to."

"It's a completely different lifestyle, living in the country. Must be lonely for you, especially since your parents have to be out of town like this," he said.

"I enjoy the solitude." She shrugged as she scooped ground coffee into the filter.

"Really? A young, beautiful girl like yourself wanting to be all alone out here in the middle of nowhere?"

She looked away, embarrassed, feeling her cheeks burn—not entirely unpleasantly—and flipped the switch on the coffee maker. Was he being sincere, or just trying to flatter her? There was a pause and Justine found herself suppressing a smile. She turned toward where she thought he was standing only to find him seated at the kitchen table, like a magician disappearing and reappearing somewhere else. Strange.

They smiled at each other, and Justine found that she liked the way he looked at her. She liked the feeling of his eyes on her.

"How old are you, anyway?" he said.

"I was born the year of the dragon." She smiled.

"Really. Maybe more like the year of the joker, huh?" He laughed.

"I just turned eighteen. Perfectly legal now."

"Good to hear it...so, have you gotten to know anybody up here?"

"I don't know if you've noticed, but it's not exactly like we have any neighbors."

"Well, then I'm the first friend you've made. You can consider me the Welcome Wagon." He smiled and then asked, "Have you been into town much?"

"We go in to the supermarket about once a week and my dad has been in quite a bit to the hardware store, but that's about it."

They talked for a few minutes about the town and local attractions and happenings. She took coffee mugs from the cupboard and set them on the counter.

"So, you said you're Irish, right?" she asked.

"I was born and raised in Belfast, but I'm not Irish. I'm a British citizen."

"Oh." She looked at him, confused. "How are you British, if you're from Ireland?"

"A lot you Americans know about our island. Northern Ireland is a province of the United Kingdom, as are England, Wales and Scotland. That makes me British."

"They didn't teach any of that in my history class." Changing the subject, she said, "You know, I feel kind of bad, knowing that we bought this house and that, well, it's not as if you sold it willingly."

"You've got nothing to feel bad about, girl. It's not you who took it from me, now is it?"

"I know. I just can't help feeling…awful. I heard that you were looking into trying to get it back, actually."

"Aye," Rory said. "I went to see a lawyer, but it's not that easy to overturn a foreclosure, I've since discovered. So I've got to come up with another plan."

"Another plan? What do you mean?"

"That's top secret information. If I tell you I'd have to kill you, too," Rory said grinning, shaking a finger at her.

Justine laughed off his comment. Yet, there was something in that statement that caused her to pause. She poured their coffee, stirred a spoonful of sugar into his, and handed him a cup. Abigail was asleep in her swing as Justine peeked into the living room. Duke was sleeping on the rug; all fours sprawled out as he lay on his fat belly. She was awed by how easily the both of them could fall asleep.

"So, before you became a mother, what was Justine all about? Did you have a career?"

"I worked in a music store part time and I used to sing."

"You're a singer? That's amazing? Original stuff?"

"I have about twenty original songs. I toured a little bit with my band, and I put out an indie CD."

"That's fantastic. What type of music?"

"Jazz with a bluesy-rock edge." Justine sipped her coffee, studying him over the rim of her cup, allowing the tension in her shoulders to relax.

"So what happened? Are you still with the band or did you give it up?"

"Well, I wouldn't say I've given up singing or music," she said, approaching the table and sitting down across from him. She studied the way he slouched in the chair, draping himself over it so comfortably, as if he had the self-confidence of a king. "I still play my guitar and I write stuff," she continued. "but I had to give up the band once Abigail was born. I wasn't planning on it, but it's just the way it's turned out. I couldn't very well go on tour and be away from her. Being a mother is my priority."

"So you play acoustic or electric?"

"Acoustic mostly, but I have an electric guitar."

"Show me," he said.

"Do you play, yourself?"

"No, not me," Rory said, following her into the living room with their coffee cups. "I don't have a musical bone in my body, but I appreciate it in others."

"It's a little dusty." Justine laughed as she stared down at the guitar she had set up by the wall of windows.

"Play something for me."

"Oh, no." She shook her head and laughed, thinking she might be too rusty for an audience.

"I'd love to hear you sing something. I bet you've got a fantastic voice. Go on, play something for me."

Justine picked up her guitar and sat down on the edge of the coffee table. Rory sat across from her in a chair. Her fingers found the familiar notes on the strings as she began to play. She glanced over at him as the music rose up in the air and seemed to encompass them. She watched as he closed his eyes. The music spiraled down inside of her, into that deep, private place she hadn't visited in so long. Her voice found the notes and melded into the harmonies, the words, and the sensation. Justine sang with abandon, consumed by an intensity that expanded outward, and then softly she let the notes die. She raised her eyes and looked at him. She smiled broadly, then laughed and stood up, feeling elated.

"That was beautiful, Justine."

"You like it?" she asked feeling like a child, a little girl consumed with her own magnificence, her own joy of being alive in the world.

"Very much."

She looked at her baby and saw that her eyes were open and she had a happy little smile on her face. Justine replaced the guitar in its stand and lifted her baby from the swing.

"Thank you for that, Rory. I haven't played in so long." She turned to him grinning.

"No, thank you for the performance, I enjoyed it. It was grand." He stood up, coffee cup in hand and moved toward the windows to look out at the lake in the distance.

"What are you doing this evening? Why don't you join me for dinner?" he asked.

There was a charged look in his eyes. She felt a sweat break across her palms. Her face flushed. There was something compelling about Rory, something that fascinated her.

"Oh, I don't know if I can do that."

"You're not allowed to go out and enjoy yourself with a new friend?"

"We have escalated from acquaintances to friends now?" She raised an eyebrow at him. "That's pretty quick isn't it?"

"Sometimes that's just the way it happens and we have no control over these things."

"Well, thanks, but I've still got so much to do here with decorating and I'm still not finished unpacking."

Rory stared at her and she knew he didn't believe her. It was true; she realized suddenly, she was lonely out here. She was homesick for Manhattan and all that was familiar to her. She missed the life she'd had before becoming a mother. She missed the stage, the lights, and the fans. She missed the jam sessions, the writing and recording. There were times she couldn't help wondering how far she might have gone. She hadn't known how motherhood would take over her life. And now, here she was having coffee with some stranger she'd let into her house. Was she that desperate for company and just didn't realize it?

"I should feed her." She tilted her head and shrugged.

"All right. I'll leave you two to your mother and baby business. But you know something? I don't think you belong here, girl. You don't belong here all by yourself hidden out here in the middle of nowhere."

She stared at him, uncertain what to make of his words.

"Thank you for the coffee," he said. "I'm going to leave my number and address with you. I'd like to show you around the area. Like I said, consider me the Welcome Wagon."

In the kitchen he wrote his information on a piece of paper for her. She walked him to the door, and felt surprisingly sorry to see him go.

Chapter
TWENTY-ONE

Rory sat in the armchair looking out at the street below his apartment, and rolled himself a spliff—a blend of cannabis and Marlboro light. He licked the paper and pressed it closed, and then lit the end with a flick of his Zippo. He took a few deep drags, awaiting the buzz that would arrive momentarily and chase away the swelling darkness within him. Then he lifted the receiver and dialed the same number he called every year at this time.

"Hey, Gilmour, Rory Madden here. How have you been?"

"Rory! Christ, Rory, I've been trying to get a hold of you for a bloody fortnight. Your phone's been disconnected and I don't have any other numbers for you, man." He laughed. "But, I parked my arse at my desk today 'cause it's Frances's birthday, so I knew you'd be calling."

Gilmour sounded excited. Usually he was sedate when Rory called once a year, or sometimes more often. It was more a perfunctory act than something he thought might actually bear fruit. They would chat, mostly small talk. Gilmour would fill him in on the local happenings, and the Troubles around Belfast and the peace talks of more recent years. Rory would talk about his renovation business, the custom homes he was working on in the Finger Lakes area. They would end the same way, with Gilmour saying he should come out for a holiday and do some fishing. He would promise to keep Rory updated on any new breakthroughs in the case. And that was it.

Gilmour was the one who was instrumental in helping Rory relocate. He was a good man, and one of the few people—a cop, no less—whom Rory trusted. He was a diehard Loyalist.

In his mind, Rory could picture his twelve-year-old self the day two policemen came to the door after Frances disappeared; big men with dour, pasty faces, their presence foreign and somehow sinister. They asked to search the Madden's home. The one named Gilmour shook Rory's hand and smiled. He asked Rory to show him around. Rory watched the two of them look into cupboards, underneath the beds, behind doors, as if they expected to find his sister in some bizarre game of hide-and-seek. His mother waited on the settee, a tissue pressed to her nose. Their neighbor from up the street, who used to mind them on occasion after school when Rory and Frances were younger, held her hand. His mother's boyfriend, Dwayne, walked to the pub. Rory remembered knowing that Dwayne would undoubtedly return drunk sometime during the night, stumbling into furniture, knocking things over, and waking Rory from sleep.

"Did your sister have a row with anyone yesterday?" Gilmour had asked, as he peered down at him with gentle eyes. He bore the reddish hair and muttonchops of a Scotsman.

Rory sat on the edge of his bed; arms folded, and looked up at the man from behind the hair that hung across his eyes. He shook his head. It was the middle of the day, and the light was on in his room. His bedroom window was boarded up. It was smashed a week earlier during a night of riots. That same night, their neighbors across the street were driven from their home when a petrol bomb went through their living room window and set their house on fire. The riots were not as bad as they had been a few years earlier, when Rory would watch coffin after coffin go down the Shankill Road. Things had settled down in recent years, although the anger and the hatred of the Troubles were always there, just beneath the veneer of relative calm, ready to break through at any moment.

"Do you have any idea what would cause her not to come home, son?"

He shook his head again.

"Any thought as to where she might be?"

"No." Rory sighed.

"Did she get on well enough with your mother and step-dad?"

Rory shrugged. "Aye. They get on right enough."

"If you know anything that might help us find her, can you give us a ring? You can call me yourself, son. Anything you might remember that can help, just give me a ring, all right? No matter what it is," he said and handed Rory a card with his name and number. There was a look in his eyes that spoke to him louder than any words, conspiratorial, as if they shared some understanding.

Today there was energy in Gilmour's voice like Rory had never heard before. It sent a little seed of electricity coursing through him. Had something actually happened after all these years? It was too much even to wish for.

"What the devil is it?"

"A witness," Gilmour said. "Well, not somebody who actually witnessed anything. A woman who says she met someone online who was communicating with her about the case."

"And?"

"The woman had been seeing this guy for a few months when he confessed something to her."

"Confessed what?"

He could hear Gilmour hesitate for a moment, and pictured the man leaning back in his chair; his muttonchops now white with age. When Gilmour spoke again, it was in a subdued voice. "He confessed to killing a wee girl from the Shankill Road in 1995."

Rory felt something inside of him shift, as if all the organs were voluntarily moving and realigning themselves within his body. His heart picked up speed. He sat up on the edge of the chair, the joint burning forgotten in his fingers. He felt his mouth go dry.

"Did he say it was Frances?"

"He hasn't given a name."

"So, what happens now? How do we find out?"

"The woman has agreed to help us. She's going to wear a wire and see if she can get him talking."

"Who is it? What's his name?"

"Randal Trowbridge. He's got a few priors from way back, like in his teenage years. Disturbing the peace, drunkenness, nothing serious, and nothing in years."

Rory was quiet as the name sank into his brain. Randal Trowbridge. Why did that name seem familiar? He felt his blood pressure rise and realized his stomach was quivering from the adrenaline that had surged into his veins.

"And is he from Belfast? Did he live in the area at the time Frances went missing?"

"Aye, he did. He lived just two streets over from youse."

Rory sighed and crushed the joint in an ashtray. His vision narrowed. He felt like he might be getting light-headed. He thought of that woman living in his house. Was it possible she was Frances? How likely was it that woman could actually be his sister? What were the odds? Maybe this guy had murdered some other girl, not his sister, and maybe Frances was still alive.

"You know, Rory, this could just turn out to be bullshit. It could just be some fanny who remembered the wee girl who went missing in his neighborhood and now he wants to claim responsibility for her disappearance to get some kind of recognition. It's not uncommon for people to make shit like this up. There's plenty of whackos out there who do."

"Aye, I know," he said, feeling his hope weaken in spite of Gilmour's words.

"Remember that kook who used to call us all the time after Frances disappeared saying all kinds of weird shite about her joining some devil-worshipping cult in California and drinking pig's blood? He was round the bend, that one. Claimed he was a psychic. And then there was that old man who said she was abducted by a space ship and claimed he had photos. We checked it out and it was pictures of his dead dog that he said had told him. And then he asked if we wanted to buy the dog's soul for twenty pounds." Gilmour released a high-pitched laugh, bordering on a cackle.

Rory laughed, but it felt forced.

"There's no shortage of these jerk-offs out there. But listen, Rory, we're going to follow up with this. I'll let you know if anything pans out. You never know, it's the only lead we've had in years."

"Thanks Gilmour, for all your dedication. You're the only one who gives a shit anymore, you know?"

"If it turns out he's not lying, Rory, we'll nail the bastard."

"Aye, keep me updated."

"Where can I reach you? You move again?"

"I was in jail, actually."

"Jail?"

"Don't ask, Gilmour. You don't want to know."

"You got yourself a good lawyer?"

"Aye, I do now. It's all under control. No worries."

Rory gave him his new phone number and hung up.

He stood up and looked out the window at the passing cars on Main Street. He noticed how grimy the windowpane was up close. He could see clearly at this proximity, that the grime was not only on the outside, but on the inside as well. He traced an index finger in the dirt and an image of Frances played inside his head like an old film reel. She was drawing flowers on the dinner-steamed glass of the window in their kitchen. He turned and looked at the smiling photograph of the woman that was sitting on the end table, propped against the lamp. Rory knew it had only been wishful thinking.

A knock at his door startled him out of his reverie. In bare feet he crossed the cool wood floor and hesitated at the door.

"Who is it?"

"It's Deputy Sheriff Gus Linden, Rory. Open up, son, I'd like a word with you."

Wow, two cops in one day eager to talk to him. Rory cursed to himself, knowing this visit was about as friendly as gunfire. He looked around his apartment to see what might be in plain sight that needed to be hidden from prying eyes. He spied a handgun sitting on the coffee table and crossed the room to grab it.

"Just a sec," he said. Hastily he put it under the chair cushion.

Rory turned the dead bolt and opened the door a couple of inches, leaning out shirtless.

"What up?" he said.

"How you doing, Rory? Everything okay with you?" the old cop asked with a half smile under his trimmed moustache, one thumb hooked into his thick belt. He chewed on a piece of gum, looking Rory over as if he expected to see something wrong.

"Sure. Why wouldn't it be?"

"Just checking up on you. Figure it's got to be tough, you just getting out of jail and trying to get on your feet and all. Just wondering if there's anything I can do for you, son?"

Rory's eyes narrowed, and then he started chuckling. He folded his arms and leaned against the doorframe. "So the PYPD is making house calls, now? How about some beer? Can you bring me 'round a case, 'cause I could sure use a drink."

Linden laughed like they were old friends. "Well, it's good to see you haven't lost your sense of humor in lockup, Rory. You think I might be able to come in for a moment, and have a chin wag with you?"

"I'm kind of busy, to tell you the truth, and I wasn't expecting any guests so I've given my maid the day off. Just wouldn't be proper having one of New York's finest in for a visit with the state of things." He smirked.

"Hey, no problem, I understand you don't want the cops in your place snooping around. I was just concerned about you is all, son. Thought I'd drop by."

Rory sucked his teeth and gave him a level stare, the smile now gone.

"Fishing season's just around the corner now. You planning on doing any fishing this year, Rory?"

"Why don't you get to the point, Linden? What are you really doing at my door?"

"Well, I been thinking about how you lost that house out on Welker Road. And I heard tell you was trying to get it back."

"So what if I was? What's it to you?"

"I was just hoping that you would be taking a legal route in that endeavor and not be thinking about muscling your way in on anyone," Linden said. "Namely, that new family that's bought your place, Rory. You wouldn't be thinking of approaching them directly I hope. 'Cause I don't think they came up here looking for any trouble. And as I see it, it's not like they're the ones you should have the problem with. Your business would be directly with the bank that foreclosed on your mortgage, not this nice family."

"That so?" Rory said.

"It's best you move on, son. Put all this bullshit behind you. Focus on rebuilding your life and not making any trouble for yourself or anyone else. And you know, I'm not here to judge anyone. My job is in peace-keeping. So, if you need anything from me, anything that I can personally do to assist you in getting on with your life, you just let me know."

"Well, I'll be sure to keep that in mind." Rory gave him a dead stare. He took a step back inside his door.

"You've got a second chance here, Rory. Don't go and blow it doing something stupid that's going to land you back behind bars, now. I sure don't want to be coming to arrest you. But if it comes to that, well, it's not going to be pretty."

"Now that sounds distinctly like a veiled threat," Rory said.

"Take it how you want to. My job is to do all I can to keep this town safe. And I'm sure you're smart enough to understand what I'm trying to say. Don't let me see you getting yourself in any more trouble round here, son."

Rory was about to close the door on him without another word when Linden held up his hand.

"Oh, one more thing. Your old lawyer was found shot to death out by the lake. Larry Blackmore. You hear about that?"

Linden place his hand on the door frame and closed the gap between them. Was he trying to intimidate him, Rory wondered?

"Aye, read it in the paper." Rory snorted, and folded his arms.

"He was your first lawyer, wasn't he?"

"Aye, he was."

"So what was the deal with him? You fire him or what?"

"That's right."

"Why's that? You two have a falling out?"

"Proved himself to be incompetent," Rory said. "Firing him was the best thing I could have done for myself as it turns out."

"You don't say. Hey, when was the last time you talked to Larry, anyhow?"

Rory shrugged. "Why you bothering me with this? You liking me for his killing, are you?"

"Ah, you know me, always looking under rocks." Linden narrowed his eyes, and stared hard at Rory.

Rory snorted again, wanting to coldcock him one in the mouth. He closed the door on him, and locked it.

"You have yourself a real nice day," Linden yelled from behind the door.

Chapter
TWENTY-TWO

"Have you had breakfast?" the man on the phone asked, and she knew immediately who he was.

"What?"

"Breakfast. You know, that meal people usually have first thing in the morning?"

"I'm not quite out of bed yet."

"Did I wake you? I'm sorry. Do you like eggs Benedict?"

"Rory, I—"

"A simple yes or no will suffice," he said.

"Yes, but I can't go out for breakfast, I have to—"

"No worries, I'll bring it 'round to you. Say in half an hour? Make sure you're decent then," he said.

"I'm always decent."

Rory's laugh was a deep, rich sound in her ear. "That must be what I like about you," he said. "See you shortly."

She put down the phone and sat staring at the flickering sunlight spilling in between the gaps in the curtains, warming her room. Outside, she could hear a bird singing. It made her smile. A tune was running through her head. Yesterday, after he'd been over, she sat down with her guitar and wrote a new song. She thought of how Rory had insisted she play him a song. It felt amazing. And today she was grateful that he had asked. It was now apparent that she must get back to her music. She needed it to stay happy, to keep her buoyant. Keep her sane, in fact. It occurred to her that her life was lacking a sense of balance. She had become so consumed with taking care of the baby that she had completely forgotten about taking care of herself. Surely, that wasn't healthy. A woman needed a sense of her own identity outside of being a mother.

Something sharp jabbed her in the shoulder as she shifted to look over at the baby. She sat up and pushed aside her pillow. The kitchen knife she'd hidden there the other night had just pricked her, and she realized how unsafe it actually was to sleep with a knife in bed—a bed where she routinely nursed her baby. She lifted the knife by the handle, and shoved it into the baby bag on the floor, burying it in the bottom.

She dressed in yoga pants and a T-shirt and pulled her long hair into a braid. In the bathroom, she washed her face. She turned up the volume on the baby monitor next to Abigail's cradle and left her to sleep.

A few minutes later, Rory greeted her at the front door with a plastic bag, a tray of coffee, and a phone book.

"Compliments of the Welcome Wagon," he said, extending the phone book.

Justine laughed. "Thanks, that's awesome. Come on in."

Duke bounded out the door before she could close it. Then remembering the nest above the door, she looked around for the mother bird but didn't see her. Maybe Rory had frightened her off.

"Little bugger," she said, looking at Duke and then closing the door. "I just have to remember to let him back in again. Sometimes I forget and he's out there for an hour."

"There's a lot to explore out there."

"I hope he knows his way home again. Here let me help you," she said, taking the tray of coffee.

"I wasn't sure how you take your coffee, so I just got yours black with cream and sugar on the side."

"This is so nice of you to bring me breakfast, but completely unnecessary."

"Since when has eating become unnecessary? Are you on one of those Hollywood diets?" He followed her into the kitchen. "You sure don't look like you need a diet, to me."

"You know what I mean," Justine said.

"Aye, I know what you mean." He grinned. "Where's the other wee one this morning?"

"Sleeping. Not for long I'm sure; she was up at six this morning, so she'll be up again soon. If we're lucky, we'll be able to eat without being interrupted."

They sat across from each other at the kitchen table, by the window that overlooked the trees, and ate breakfast. A cheerful, jesting conversation quickly developed between them, as though they'd known each other for a long time. Justine had the sense that it wouldn't matter what they were doing or where they were. Just sharing time felt satisfying and extravagant.

"So what is your tattoo?" She pointed to his arm.

"It's an Oriental dragon." He put down his fork and pushed up his sleeve to show her.

"It's beautifully done. Does it cover your entire arm?"

"Aye, and my chest." He opened the neck of his shirt to expose the face and a claw covering his chest. He was lean and muscled, his chest near hairless. She could see that he was in great shape. She studied his face, that one crooked tooth, the stripe of beard on his chin. A warm scent emanated from him, rich and spicy, faintly sweet, like cinnamon.

"And who's Frances? Is she the love of your life?" She smiled playfully and touched the cross on the inside of his forearm with her finger, letting it linger there. Was she flirting with him, she wondered? It's not that she had intended it; it just seemed to rise up in spite of her.

"Aye, that she is." His eyes were downcast, staring at his tattoo. She studied his expression. She could see there was pain there that he kept in check.

"Your girlfriend? Wife?"

"My sister. Frances is my sister." He gave her a tight smile, took a sip of coffee and looked at something out the window in the distance. "She went missing when she was a child, abducted, we think. Haven't seen her since. It's been fifteen years. She was eight years old. I was twelve. And she just didn't come home from school one day. There's been no word of her since. We thought perhaps my father had taken her and brought her to the States. He lived in New York. But when I came over, I tried to track him down. But he was dead by then, and there was no trace of Frances."

"So, is that why you emigrated from Ireland, to find her?"

"Aye, it's why I came to New York." He gave her a steady gaze. "Actually, you might find this a bit strange, but when I first saw you that day out by your mailbox, I thought you were Frances all grown up. You look quite similar."

"Really," Justine said. She felt the blood rush to her face as the news hit her, wondering what this meant. "Do you have a picture of her?"

He pulled his wallet from his back pocket and produced a small, worn snapshot of a skinny girl with a head of wavy, golden hair. She thought about the picture of herself that had been removed from its frame. Had Rory been in their house and taken it? Was that why he broke in, to look for evidence that she might be his sister?

"Yeah, I can see a resemblance. I looked a lot like this when I was her age." She handed the picture back to him.

"I haven't given up trying to find her. In fact, there might be a new lead in the case, I just learned. I'm still in touch with one of the cops who investigated her disappearance, and they've got new information. He should be getting back to me soon about it. I know it might turn out that she's dead, but then at least I'll know. The not knowing is the worst."

"That had to be so tough on your family, Rory."

"Aye. Was the worst."

She sipped her coffee and gazed out the window, aware of his eyes on her. Turning to him she said, "Thank you for asking me to play for you the other day. I realized I hadn't picked up my guitar in weeks, and it's exactly what I needed. So, I just wanted to say how grateful I am. You've inspired me."

"You're an amazing singer," he said. "I don't know why you would stop. I suppose being a new mom has sort of taken over a bit, has it?"

"It has. But I think I have to stay connected, too, to my passion, which is my music. It makes me feel alive."

She liked the look of his dragon tattoo peeking out from his shirtsleeve, the way it covered his skin entirely. There was something provocative about it. And then she wondered suddenly, what was this man doing in her house while her parents were out of town? She knew they wouldn't want Rory Madden, the man that used to own their house, to be in their home. They would see him as an enemy. But somehow, this gave her pleasure.

Abigail began to cry over the baby monitor.

"Look, you go take care of your wee angel and I'll clean up around here," Rory said. "And then maybe I'll go out and look for your wee pup before he gets himself into trouble."

"Sweet. Thanks." She smiled and went to attend to Abigail.

Once the baby was fed and changed, Justine emerged from the bedroom with Abigail over her shoulder, to find Rory coming through the door with Duke in his arms.

"He's covered in mud. Found him digging out by the road. I'll give him a bath for you."

"Duke, you bad boy. We really should use the dog kennel out there."

"That might be a good idea. Then he wouldn't be able to run off."

"Did you put that in yourself? The dog kennel?" she asked, following him into the laundry room.

"Aye, for my dogs. I had two Rotties, just a bit older than this wee fellow here."

He ran water in the laundry tub and she watched the gentle way he handled the pup, talking to him in a soothing voice. The dog looked up at him with worried eyes, his ears back and his little tail between his legs.

"Have you got some shampoo we could use?" He rolled up his sleeves.

"I'll go get some."

After she put the baby in her swing, Justine went to retrieve some shampoo and a towel from the bathroom and returned to the laundry room.

"Have you got him treated for ticks? There's some out in those woods," he said as he massaged the shampoo into the dog's fur. "Found them on myself after I'd been out there. Must have carried the little bastards home on my pant legs. One climbed up on me and burrowed into the back of my neck. The dog ticks aren't so bad, just a nuisance, but the deer tick can carry diseases. Spring is the season for them, too. You should check him over when he comes in. You don't want these little fuckers infesting the house."

"I'll talk to the vet when I take him for a check-up," Justine said.

"Stick around, girl, I'm a wealth of information, some useless, some not so useless." He grinned.

Justine watched him wash Duke, fascinated by the way his hands touched the pup.

"Don't wash off his smell," she said.

"His smell?"

"His 'new puppy' smell."

Rory tossed his head back and laughed. He dried the pup, rubbing him vigorously on the floor until his fur was nearly dry. Duke grabbed the towel excitedly in his mouth and played tug-o-war with Rory. They laughed so hard as the dog growled and sneezed, trying to show that he was fierce, that they were nearly in tears.

Justine went back into the living room to check on Abigail. Rory followed her in with Duke snapping playfully at his heels.

"I think you've got a new best friend," she said, watching the dog as he sat down and stared up at Rory, panting.

"Aye, I think you're right. He could use a little training. Maybe I'll teach him a few tricks sometime, from one dog to another."

Justine turned to look out the window at the lake. "It's nearly all melted out there."

"Aye. It's finally starting to warm up. Winter is pretty desolate out here."

He moved beside her, standing only inches away and she could feel the heat of his skin.

"That's a good word for it." She turned to him and looked up to study his face. "It's barren out here, like the arctic."

"Aye. It seems impossible to think that the spring could actually come, doesn't it? Everything looks so dead right now. Summer is the complete opposite. It's like night and day," he said, his gaze meeting hers. "It's like a little piece of paradise here, then. I know you wouldn't believe it now, looking at all those bare trees out there, but I promise you, in a few more weeks you'll see what I mean."

Rory reached up a hand and gently wound a finger in a tendril of her hair and released it. She watched his expression, his eyes, as they studied her face, the smile curling up the corners of his lips, causing the lines on his cheeks to deepen. She felt something in the silence between them as they looked at each other, something that caused her heart to beat faster and her breath to quicken. She was conscious of being drawn to him and she wondered what his hands would feel like on her skin. She felt eager for life, for all the simple details that seemed suddenly beautiful and mysterious.

"So, tell me how a man with such a beautiful girl as yourself and a wonderful wee baby abandons you both to these parts?" he whispered.

She cocked her head to one side and gave him a half smile, not sure how to respond. Instead she turned to study the horizon, the steel-colored clouds hiding the sun, looking like they might dump a load of snow, dashing everyone's hopes for an early spring.

"It was not the fairy tale I thought it would be," she said. "It lasted only a few months."

"A damsel in distress, then." He grinned and she couldn't help but smile. "Have you ever had a sitter come mind the baby and let you get out?"

"I have trust issues."

"Trust issues? Aye. Well, who can blame you?" He looked down at the baby in the swing and smiled. "But if you ever think you might like to get out for an evening, I've got a friend of mine whose sister works with children and sometimes she does babysitting. I could see if she's free this evening so I can take you somewhere for dinner and then for a few drinks, maybe let you beat me at a game of pool."

"*Let* me beat you?" She laughed and playfully poked a finger at his side, noticing how solid his body felt. "You think I need a man to *let* me beat him?"

"Well, I'm pretty good," he said, grabbing hold of her hand, preventing her from poking him again. "It might actually be hard to beat me."

Rory lifted her hand and looked at the gold ring in the shape of a heart on her pinky finger, caressing it with his thumb.

"My father gave that to me for my fifteenth birthday." She smiled. "I was in the loony bin at the time, incarcerated against my will."

"The loony bin. Well, that explains everything then," Rory said.

"Really?"

"Aye. I knew you were round the bend."

She gasped at him as he threw back his head and laughed.

"Don't worry, girl, it hasn't scared me off, you being crackers and all."

"You are so funny. I can't believe you."

He was still holding her hand, his thumb caressing the back of it, when the phone rang. Leaving him at the window, she hurried into the kitchen, and disappointment welled up inside of her when she saw her father's cell number. She snatched it up. Instantly, her mood changed and the whispering inside the walls commenced. But it was louder now, more insistent than it was previously. It was terrifyingly loud.

"They're going to send you back! They're going to kill the baby! You've got to stop them! You've got to save yourself!"

Justine broke out in a cold sweat as she hung up the phone and went back to the living room. Through the window she could see crows in the tree branches. They were agitated, cawing angrily.

"My dad, he's on his way home." She was aware of a quiver in her tone and realized she was shaking.

"You'd prefer they didn't come home, then? You've got issues with your parents," he said. "I can see it in your face."

"Issues? More like the whole damn subscription. I just turned eighteen years old, a mother myself now, and my parents treat me like I'm still a child. I think they...they want to send me back." She looked out the window at the lake.

"Send you back? To Manhattan, you mean?"

"I wish. To the hospital, to the psych ward."

"Really? Well, then they're the ones who are crazy."

She smiled sadly and said, "Sometimes I wish the earth would just open up and swallow them down and then close back up again. I wish sometimes they wouldn't come home at all, that they'd just disappear and leave me alone."

"Wow, that bad, is it?" He laughed as if trying to make light of it for her benefit.

"Listen, I'm glad you came out today, Rory," she said. "But I think I'm going to get the baby ready and go run some errands. I just need to get out of the house for a while before my parents get home. I need to think about what I'm going to do."

"Sure, I'll be on my way then." He stared at her for a moment, and then said, "Are you really worried about that? That they want to put you back in the hospital?"

Justine's eyes flitted around the room as she nodded in response. She felt the walls closing in and an overwhelming terror building inside of her. She felt as if her entire being was about to explode into a thousand pieces and fly away. She fought to hold it together, to hold onto something and stuff the anxiety back down. This was no time to fall apart. She needed to be strong and protect her daughter. That's all that mattered now, that she stay strong for her baby. That she keep it together.

"Don't let them win! Don't let them get you! Don't let them get the baby!"

She walked him to the door that opened onto the deck, disappointed that he was leaving.

"There's a bird's nest above the front door with three eggs inside," Justine said. "The mama gets a little twitchy whenever we open the door, so let's save her the stress, just this once."

"A bird's nest? Above the front door?"

"It's an Eastern Wood Pewee, I think," Justine said. "I looked it up on the Internet last night."

"That so?"

She smiled at him.

"Lots of wildlife around here," he said. "Had a couple of barn swallows build nests in the garage last spring. I had to keep the doors open so they could get in and out."

Justine laughed and cocked her head at him. She was sorry to see him go, and suddenly felt anxious that he was leaving.

"Thanks for having me over," he said. "I enjoy your company. Call me if you ever need anything, all right? Call me if you need my help. Anytime."

"Thanks Rory," she said, feeling comforted that he mentioned this. Impulsively she flung her arms around his neck and hugged him tightly.

She would be okay. Somehow, she knew he had come into her life to protect her and the baby. Just being in his presence made her feel safe.

Closing the door, she watched him through the window as he hopped down the steps and then disappeared around the side of the house. She turned back to the living room. Abigail was asleep. The house felt oppressive. Her heart pulsated throughout her entire body, pounding in her head like hammers. The walls pressed in on her and the crows outside grew more aggressive.

All the memories could still bring her to tears, the silent scream within her soul, demanding to be heard. But as she looked out at the birds and the trees just beginning to bud, she thought of Rory and felt a sense of hope come over her. It felt as if a door in the darkness of her very depths had cracked open, and a sliver of light was shining in; as if her heart was seeking its own healing.

But then the gray people screamed at her, and immediately doused that little spark of hope, sucking her down into a vortex of anguish.

Chapter
TWENTY-THREE

Gus Linden sipped a glass of Merlot and looked out between the trees at the lake. A fog lifted off its silvery surface, and he watched as it lingered, hovering coldly at the edge of his property, nearly engulfing his fishing boat tied at the dock. He had the sensation that something heavy was crouching at the perimeter of his mind, ready to spring out at him when he wasn't expecting. What was it that was needling him?

The sounds of his wife in the kitchen preparing dinner drifted through the screen door onto the deck where he stood, and mixed with the sounds of whales set to music from the stereo. He found it interesting; the music itself was peaceful, yet he thought the whale noises were a bit haunting. They sounded lonely to him as they cried out, almost like babies. And he wondered what message they would be sending if the sounds could be interpreted. Did they watch us from their deep watery home? Did they see the way humans dumped toxins and oil into their oceans and want to warn us of the planet's pending disaster? Is that what they would tell us if they could communicate with us?

The sun was a residue of orange in the sky beneath distant clouds rolling darkly over the hills. The temperature would drop tonight after an unseasonably warm day. It was too early in the season for bugs, but Gus was thinking about screening in the deck soon. With the number of trees on the property and being so close to the lake, the bugs could be killer out here. He and his wife enjoyed spending time on the deck, looking at the lake, and listening to the birds. Sometimes, while he read, Anna would sit with her knitting, working away on a baby sweater or booties for somebody's pending birth. Or she'd be knitting the Christmas sweaters for the grandkids she liked to start on in July.

His official retirement was seven months away, and he was looking forward to it. To all the travel plans he and Anna had; Europe, Hawaii, and she'd talked about going on cruises. They had stacks of pamphlets and travel magazines in nearly every room of the house. There would be plenty of time for all of the building and woodworking projects he wanted to do then, as well, but the screen couldn't wait another season. Maybe he'd start on it this weekend; take measurements at least, figure out what he needed, perhaps price it out at the hardware store.

He felt the shadows at the edge of his mind leaning on him, and he turned his thoughts away from the pending project. What was it that was bothering him? And then, a moment later, it became clear as an image of Rory Madden pushed into his mind. Of course, that was what was taxing him. There was something about that boy that just wasn't right. He had a bad feeling about him.

Gus shook the thought of Rory from his mind. He didn't want to dwell on him now. With a fingernail, he picked at the flaking paint on the railing of the deck. Painting the deck was another thing he would need to do before the summer started. He loved this house. Loved its warm, log cabin feel with all the natural wood and high ceilings, and its picture windows with the view of Keuka Lake. He loved fishing on a summer evening and bringing home their dinner; or early in the morning as the sun was rising and the lake was still, its mirrored surface reflecting the sky and the hills. He loved the woods that surrounded them, the peace and quiet of the lake—at least until the tourists descended. He loved that they had lived here nearly forty years and raised their three children in this house.

For a while, they had tossed around the idea of selling once his retirement came in, moving down to Florida, St. Pete's Beach, but the thought of leaving their home and leaving Penn Yan was unimaginable. He'd lived in this town all his life, grew up on Court Street playing cops and robbers with his older brothers. Funny, how they'd always made him the cop, and look what he'd grown up to be. Fortunately, his brothers hadn't taken their childhood roles into adulthood. One had become a teacher and the other a boat builder. And they'd all stayed right here in Penn Yan, married and raised their children.

Leaving Penn Yan was not in the cards for Gus. It was best to stay put and just do some traveling. They were happy here. There was no reason to leave and too many to stay.

Gus drank his wine and watched the fog hovering around the dock.

"Dinner's ready," Anna called to him from inside. He turned and watched his wife carrying two plates of pasta topped with her homemade sauce. A ruffled apron was around her middle.

Gus moved back inside the house and closed the screen and the sliding glass door behind him.

"It's your favorite, spaghetti," she said, laughing, her blond curls bobbing, and set the plates down on the dining room table.

"You mean *your* favorite, don't you?"

"Spaghetti's not your favorite?" She adjusted her eyeglasses and pouted. "You couldn't have told me that when we first married, Gus?"

He made an exaggerated show of clearing his throat, "What do you mean? It's always been my favorite. Boy, oh boy. Bisketi again!"

They laughed at their shared joke about the spaghetti, which she served them at least three times a week. Every Sunday, she would make a new pot, adding fresh herbs and spices. Sometimes they would have other pasta—rigatoni, penne, or linguini. Mostly it was spaghetti.

Gus lit the candles on the table and sat down across from her. He shook Parmesan over his plate and buttered a piece of bread in silence as Rory Madden's face drifted into his mind. He wondered if he should give Liz from Blackmore's office a call, and see if she knew when Rory last contacted him. Liz, being Blackmore's secretary forever, knew everything there was to know about the man. She was also a good friend of Anna. If anyone knew Blackmore's life, it was Liz. Probably the state investigators had already talked to her. But it wouldn't hurt, him giving her a phone call. The investigators probably didn't know to inquire about Rory.

"Got something on your mind?" Anna raised a thin eyebrow at him and sipped from her wine glass.

"Just work." He turned his fork in the middle of the plate, winding the pasta around it.

"Bringing it home, are you? Is it the Larry Blackmore case?"

"Sure is. Got our hands full with that."

"I feel so sorry for his wife. Their daughter is expecting her first baby. She's due any day, and now this." Anna took another sip of her wine, not yet touching her food. "I went round to the church today for our strawberry tea and Joyce was there. She's heartbroken, Gus. I didn't know what to say to her. They've been married twenty-five years."

"It's a shame. Especially the way it happened. Shot like that and just left to die. Nobody deserves that, least of all Larry. He wasn't a bad guy."

"For a criminal lawyer." She smirked. "Strange partnership that is, you catching them and him getting them free. Isn't that how it works?"

Gus laughed. "Yeah, something like that."

"You always see the good in people, don't you Gus? It's an odd quality for a cop, you know?"

"You've told me that once or twice. It's the town, is what it is. I'd be a whole other breed of cop if I'd have been stationed in New York City now, don't you think?"

"Got any idea who killed him? Any suspects?"

"Got my eye on one," he said. "That Rory Madden fellow who lost the house out off of East Lake road, there. Larry Blackmore was his first lawyer, and then they had some sort of falling out and Madden fired him. I'd really like to know what all that was about. You know, I just get a bad feeling about that boy. Something not right about him."

He chewed a mouthful of spaghetti and then said, "So, you liking this new CD you got?"

She eyed him over the top of her eyeglasses, and then they both broke into slow smiles.

"I can tell you're not," she said.

"You know me, Anna. I'm a Sinatra fan. This New Age crap don't do nothing for me. I'd even take your Andrea Bocelli over this."

"Bocelli it is," she said and lifted the remote control from the buffet beside her, then switched the CD. "We'll go visit his hometown when we're in Italy."

"Sounds good to me. You think they make spaghetti sauce as good as yours in Italy?"

Her lips twitched and she patted her curls. "I could teach those Italians a thing or two, couldn't I?"

"You sure could, Anna." He winked at her.

Rory's face tore at his thoughts. If he had anything at all to do with Blackmores's death, Gus was going to find the evidence and bring the son of a bitch in. Before he officially retired, he would make it his mission to make certain Rory Madden paid.

Chapter
TWENTY-FOUR

"Hey Rory, how's it going, buddy? Hope I'm not calling too late, but when you're an insomniac like me, two in the morning is still early," Douggy Chambers said over the line.

"What up? You find out anything on the Jameson family?"

"Well, yes and no. It's complicated. I couldn't find any birth records for Justine. It appears she was adopted or something by Brett Jameson when she was just eight years old. Pamela Jameson is not her real mother, though, it's her stepmother."

Rory slouched in his chair with the glow of bluish light from the television washing over his shirtless body, and lit a cigarette. "What else?"

"She had a stepsister who died about four years ago. They were raised in the Upper East Side, attended the Spence School for girls. Then it seems Justine went loony tunes and spent a year inside a private psychiatric hospital when she was just fourteen. She moved home after getting out, graduated high school and worked at a music store in mid-town. Her father owns a footwear company, makes specialty boots for arctic weather. Looks like it's on the brink of bankruptcy; he's got creditors on his ass."

"And where was she before Brett Jameson adopted her? What about all that?"

"Well, that's the strangest thing. I can't find any info on her. It's like a dead end, like she didn't exist before. If I could get a hold of the adoption records, then—"

"I don't think she's Frances. I think I was grasping at straws. She's not even the same age." Rory flicked the ash from his cigarette onto one of the teacup saucers he was using as an ashtray and watched the faces on the TV screen.

"I'd have to agree with you on that, buddy. You want to hear what I dug up on this Pamela woman? There's a lot."

"Aye, I suppose." He let out a breath, feeling his interest waning.

"Well, I'll start with the boring shit. Pamela is originally from Watkins Glen. Her mother still lives there, and it looks like she's not long for this world. Lung cancer. That's a certain death sentence. So it appears they moved up this way to be closer to her. Anyway, Pamela pays for a shit load of nurses for her, and guess how she finances it? Mrs. Jameson is a member of the world's oldest profession."

"Now what could that possibly be? Dinosaur-slayer?"

Douggy let loose one of his best hyena laughs. "Okay, so maybe there's other professions just as old. She's got a Web site. Calls herself Stephanie. Stephanie of New York dot com. Check it out. There's lots of pictures. She doesn't even hide her face. Probably not the smartest thing to do for a woman who's married, unless of course her husband knows she's sucking dick for a living, but I get the impression she's doing this on the sly."

"No kidding," Rory said. "Well, you just never know what's behind that happy façade of domestic harmony, do you?"

"It doesn't end there, my friend. I got some dirt on Mr. Jameson. Check your email. I sent you some pictures, and plenty of them," Douggy said. "Buddy of mine in the city put a tail on him. Brett Jameson hooked up with some broad for dinner at Marseille on 9th Avenue, and then went back to her apartment on the Lower East Side. Goes by the name Lorena. She's from South America. Works as a dancer at Stringfellows."

"Your friend able to shoot any intimate moments?" Rory stood up, crossed the room to the kitchen table and clicked on his laptop, accessing his hotmail account.

"Does swapping spit and grabbing her boob qualify as intimate? They look real friendly, if you ask me."

He opened Douggy's email and downloaded six pictures.

In the first one, Brett was walking along the street with a dark-haired, lanky woman in heels and a short dress, wearing a raincoat. In the second one, he was hugging her playfully and they were smiling. In the next one, they were engaged in a passionate kiss and his hand was on her breast. The other ones showed them kissing and heading inside an apartment building.

"Aye, he's been a naughty little boy, all right," Rory said, grinning. "Good work, Douggy."

"There's more. The apartment she's living in is registered in Brett's name, looks like he pays the rent too."

"His wife's not going to be happy about that."

"Well, it's no surprise to me, the shit I see. So you need anything else on this Brett guy? Or the broad he's been doing the horizontal bop with?"

"That should be all the info I need for now, Douggy. Let's have a drink tomorrow at O'Leary's."

"Sounds like a plan," Douggy said. "See you then, buddy."

Rory put down the phone and measured out two lines of coke, moving them around on the kitchen table with his bankcard as he studied the pictures. He wondered how he should approach this. How much did Brett Jameson want to keep his lover a secret from his wife? Enough to give up the house? Sign it over to him in exchange for the pictures? Maybe. Maybe not. And what about Pamela Jameson? Was she keeping her double life a secret? Would she pay for it to remain that way?

Rory sucked the coke up each nostril through a short straw. The woman was a prostitute. It was possible her husband didn't even know. What kind of fucked up people was he dealing with here? How could a woman keep something like that secret from her husband? As he turned this information over in his mind, the beginning of a plan developed. He'd have to give this some more consideration, see how it could benefit him.

A half moon paraded in the frame of a darkened window as if peeking in at him, communicating silently about the secrets it kept. He could see his plan as it unfolded before him. He just had to play it right, be patient and wait for the right opportunity to reveal itself. It wasn't something he could force. Timing was everything. He would stay centered, and then everything he wanted would come to him effortlessly. The moon's presence seemed to confirm this.

An image of Justine playing her guitar fluttered into his mind. What was it about this woman that captured him? He knew it wasn't just her physical beauty that struck him, her long mass of wavy hair and her smooth, clear skin. And it wasn't just her rich, soulful voice, reminding him of a summer breeze wafting through the leaves of trees or a field of tall grass. It wasn't just her abundance of natural talent that impressed him. It was the warmth and gentleness in her heart, an inner light she possessed and strength more spiritual than that of anyone he had met. Being around her made him feel good. That was what he liked about her. How he felt about himself when he was in her presence. Was she the woman he was waiting for? Was she the one? He turned these questions over inside of him, thinking that he might be falling for her. And yet, only a short time ago, he had wished for her to be his sister. It was so peculiar. If felt almost depraved.

He held one nostril closed with an index finger, and inhaled another line, and then one up his other nostril. The intensity of the drugs swept through him like a rush of brilliance; that sublime, peaceful feeling, facilitating a sense of enlightenment. The shadows inside of him faded to the background. A sensation of bliss expanded in his veins, pulsating in his blood. He felt the wings of the great mystical bird pulling inside of him, rushing up from his soul, connecting with the heavens. It spoke to him in the pure silence of his being, without words.

The next morning, Rory was up at seven. He made himself a coffee, lit a cigarette, and sat down in front of his laptop. He clicked on the incriminating pictures of Brett Jameson on his clandestine little tryst with some stripper who looked half his age, and grinned. He did an Internet search for Brett's company and found his email address. He formulated a cryptic letter that Brett should easily be able to decipher and read it back to himself.

Dear Mr. Jameson,
I have something you want. It pertains to your meeting at Marseille Restaurant the other night. Let's see if we can meet and come to an agreement that would benefit both of us.
Rory Madden

Rory included his cell phone number in the email. After his coffee, he put on his sneakers and track pants and went for a run outside. His cardiovascular system had weakened due to lack of exercise and he hacked up phlegm along the way, knowing that either the tobacco or the exercise would have to go. Back at his apartment, he showered, dressed and walked down to Angel's Diner for something to eat.

His cell phone rang and he looked at the unfamiliar number before he answered.

"You sent me an email this morning," a stern voice greeted him. "What do you want from me?"

"Brett, how nice of you to call me."

The waitress set a plate on the table in front of him.

"Cut the shit. What is it that you think you have?"

"Would you like more coffee?" she asked. Rory nodded.

"Pictures."

"Pictures," Brett repeated. "What pictures?"

"You and that hot wee stripper you're running around with on your wife."

The waitress splashed coffee over the rim of his cup.

"Oh, I'm so sorry!" She mopped it up with a dirty rag.

Annoyed, Rory shooed her away, giving her a scowl. She looked embarrassed as she hurried off.

"What are you talking about? You're crazy." Brett laughed.

"Shall I email them to you, then? Or maybe I can send them to your lovely wife."

Silence.

"Bet she'd be pissed about you footing her rent, now wouldn't she?"

More silence.

"Are you still there?"

"All right, what the hell do you want?"

"My house. I want my house back."

"It's not your house. You lost that house and we bought it fair and square from the bank."

"I'm afraid I was ripped off, you see. I was unjustly treated by a number of people, from the police who did an illegal search of my premises, causing me to be incarcerated, to my lawyer who pilfered my savings and prevented me from paying my mortgage."

"Your hard luck story is not my problem," Brett said. "And this is not your house anymore, so you're just going to have to get over it."

"Aye, it is my house. I fucking built it myself and it's just a matter of time before I get you out. Now, are we going to play ball or shall I just pass on my information to your missus?"

"You're not getting my house," Brett said. "You're crazy if you think I'm just going to give you my house."

"All right then I guess this conversation is over."

"Wait!"

"What, then?"

"There must be something we can do."

"I only want one thing. That's it."

"But I can't. It's ridiculous. I mean I can't just give you the house. There's legalities. I can't just do this. It's not so simple."

"You seem like a man who can make things happen, Jameson. I'll give you a day to work out the details. Get back to me by this time tomorrow or one click on my keyboard will delete your happy wee life as you know it."

Chapter
TWENTY-FIVE

Justine opened her eyes. Something had awakened her. A voice. A loud voice. Someone had screamed. She blinked and looked around. Her room was dark. She looked at the baby and could see the outline of her chubby face. Was she breathing? Justine placed a hand on her chest and felt the subtle movements of her lungs. She released her own breath and lay back on the pillows, her heart pounding, her body cold, clammy.

"You're not safe here. They're going to get you." A voice whispered.

Justine turned and was startled to see the people inside the walls emerging. They were bursting forth from the plaster as if it was mere plastic, coming out of the walls! They were coming into her room!

"You'll die if you don't listen to us! Your baby will die if you don't listen! Why don't you listen?!" The voice was neither male or female. Just loud, angry.

"Who are you?" Justine sat up, staring in disbelief. An odd feeling of delirium made her dizzy. Was she dreaming? She reached for the knife under her pillow, her hands shaking. Where was the knife? Where was the goddamn knife!

Two of them had broken free from the wall, their naked figures gray and grotesque in the shadows of the room. They stepped toward her, moving as if their limbs were made of stone, pieces crumbling, falling away from them. More were following. All around the room. From every wall, they emerged. Huge, faceless creatures, closing in on her.

"Get out! Get out!" Justine screamed at them, feeling around for the knife. She was sure she had put one here! Where the hell was it?

"They're going to get you! They're going to kill the baby! Give her to us and we'll keep her safe."

"Justine! Justine! Wake up!" Pamela's face appeared before her, eyes round, glaring. Justine let out a shriek and drew back from her.

"You were dreaming. It's a dream, Justine. It's all right, it's just a dream." She shook her head and a lock of bleached hair fell across her face.

Justine sat up, her gaze darting around the room. Light crept around the perimeter of the curtains, sunlight assaulting her eyes like a thousand razor blades. The room was silent. The gray people were gone.

"What the hell is this?" Pamela lifted a knife from beside Justine's pillow.

"Can you not use bad words around the baby? I promised Dad I'd stop, so you can't be doing it either." Justine lay back on the pillow feeling exhausted, like she could sleep for days.

"Tell you what," Pamela said. "I'll stop swearing around the baby if you stop carrying knives around her."

"Oh, for fuck sakes Pam, I'm not going to pull an Andrea Yates if that's what you're thinking."

"I thought we weren't supposed to use bad words around the baby."

Justine gave her a look and turned over.

"This is really unsafe, Justine. Why would you have a knife under your pillow? Actually, it wasn't even under the pillow. It was more like beside it."

"Do you even have to ask why I would have a knife in bed after what happened?" she whispered, trying not to disturb the baby. "And what are you doing in my room, anyway? Don't you know how to knock?"

"You know, it wasn't that long ago Brett came home to find you in tears, all freaked out about the knives in the kitchen and worried that they could hurt Abigail. Now you're sleeping with one underneath your pillow. This doesn't make any sense to me, Justine. This is just you being stupid and careless, as usual. I thought you had become more mature, but it's obvious you haven't."

Justine pushed the covers aside and got out of bed. So much for sleeping. She was wide-awake now.

"What doesn't make sense to me is you questioning me about sleeping with a knife after the break-in we had," Justine said. "Oh, that's right, you don't really believe me. My fault, I forgot."

Pamela tsked and stalked out of the room. Justine listened to her retreat and head down the stairs, probably to replace the knife in the block in the kitchen.

The fleeting idea of leaving occurred to her. What would she do? Go back to Manhattan? She could pack up her things in her Jeep and go stay with her friend, Diane, in Brooklyn. She could find a job and support Abigail herself. Maybe they would even hire her back at the music store. No, she couldn't live with Diane and her kids. She would go crazy, for sure.

Maybe she could rent a room somewhere, at least temporarily until she got her own place. She needed to talk to Keith about child support payments, too. Justine was an independent, educated, resourceful woman. What did she need her parents for, anyway? Women raised babies single-handedly all the time these days. Her own mother had been a single parent. Maybe she should have a backup plan just in the event they tried to put her away again in a hospital. Wasn't that just being cautious, planning for the worst? Like buying life insurance?

Justine took a deep breath. She heard the puppy barking excitedly as he was let out of his kennel and taken outside for his morning pee.

"I found the other ones," Pamela announced, entering the bathroom a few minutes later where Justine stood brushing her teeth. Duke wandered in and began sniffing at the garbage can beside the sink. "The ones under the sofa cushions? There's one more missing from the block, though. Where did you put it?"

Justine spit in the sink. Pamela was treating her like a child.

"I don't know what you're talking about."

"Justine! You know exactly what I'm talking about," Pamela said. "What is wrong with you, hiding knives all over the house? Next you'll want to get a gun."

"Actually that's not a bad idea. Isn't that what people do out in the country, anyway? They have guns? Boy, things are getting real exciting around here, aren't they?"

Pamela frowned and ran a hand across her forehead as if the beginning of a migraine had assailed her. She looked odd without her makeup; all pale and creepy, like a being from another planet.

"How are the pills working out for you?" Pamela said.

"Fine."

"Really?"

"That's what I said."

"So, they've been working fine. You feel okay taking them?"

Justine turned away without answering.

"Well, that's funny, because you ran out of them weeks ago. I checked the dates. What's the matter with you? Why haven't you refilled the prescription? This is just completely irresponsible of you," Pamela said. "When are you going to grow up, Justine? Tell me when?"

"Whatever. You need to leave me the fuck alone now."

"You're fine? Really? Cause I swear I don't know who you are."

"Oh, please. You've never known who I was, Pam. That's nothing new." She snorted, giving the dog a less than gentle nudge with her foot, away from the toilet he was stretching up at.

"You haven't been the same since you had the baby. You're not the same."

"I'm crazy right? That's what you think isn't it? Want to lock me up again and try throwing away the key this time? 'Cause I'm a fucking lunatic who imagines things, sees things that aren't fucking there! Monsters living in the walls—"

"What? Monsters?"

Justine said nothing, afraid Pamela would think she was mad. Maybe she really was losing her mind. Was it normal to see people emerging from the walls? But wasn't it true that people who were crazy didn't know they were crazy? So if she actually thought she was nuts, then maybe that meant that she was really okay.

She needed to meditate, do some yoga, release all this tension.

"Are you seeing things?" There was a little quiver in Pamela's voice and Justine found that she liked the sound of it.

She turned away without saying anything and walked out of the bathroom.

"Tell me what's going on," Pamela said. "Don't shut me out!"

Pamela followed her into the bedroom, as she pulled a summer dress and a cardigan from their hangers in her closet. She could feel Pam staring at her. The silence hung between them like a pit, a giant dark hole that wanted to suck them in.

"Justine, you're not okay. I can see that you're not, and so can your father. Now you've got to start talking, you've got to start telling us what's going on."

"I don't need any pills or doctors or hospitals. Leave me alone, I have to get dressed, " Justine said. She peeked in the crib to see the baby still asleep.

"You know, it's like you live in your own universe." Pamela threw up her hands. "You've always been like that, thinking you know everything. You know so much more than everyone else on the planet, right? Well, if you're so goddamn smart, why can't you support yourself like everyone else, huh? Why did you let your relationship fall apart, if you're so smart? Why are you back living with us if you're so goddamn smart, Justine? Just look at the mess you've made of your life!"

Justine took a deep breath, released it slowly, and said, "Keep your voice down please, I don't want you upsetting my daughter. You and I have nothing more to talk about."

"I'm trying here, okay? It hasn't been easy for me, but I'm really trying. I don't like this situation, but I'm trying to be supportive. I know you're feeling isolated out here. Brett told me. And I know you've had some things to deal with being a new mom. But can we at least try to get along?"

"Why the fuck do you suddenly care?"

"I've always cared, Justine." Her voice sounded tired.

"Excuse me while I stick a finger down my throat, cause I'm gonna retch." Justine thought about that text message from Russ. She wondered if her Dad had confronted Pamela with the information. "All you've ever cared about is yourself and Allison," Justine said. "You never gave a shit about me. Allison was your whole world, and there was no room left in it for me. I was an inconvenience to you. And as soon as she died, you were on a mission to get me out of the house, locking me away in that medieval torture chamber they call a fucking hospital."

"Justine, I didn't—"

"And honestly, Pam, I don't think you even love my dad. I don't know why the fuck you ever married him in the first place. I guess he had money at the time, didn't he? So now that he's broke, what the hell are you still doing here? Why don't you just leave?"

Pam was quiet for a moment, and when she finally spoke, her voice was soft and trembling. "That really hurts me. You have no idea what I've been through," she said. "And you have no idea what I'm going through with my mother right now being ill, and now your father's business going under. You think I've had an easy time of things? You don't know anything."

Justine stood with her arms folded, saying nothing, and waiting for Pamela to leave so she could get dressed. There was a pause for what felt like forever.

"Can we call a truce?" Pam asked, sniffing back tears. "Can we try and be friends? All this hostility just kills me. Why don't we go into town tonight and have dinner or something? We need to hit the supermarket, don't we? Let's be friends, Justine. That's what I really want is for you and I to be friends."

Justine felt beaten down, exhausted from the insomnia. Still, she wouldn't allow herself to give in. Pamela was the enemy.

"I've just got to stop in on your Grandma and then go into the office for a bit this afternoon. I should be home around six." She turned to walk away and then stopped. "Justine?"

"What?"

"I want you to keep the appointment Brett made for you with that doctor in Manhattan."

"I'll think about it," she said, knowing there was no way in hell she was letting them take her to a shrink. She was offended that her father went ahead and made an appointment for her when he knew how she felt about doctors, psychiatrists in particular. Knowing what she had experienced and her deep mistrust of doctors, how could he simply go ahead and do that? Did he have some plans she didn't know about? Plans to have her locked up somewhere? Is that what her parents had in mind for her?

Justine could feel them conspiring against her. They wanted to put her away and steal the baby. And then what? What sick and vile things did they have in store for Abigail, the bastards? She shivered at the thought.

A moment later, everything inside of her shifted. Her mind cracked, like a door had opened. She understood fully the absurdity of her thoughts. What had she been thinking? Where had all this paranoia come from? Maybe she really was losing her mind. If she could just figure out a way to hang on to this moment of coherence, live inside this awareness, she would be fine. Everything would be fine. She would be normal.

Chapter
TWENTY-SIX

Rory felt euphoric, fired up like an engine straining at full speed. It stretched through him, inside every bone. And strangely, he felt centered, knowing he had found the answers he had sought for fifteen years. Fifteen years since the pivotal event that had shaped his very existence. Fifteen years of suffering; a black hole of pain that defied human understanding. The crust of terror that bound him, sealing him inside, was finally cracking and breaking away. He could feel a tearing at his soul and a sense of release as if all his senses had come to life.

The ringing of the phone pierced the silence of his apartment. Rory snatched it up immediately.

"Rory, how you doing?" Gilmour said. "I got your message that you called. Something urgent?"

"Randal Trowbridge. I know who he is. He was called Randy. My sister wrote about him in her diary."

"Really? She had a diary? We didn't find any diary in her room, though I remember looking for one, in fact."

"You didn't find it because you didn't know where to look." Rory lit a cigarette and puffed as he paced the wooden floor. "There was a loose floor board in her room, inside the closet. I used to read it sometimes when she wasn't home. Randy was some guy she knew that she had a crush on. He was quite a bit older. Fifteen or sixteen, I think."

"It might be the same guy, but then again, Randy's not an uncommon name."

"Sure, but it's possible right? She referred to him as her boyfriend in the diary and she talked about how she was in love with him," Rory said. "It was all little girl crush sort of stuff that she wrote. I only remember some of it and it's pretty vague at best."

"Really. This would have been helpful at the time if we had this information, Rory."

"Aye, I know, but what can I say, Gilmour? I was just a kid at the time. I was in shock over her disappearance."

"It didn't occur to you then that this might have been significant information?"

"Fuck no. Frances was also in love with Mr. Harmon, her gym teacher the year before. He was like forty or something, so when I read about this guy, Randy, being a lot older, I just thought it was innocent; just Frances with her head in the clouds again. You know, I just assumed all this time that—well, I assumed a lot of things, but I thought this was just some guy she had a crush on and that was it. I didn't think he was returning the feelings. You know, I was twelve fucking years old then, Gilmour. What the fuck did I know about anything?"

"Aye, okay. Okay." He sighed.

"Do you think it's possible she ran off with this guy? You know, maybe he didn't kill her; maybe he's just making that shit up, like you said. Maybe she's still alive." Rory moved over to the window, and leaned on the frame, trying to see the hills in the distance that were obscured by fog.

"We have to look at all scenarios. Do you still have her diary?" Gilmour said.

"I never kept it."

"Any idea what might have happened to it?"

"We moved only months after she disappeared. I came out of school one afternoon and my mom was there waiting for me with the car all packed up and we just moved right then to another flat across town. My mother packed up all Frances's stuff and just put it in a storage locker in the basement, but I'm sure she didn't know about her diary. I was never able to go back to our house again. Maybe it's even still there."

Gilmour was silent for a moment. "Maybe. It's a possibility. What else did she write about this guy? Can you think of anything else?"

"He drove a car and he smoked. That's about all I can really remember. She just drew a lot of little hearts and pictures and stuff. I love Randy, true love always, you know?"

"Rory, can you remember when you read this stuff about Randy? When was it in relation to her disappearance?"

"It was a couple of months before she went missing. I had only read it just a couple of times, maybe three, at the most. I guess I just didn't find it all that interesting."

Rory butted his half-smoked cigarette in the teacup saucer and rubbed his eyes. He sat down and laid out a line of coke on the coffee table. He licked an index finger, enjoying its bitter taste. "So, what now? Where do we go from here?"

"The woman who contacted us about him has agreed to help us. She's going to wear a wire and try to get him talking about what happened. He hasn't even given up her name yet, that it was Frances. But the MO matches Frances. We just need him to admit that and then we'll bring him in."

"Good, okay. That's progress, at least. How long do you think this will take?"

"A couple of weeks, maybe. She's been seeing him quite a lot. He's asked her to marry him, so he trusts her and she's willing to play along. Brave woman. Without her, we might never crack this thing. So, I'll keep you updated, Rory."

"What about Frances's diary? Will you try and see if it's still in the old house?"

"I'm definitely going to look into it." Gilmour said. "You can count on that. It's evidence we can use against this guy. If he did what he says he did, and the more we can lock this case up tight, the better chance there is of a conviction."

"Okay, call me when you know more."

"For sure. So hey, everything good with you, Rory? You keeping yourself out of trouble?"

"Aye, no worries. Things are looking up."

"Good, that's good to hear. We'll talk soon."

Rory hung up the phone and snorted a line off the table. He relit his cigarette. Yes, things were definitely looking up. He could feel himself flowing freely into everything around him, breaking from the darkness, rising up as a phoenix from the black hole inside of himself, awakening to a new sense of power. Yet, he wondered, as he inhaled another line, if it was the coke creating these feelings of invincibility. Maybe he needed to slow down. Lay off all the drugs.

He thought of Justine. He had wanted so badly to believe she was Frances.

The black hole where his heart had been beckoned to him; he knew if he let go, if he gave in, it would suck him down and he might never emerge. He also knew that if he found out what happened to Frances, he would be complete somehow. The hole inside of him would fill in and bury his pain forever. It would free him.

Rory sucked in another line of coke through the straw, checked the magazine in his handgun for bullets, and stuffed it in the back of his jeans. From the closet he retrieved his leather coat, and then pulled his cap over his head. He would take care of some unfinished business in the meantime, and chase away all this frustrations.

A chill rain fell in splotches, lifting the smell of earth and concrete into the air as Rory walked along the sidewalk on Main Street to the convenience store two blocks up. The sky above was a jailhouse gray. A crack of thunder echoed across the clouds as he stood in front the pay phones and dialed Brett's cell phone number.

"You've had more than enough time to take care of this problem we have."

"Was that you who smashed my car's windshield, Madden?"

Rory laughed.

"You asshole. Stay the hell off my property or I'll have you charged with trespassing."

"Sounds like you're not willing to be cooperative. And here, I thought you were a reasonable man, Mr. Jameson. I would have thought a family man such as yourself would be a little more careful about the decisions he makes, so as not to bring anything onto his loved ones unwittingly. I'm sure you don't want that type of complication in your life, Mr. Jameson."

"I don't care what you do with those pictures, but if you think you're going to blackmail me or threaten me and my family, you've made a big mistake."

Rory watched a PYPD cruiser pass by, staring at it until it turned down Maiden Lane. "All right, then. If you don't want to play ball that's your choice," Rory said. "But you're not going to like what's coming next, buddy."

"I'm going to call the police if you don't back off."

"They can't help you." Rory said and quietly replaced the phone.

Chapter
TWENTY-SEVEN

Pamela stood looking out the window at the little girls playing on the street in their pink battery-operated car, the sound of gravel crunching under its plastic tires. Their screeching voices pierced the air and flowed inside the house, surrounding her with memories.

The smell of burned toast wafted in the air and Pamela turned, annoyed. That new nurse she hired was a retard. She should look into getting a replacement. Pamela noticed that her mother's eyes were closing, and she moved over to her chair to push on the back of the recliner so she would be more comfortable. She stroked her wispy hair, soft as Abigail's, and pulled the crocheted blanket over her chest. She remembering her mother making the blanket in this very house. Pamela had been fifteen then, and pregnant with Allison.

Her father had been disgusted that she was pregnant. But he seldom came around the house then. Eventually, he didn't come around at all. He just disappeared, and they all assumed he drank himself to death—a long overdue miracle in their lives.

She walked over to the window again and peered out at the lawn. The grass was starting to green up and would need mowing soon. She should see if the kid next door was still willing to do the yard work again this year. In the flowerbeds, the daffodils were in full bloom and the tender shoots of tulips were pushing through the dirt.

She watched the little girls, and thought of Allison playing on this very street with her friends, skipping, tossing a ball, or chasing each other in a game of tag. In her memory she could see her sandy pig-tailed hair bouncing like two springs as she ran, her skinny legs and arms pale in the afternoon sun, slathered in suncreen.

It was a Sunday in early spring when Allison, who was just fourteen, made dinner for the family—something she often did. They sat at the dining room table—herself, Brett and both girls—eating stuffed roast chicken, broccoli with cheese sauce and Parisian potatoes. They drank cold glasses of tomato juice and talked about going on a skiing vacation in Vermont at Christmas. Neither of the girls had ever been skiing. The mood was cheerful, happy.

Allison's cat jumped up on her lap and surprised her, causing her to draw in a sudden breath. Pamela asked what the matter was when it looked like she was trying to say something but for some reason, couldn't get the words out. Then Brett jerked to his feet, bumping his plate. A fork clattered on the wood floor as he lurched forward and started patting her on the back. Then he began slapping her back hard. Allison shook her head. Her hands clawed at her throat. Her face turned red, then deeper red. Pamela stood up yelling at Allison to cough it up. Brett tried to stick his fingers down her throat. Allison's face turned purple. Her eyes rolled back in her head. Pamela hurried into the kitchen and called 911.

Pamela screamed into the phone for an ambulance. Justine sat as if in shock, her eyes wide and staring. The operator began instructing her on the Heimlich maneuver. Brett was kneeling on the floor with Allison face-down across his knee, slapping her back. Allison wasn't moving. Pamela was yelling at Brett and yelling at the operator and Brett looked up at her, fear in his eyes. She screamed out the instructions as Brett struggled with Allison's limp body, falling under her weight. Finally he got his arms around her and began to push with his fist in her solar plexus. He was sweating, fumbling with her. Her face had turned a chalky color. Her eyes were closed.

Everything happened so suddenly and so quickly. It was unthinkable. How was it that one minute they were all enjoying dinner around the table and in the next, a potato had lodged itself in Allison's throat, and she had asphyxiated? How did that happen? It defied reason.

Sadly, now they all knew the Heimlich maneuver.

Pamela watched the droplets splatter on the windowsill and she touched her fingers to her face, feeling the moisture of her tears. She felt something swirling in her stomach, something that wanted to come up. Taking a few deep breaths, she closed her eyes, willing the sensation to pass. She wanted to just go home and crawl under the covers of her bed and cry until she felt nothing and then went to sleep. But she couldn't. A customer was expecting her in half an hour. She looked down at her watch, knowing she needed to pull herself together. She thought of her bank account. She wasn't sure how much she had managed to squirrel away into her savings since the move, but she knew she had twelve thousand dollars in a coffee can in the kitchen cupboard. When would it be enough? She didn't know. Probably never.

Pamela went into the kitchen where the nurse was busy buttering more toast. She placed her check on the counter.

"The doctor's coming to see her this afternoon. Her chest seems congested and she's not eating," the nurse said. "She probably won't even eat this, but all I can do is try."

"It might be just a cold she's got," Pamela said.

In the bathroom, Pamela looked in the medicine cabinet. There was a bottle of Percocet sitting on the shelf. She opened it up and shook half the bottle into the zippered pouch inside her purse. Her mother couldn't swallow them anyway, so nobody would miss them. Back in the living room, Pamela kissed her mother on the forehead, brushing back her soft hair as she slept. It seemed like only this morning that her mother had been in the kitchen peeling apples for her pies, and Pamela just home from school, had been eating those sweet strips of apple skin as they came off her peeler, sometimes the entire skin in one long strip, listening to her mother sing, her voice strong and full. How had time moved so quickly and eroded her into this sick old woman? In a matter of months, weeks even, her life would be gone. Pamela felt her heart restrict.

The thought of losing her was frightening. Who would she have then? Brett? She thought of Allison. It had been more than four years since her death. Maybe it was time to let go, time to forgive Brett, and try to repair all the damage done. Pamela swallowed down her tears. She had cried enough today. She had to be strong. She had to keep putting one foot in front of the other. What other choice did she have?

"I love you Mama. I'll be back in the morning."

The drive to Rochester was forty minutes from her mother's house. She made it in twenty-five and pulled her Lexus into the parking lot of the motel where she sat for a moment powdering her face and reapplying her lipstick in the visor mirror. She took a deep breath and summoned a smile, getting herself into character.

The shirtless man who opened the door of room number 156 looked at her with round eyes behind bifocals that were sliding down a pinched nose, and gave her a sloppy grin, his lips slick with spit. She could smell whiskey mixed with garlic on his breath as he greeted her. He was tall, skinny, and stooped, the shape of a snake that had just dined on a rabbit, with his pot belly hanging over wrinkled shorts. His hair was the color of moldy candy floss, long and wiry, and stuck up in clumps like some stereotypical mad scientist.

She gave the room a quick scan as she sauntered in, noticing the bunched up sheets and striped comforter on the bed, his clothes hanging over a chair beside a round table by the window. The curtains were drawn, the TV in the corner on with the sound turned down. The furnishings were cheap maple wood, the decor bland and functional—exactly what she'd expected. The only thing that ever changed was the faces of the men, although like the rooms where they met, they were all much the same. When she turned around, the man was holding a camcorder and touching himself over his shorts. She held up a hand to block the lens.

"Come on," he said and reached into the front of his shorts, pulling out a limp penis. It hung there pathetically, like something dead. His fat stomach jiggled as he jerked his hand, trying to hold the camcorder steady.

"Turn off the camera, please," she said, attempting to be polite.

"Take off your clothes."

"Not until you turn that thing off."

"Hey, I'm paying for this, aren't I? Nobody's going to see it but me. Now take them off, bitch." His speech was mumbled like his tongue was too big for his mouth.

"This isn't going to work out. You can just call someone else for your little games."

He lowered the camcorder, his fat lips actually pouting like a little boy who couldn't get his way. "The other girls let me."

"Sorry, not this girl."

He put the camera on the dresser and looked her up and down.

"You have nice breasts. Are they real?" he asked, reaching out a bold hand and squeezing one, his dick still hanging out the front of his shorts.

"Can we take care of business first?" she asked, stepping back.

He sighed, crossed the room, pulled a wallet from his pants, and handed her a fold of bills. She sensed him moving closer, teetering on his feet, the stink of his heavy breath in her nostrils, as she counted the money.

"There's only three hundred here."

"So?"

"So it's five hundred."

"Three hundred is all I pay."

"Not for me."

"What makes you so special?"

"Unless you come up with another two hundred bucks, you're not going to find out, are you?"

"Three's the going rate. You're lucky to get that too, bitch, you're no spring chicken. Pussy's not so tight at your age anymore. Your ass still tight, I hope?"

She tossed the bills onto the bed, watching them flutter as they spilled over the messy sheets.

"Wait, I'll give you another two. Holy cow."

Gathering up the bills, he took more from his wallet and pressed them into her hand. She sucked in a long breath through her nose and took a moment to count them all.

"It's all there, but this better be worth it, bitch," he said and smirked at her.

She stuffed the bills into her purse, removed a bottle of lubricant and turned to him with a smile, trying to regain her bubbly façade.

"Okay, baby, let's have some fun. Sit back and I'll take care of you, baby." She moved over to him, placing a hand on his forearm, backing him up toward the bed. She eased down his shorts, letting them fall to his feet and then without allowing him to step out of them; she immediately pushed him down into a sitting position on the edge of the bed.

She saw that his cock was starting to firm up. She pulled off her top and bra, letting him touch her breasts as she got down on her knees between his legs, squeezed some lubricant into her palm, and began to stroke his cock. The man closed his eyes and moaned deep in his throat as she continued to stroke him.

"That's it baby; get it nice and hard for me now. I'm so horny for you." She began to move her hand faster when she saw how much he was enjoying it. She could tell he was getting close, in spite of his alcohol consumption. Old men like him didn't last long. Two or three minutes were about all they could stand. Sometimes she timed them on her watch over their shoulder, making bets with herself.

The man looked down at her with damp eyes, the glasses still balanced on the end of his nose.

"You better stop, I'm going to—"

She moved back as he came, careful not to get any on her. She stood up, releasing him, turned, and pulled out some wet wipes from her purse, cleaning off her hands, and tossing it into a wastebasket. Her movements were quick, determined. She reached for her bra and blouse on the end of the bed and put them on.

The man looked up at her with a lopsided grin like a giant infant, waiting to be tickled.

She straightened her skirt, grabbed her purse and smiled. "Thanks, baby."

"Where you going?"

She shrugged. "We're done."

"No, we're not. You just jerked me off, that's not what I paid for!"

"You already came. The party's over." She smiled and turned to leave as he got to his feet.

Obviously forgetting that his shorts were still around his ankles, the man took one step and landed on the floor on his fat belly with a thud.

Pamela hurried toward the door.

"Call me," she said over her shoulder and let the door slam.

For every five customers there was usually one asshole like him. She'd learned quickly, as a sixteen year old girl, how to take control of the situation and not allow herself to become a victim.

One cigarette, one Percocet, and one coffee later, she was knocking on the next hotel room door. When it opened and she looked up at the man on the other side, she was struck by his good looks and piercing blue eyes.

"Hello, Stephanie," he said. His face broke into a smile and she noticed a crooked tooth that stood out, bestowing a charming quality.

Chapter
TWENTY-EIGHT

"John, is it?" She gave him a coy smile as she stepped inside the shadowed room. He closed the door behind her.

"Aye, it's John." He laughed.

"How appropriate." She looked him up and down, observing the T-shirt stretched over broad shoulders and an athletic frame, pleased at how good looking he was, knowing that for a change she was about to enjoy herself.

The man said, "You're just a wee thing, now aren't you?"

"Excuse me?"

"I mean you're petite. From your pictures you look taller."

"Well, I hope you're not disappointed."

"Not at all, you're gorgeous."

The room smelled of cigar smoke. She would have to think of something to explain the scent that would undoubtedly cling to her clothing and hair. The low bass of a dance song pulsed from the television and she could see Beyonce on the screen across the room. She felt the man's eyes on her as he circled her like prey.

He stood towering before her in bare feet and jeans. She could feel the heat of him in the space between them. His musky scent filled her nose and unfurled inside of her, amplifying something fevered. She felt captivated by the unexpected beauty of him. Lifting a hand, he touched her hair and then she remembered why she had come here.

"Let's square up first, okay?" She smiled, trying to make it sound off-handed, as if the money didn't mean anything.

He turned and lifted a bottle of Budweiser from the dresser, in no particular hurry, took a long swallow, set it back down, and then reached into his front pocket. She counted as he tore off five one hundred dollar bills.

Pamela thrust the money into her purse as if the speed with which she hid it away could make them both forget what this was really about. She plucked two square packages of condoms from her purse.

"That's quite the tattoo," she said, turning back to him and running a hand over his arm. "What is it? A dragon?"

"Aye." He pulled off his shirt. She took in the shape of his body, the muscled pectorals with the sparse hair in the center of his chest, the prominent abdominal muscles and narrow waist. God, if only they all looked like him she might be paying them. He took a step backward, beer in hand, sat down on the bed, and looked up at her.

"Come here," he said.

"So what do you want?" she asked, stepping toward him with a provocative smile, tossing the condoms on the bed beside him.

"I want everything that I'm owed." He leaned back on his elbows, tilted his head, and studied her body as she pulled off her top, tossed it on the bed and stood before him in a black lace bra.

"Keep going," he smiled and drank from his bottle.

She unzipped her skirt, turned to let him see her from the back as she pranced over to a chair, and let the skirt fall to her feet. She leaned over and slipped out of her panties. On her tiptoes, she stepped back to the edge of the bed, naked, with her hands on her hips. He sat up, leaning toward her, and placed his beer bottle on the floor. His hands were on her body, moving over her stomach, her back, squeezing her ass. His mouth was hot against her skin, his cheek slightly rough. He licked and sucked her breasts and then pulled her down on the bed, laying her on her back.

His touch was nearly overwhelming, the strength of his body, intoxicating. It had been a long time since she had felt this way with a man. She couldn't even recall the last time. It was unusual for her to be delighted with what was on the other side of the door. Most times it was just a performance, something she had to get over with, like brushing your teeth. Of course, there were moments it was enjoyable and she actually got into it, in the hands of an expert lover, and she even orgasmed on occasion. It was really a paradox. But she couldn't recall a customer who ever made her feel this aroused before, this transported.

His fingers ignited her skin as he traced them along her neck and the side of her face, touching her tenderly. He kissed her face and then her lips. He tasted of tobacco, beer, and something sweet, warm, and familiar that she couldn't place. In that moment she wished she wasn't a hooker that he had called, but a woman he had met somewhere else, like at a supermarket, or in a line at the bank, or on the next barstool. Anywhere but here. Anywhere but how they had met. She fantasized about a life with him, leaving her husband, moving in with him. They would sleep late, make love all day, eat in outdoor cafes, teasing each other across the table, their passion detonating with a just a look, a subtle gesture, their love all consuming. She would leave Brett without a second thought for a life filled with love and passion. She longed for it with her entire being.

And then a sudden realization struck her. It had been exactly that way with Brett in the beginning. The passion and love they shared had been electric, just like this. It had been everything she had wanted. Was it possible they could ever recapture that? She loved her husband, she knew she loved him, had never stopped. It was just buried under layers of debris. Perhaps they could talk, get some professional counseling even, and dig themselves out from underneath all the shit, make their marriage happy again the way it used to be.

The light from the television flashed across their skin, a haunting blue, as the dance beat of the music flowed. The man stood up and undid his jeans as he looked down at her. She studied his body as he removed his pants, fascinated by the muscles in his arms as they twitched and flexed underneath his tattooed skin. He moved over top of her and parted her legs with his knees. She watched as he lifted one of the condom packages, tore it open and then fixed it over his cock.

She had to stop doing this. If she wanted to repair her marriage, she had to give up making her living by sleeping with other men. The time had come to start making some serious changes.

The man's tenderness was gone suddenly. He became all business. His eyes took on a chilling glow like polished steel. The lines of his face hardened along with his cock. He fucked her the way the rest of her customers fucked her, like they were trying to get somewhere, like she wasn't even there underneath him, like she could be any woman, just something to get off with, relieve them of their cum so they could get on with the rest of their day without the interference of thinking about how badly they needed to fuck something. His touch became aggressive, demanding, as he pushed her into the positions he liked, ordering her to move this way and that, pulling her hair a little too hard, thrusting into her a little too forcefully. It was as if he wanted to make it unpleasant for her.

"Slow down," she said, hoping he would realize how rough he was being.

"Shut up." He forced her face down on the mattress.

Pamela endured it, thinking it would be over soon and she could get dressed, disappointed that it didn't turn out the way she was expecting. He yanked her arms back behind her by the elbows and a sharp pain tore at one shoulder. When she cried out, she felt his knuckles strike the side of her face. A jagged fear ripped through her. And she knew she was in trouble.

"Okay, stop. This is over." She tried to pull away from him. He pinned her down on the bed, his knees digging into the back of her thighs, a hand on the back of her neck holding her. She felt another blow at the side of her head—*crack!* and then another and another. She lay dazed, the room suddenly quiet, spinning. She felt him move across the bed. He mumbled some words she didn't understand and then something hard slammed into her skull and spilled over the side of her face and onto the bed. Glass. Her mind went black.

It was mid-afternoon. Dark clouds rolled across the sky. It was beginning to rain as Rory drove back along the highway to Penn Yan. He cranked the stereo as a Disturbed song came on. He noticed how red his knuckles were. He brought his fingers to his nose. He could still smell the woman on his skin.

The screen on his phone lit up and alerted him to a call. Annoyed, he switched off the stereo and picked up the phone. It was Douggy Chambers.

"Hey, man, how's it going?" Rory said.

"I've got some news on Justine Jameson for you."

"Excellent. Give me the low down."

"Well, it seems Brett is actually her biological father. He got custody of her after Justine's mother died. Apparently Brett didn't know he even had a daughter. Then his ex-girlfriend calls him one day out of the blue it looks like, and tells him. I guess she knew her days were numbered and was making arrangements for her daughter."

Rory sucked his teeth and said, "Really."

"Sorry this didn't have the results you were hoping for Rory."

"Aye, well that's how life goes sometimes, isn't it? Doesn't come as a surprise."

"Let me know if there's anything else I can do."

"Thanks for everything."

"Any time, my friend. Stop by the house tomorrow, we're going to fire up the barbeque."

Even though it came as no surprise, Rory felt a stab of regret anyway as he hung up the phone. He had been chasing an illusion. Again.

In his rearview mirror he saw the police SUV advancing on him. He was expecting it was just going to pass him, but then its lights came on, flashing blue and red.

"Christ." He took a deep breath and eased the car over to the shoulder.

Chapter
TWENTY-NINE

Fat drops of rain pelted Gus Linden's vehicle intermittently as he pulled up behind the Challenger. Linden had just come from visiting with Liz out at her farmhouse on Carroll Road. She'd been hired to work in Larry Blackmore's office straight out of college and had been Larry's right hand. They sat at her kitchen table drinking tea, eating chocolate-chip cookies that her daughters had baked, and talked about Larry. From Liz he learned exactly what he had suspected, that Rory Madden had paid him a visit just days prior to his death. She said Larry had seemed nervous, but he wouldn't tell her what the visit was about.

What a coincidence, on the way back, to come up behind Rory Madden's Challenger heading east on Highway 364. Linden felt his heart do a flip. Where was that boy coming from?

With the holster on his belt unclipped, his right hand on the butt of his Glock, he stepped out of the SUV. The highway was deserted. He looked out at the farm fields and the expanse of sky with their storm clouds in the distance. Cautiously, he approached the driver's door.

"Good afternoon, Rory," he said as the window was lowered. "Where you coming from?"

"Was I speeding?" Rory asked, looking annoyed.

"Why, I don't think you were, son."

"Do I have a tail light out or something?"

"Not as I can see."

"Then what the fuck you pulling me over for?"

"Now, there's no need for that kind of language, Rory. I was just stopping you to ask you a few questions, is all. Nothing serious. But, you know, I swear there's a distinct smell of marijuana coming from your vehicle. You wouldn't happen to be smoking illegal drugs, now would you son?"

Rory dropped his head to his chest, then turned and eyed him over the tops of his mirrored aviator glasses.

"I think you better step out of the car," Linden said.

Rory chuckled. "This is straight-up harassment. I know my rights. You pulled me over for no bloody reason."

"I said, step out of the car." Linden took a step back and drew his gun, aiming it at Rory.

"Are you kidding me, man? Now, don't you think you're overreacting just a wee bit here?"

"You want me to place you under arrest? Get out of the car."

Rory sighed and turned off his engine.

"Put your hands up. Get out slowly."

As instructed, Rory opened the door and stepped out onto the roadside, keeping his hands up.

"Turn around."

"You mind telling me what this is about?"

"Put your hands on the roof of the car. Spread your legs."

Linden carefully did a pat up and down his legs for weapons. When he got to Rory's jacket, he felt what he knew instantly to be a handgun in the inside left pocket.

"Well, well. What have we here?" Linden pulled the gun from his jacket and put it on the hood of the car. "Looks like an illegal firearm to me, son. That's not good. I'm going have to take you in now, Rory. Put your hands behind your back," Linden said as he pulled the cuffs off his belt. With one hand he went to slip the cuffs around Rory's left wrist.

But before he could react, Rory swung around and landed an elbow to his chin. Linden heard his teeth snap together inside his skull. A hard fist caught him in the gut and knocked the wind out of him. He stumbled sideways, reaching out for the car. Another fist caught him on the nose and he felt his face burn. His vision darkened and his head began to spin. There were two quick pop sounds and then he felt something hot in the center of his chest. He dropped to his ass on the gravel, falling into the rear tire of Rory's car. The back of his head smacked painfully against the wheel well. A moment of terror gripped him as he realized he had lost control of the situation. He knew this was bad.

Linden felt himself being dragged across the gravel. He caught sight of the clouds, and then the drainage ditch as he was tossed into it. Linden thought that he should have followed Rory until they reached town, not pulled him over out here on a deserted country highway. Stupid of him. He heard the Challenger's engine fire up and then the sound of rocks as they spit from the back tires. Son-of-a-bitch was getting away.

His breath came in short bursts. He thought of Anna. She would start to worry if he wasn't home. He felt himself weakening, his lungs barely moving. He knew this was very bad. The irony of it washed over him; being a cop all his life in a small town, the risk of getting shot on the job about as great as his number picks landing the jack pot. And yet here he was, the blood flowing out of his chest, soaking his shirt. He thought of his retirement. Would he even see it? What about Italy with Anna? He pictured her at the stove, stirring the pot of spaghetti sauce. Tonight was spaghetti night. God, he loved Anna's spaghetti more than anything in the world. Had he told her enough times how much she meant to him? How she had been the best part of his life? He hoped so. In that moment, he considered his life insurance policy and their will. It was all up to date. She would be okay financially without him. And she had the kids.

Gus felt himself grow cold. He would rest here for another minute or two and then he'd try and get up. He imagined himself standing on a roof, falling over backwards and hoping the guy on the ground really was going to catch him. Was he having a hallucination? This was not how he wanted to go, alone, lying in a drainage ditch, his life trickling away. He could try screaming, but he could barely summon a whisper. Besides, who would hear him out here if he could manage to raise that kind of energy. There was nobody to hear him.

Chapter
THIRTY

Justine stood outside his door and knocked, hoping she was at the right apartment. When the door opened and he stood before her shirtless and in jeans, she drew in a breath, feeling instantly overwhelmed at the sight of him.

"Justine." He smiled at her, surprised.

"You left this at my place the other day," she said, dangling his watch in front of him. "It looked expensive, so I didn't think you wanted to just leave it lying around any old place."

"Oh, right. I took it off when I was bathing your wee doggy. Thanks. That's awful nice of you to bring it 'round. Come in," he said, standing aside to let her enter.

She hesitated for a moment and then stepped inside. He shut the door behind her.

"Where's Abigail?"

"I left her with my dad. And I'm not liking it. I think this is the first time I've actually ever left her with someone."

Justine moved into the room, examining the sparse furnishings, and wandered toward the window. "You've got a nice view."

"Not as nice as the view at your house."

She turned to him with a tight smile and watched him put on his watch, the dragon tattoo encasing his arm and chest like an affliction spreading across his skin. The top button of his jeans was undone, as if he'd thrown them on hastily to answer the door.

"I didn't say that to make you feel bad," he said, stepping toward her.

"I know."

She lifted a hand and touched the dragon's face on his chest with gentle fingers, studying the colors—turquoise, sky-blue, aquamarine, emerald, red cherry blossoms throughout with yellow centers, done in a bold black outline.

"This is so beautiful. Your artist is very talented. How long did it take to complete?"

"Probably forty-five hours, something like that."

"Was it expensive?"

"Aye. Cost me around six grand. Good tattoos aren't cheap."

"I've always wanted a tattoo. I almost got one once. I walked into this shop in Brooklyn and the guy was so rude I turned around and walked out again. That was as close as I got. I was more into piercing when I was younger."

Delicately she touched a jagged scar on his ribs with her fingers. "What's this from?"

"Piece of shrapnel hit me there when a bomb went off."

"A bomb?"

"Aye. Back in Ireland. It was many years ago now. I was nineteen, I think."

"And what's this one?" She pointed to his abdomen and a two-inch horizontal scar, just above the waistband of his jeans.

"That's from a knife."

"Someone attacked you?"

"Aye. I was coming out of a pub one night and my mates and I were jumped. One of them died. Not sure who was responsible, but I have my suspicions. I was almost a goner from that one myself, nicked my bowel and I developed an infection. I was in the hospital two weeks."

"Oh, my God."

"And this one here?" He pointed to a tiny white scar on his chin in the shape of a triangle. "That was the worst of the lot."

"What happened?"

"Rode my tricycle down the stairs at my granny's house. Nearly killed myself that time." He grinned.

She gave his arm a playful slap and laughed.

"Seriously, are those scars from all the fighting over there in Ireland? You were involved in it weren't you? That's why you've got this tattoo that says Ulster Freedom Fighters." She motioned with her chin at the red fist tattoo on his shoulder.

"Aye. I fought the war. I was in the thick of it, up to my neck."

"What's it all about anyway? Catholics and Protestants hating each other so much they want to kill each other?"

"It's a long, tangled story and you might find it boring. But it's not really about religion as some might think, other than that the Republicans just happen to be Catholics and the Loyalists happen to be Protestant," he said, inclining his head at her and folding his arms as if he was about to give her a history lesson. "Suffice it to say it's about two distinct groups of people both sharing the same territory and wanting different things, both willing to die for what they believe in. The Catholics want a united Ireland, you see? The Protestants want Northern Ireland to remain part of the UK. Neither's been willing to budge for decades and many people have lost their lives because of it. On both sides. But in recent years the politicians have been more cooperative with each other and entered into a power sharing agreement. But in spite of what's decided or voted on, there's people who won't abide by it. The conflict will go on. In fact, it's just about two years back a faction of the IRA was responsible for more killings after nearly a decade of peace. So they haven't laid down their arms at all. Well, at least not this new group of young militants. And then all the old tension rises up again in July with the Orange parades."

"Well, I'm really glad you decided to emigrate to the States, Rory."

"Aye, me too."

She turned her hand and ran the back of it down the center of his chest and across his stomach. And with that one simple shift in her touch, the mood between them altered.

She looked up at him, studying his pale eyes as his face neared hers. Their lips connected easily as if it were natural they should kiss. He stopped and looked down at her and then kissed her again; warm, tender. She breathed in his scent, an earthy smell with a trace of cologne that seemed to spiral down inside of her straight to her groin.

"I'm not your girlfriend," she said. "If I slept with you, would it make me a whore?"

"Whores get paid. I'm not paying you." He grinned.

"Okay, so what does it make me, then?"

"A beautiful, passionate girl with ordinary desires." Clasping her fingers in his, he walked backwards, leading her to another room. "A vibrant goddess who wants to experience what it feels like to be alive; who doesn't deny her feelings, but embraces them fully."

"Is that what you really think?"

"Not at all, girl. I think you're a whore."

Justine threw back her head and laughed. He hugged her and spun her around, laughing as they collapsed on his bed; a mattress on the floor with a tangle of sheets.

He looked down at her and touched her face, becoming serious again. "Of course that's really what I think. And who says you're not my girlfriend?"

He helped her out of the loose-fitting summer blouse and her jeans. His hands moved over her bare skin. His mouth explored her body, as she lay naked in his arms. She felt all of her senses awakening. He was tender, passionate, his movements unhurried, his eyes studying her. They made love with the evening sun shining in, enveloping them in its warmth. Justine felt transported in time and space.

Afterward, they lay in each other's arms, talking and joking as if they'd been lovers for years.

A moment later her father phoned with bad news. Pamela had been admitted to hospital. An accident of some kind, was all he said. He needed to leave right away and asked her to come home to the baby.

She stood and dressed, letting out a sigh of regret. "Sorry, I have to leave. My stepmother's in the hospital and my Dad needs to go to her. I have to get home to my daughter."

"Have dinner with me tonight," he said, watching her from where he lay on the bed, naked.

"Maybe tomorrow." She smiled. "Can I phone you a bit later when I get home?"

"Maybe? Did you say maybe? I'll pick you up at your house tomorrow at seven, girl."

She laughed. "I'll have to check and see if my dad can watch the baby."

"Well, you can bring her along with us if he can't."

On the floor beside his bed sat a water bottle, his cell phone, and a handgun.

"You have a gun," she said, surprised.

"Aye."

She reached for it and he grabbed it before she could pick it up.

"It's loaded," he said, "Don't want you blowing my head off accidentally, now."

"What do you need a gun for?"

"Protection. Place has got mice." He grinned and made a face, holding the gun in the air like a cowboy.

"Mice. Please. As if you need a handgun to kill mice with."

"Aye, you've never seen them. They're very big. Scare the living shit out of you, if one came at you." Rory reached up and latched onto her wrist, pulling her down on top of him, the gun still in his hand. They kissed, long and passionate.

"Can you get me one?"

"Get you one what?"

"A gun." She stroked the barrel with one finger.

"A gun? What does a girl like you need with a gun?"

"Protection. I need to protect myself and my baby."

"Oh, yeah? You got problems with mice too, have you?"

"From my parents."

He began to laugh, but when he looked at her and saw the serious expression on her face, he stopped.

"I'm not joking," she said, sitting up.

"I can see that...I thought you said you trusted your dad."

"I do, I mean—I'm trying to. But Pam...he might be under her control. I might not have any other option. What? Why are you looking at me like that?"

"I was just picturing you holding a gun, showing you how to use it. It turns me on, actually."

She smiled.

"God, you're so fucking sexy." He put the weapon on the floor and wrapped himself around her. "I want more of you."

"I've got to go."

"I'm not done with you. I'm only getting started."

She pushed him away and stood to leave. "I'll call you."

"I'm not just some cheap piece of meat you can have your way with, you know?" He winked at her. "You can go for now. I'll see you tomorrow evening at seven. Wear something sexy."

Rory kissed her at the door, a long moist kiss echoing their shared passion moments earlier.

"Will you show me how to use one?" she asked as she was leaving.

"What? A gun?"

"Yes."

"Sure, if that's what you want."

"That's what I want."

Chapter
THIRTY-ONE

In the emergency room waiting area, Brett scanned the faces, absently wondering what everyone was doing there. Except for a red-faced boy crying in his mother's arms with the saucepan fixed to his head, nobody looked particularly sick or injured.

"She has a fractured cheek bone and eye socket. We'll need to do surgery. She also has three broken ribs, multiple contusions, a gash on the back of her head that we stitched, and a dislocated shoulder," The doctor standing before him said, his eyes serious behind his frameless glasses. He seemed too young to be a doctor. He appeared no older than a teenager, with his flawless tawny skin and thick hair so black it was nearly blue. His scrubs looked like pajamas.

Brett swallowed something bitter in the back of his mouth and asked. "Can I see her?"

"In just a few minutes. We're transferring her to a room and then prepping her for surgery shortly. She'll need to stay overnight."

"Did she say what happened?"

"There appears to be some short-term memory loss, which is not uncommon with head injuries. The police want to question her, as well."

"It was an accident? Was it a car accident? They wouldn't tell me anything on the phone."

"Witnesses say she came out of a hotel room—"

"A hotel room?"

"She was stumbling and then apparently she fainted in the hallway." His voice was gentle but formal, void of emotion, as if he was describing nothing more than product that had been damaged. "She was assaulted, it appears. There were fragments of glass embedded in her skull. Looks like she was hit with a beer bottle. We want to do a rape kit—"

"A rape kit?"

"There are signs she may have been sexually assaulted, but so far she's refused to let us do the rape kit. Perhaps you can convince her. The police will have some questions for you, too."

Brett stood dumbfounded as the doctor walked away. He turned and scanned the room, certain that everyone was staring at him, that everyone knew what had happened to his wife. Even the boy with the pot stuck to his skull was looking at him, tears running down fat cheeks.

A hotel room. She had been in a hotel room. What did that mean? But he knew exactly what that meant, didn't he? Of course he did. He just didn't want to think about it. He was the master of denial, had been all his life. Always figured that if you just thought positively, everything would be all right. Why did he keep thinking this attitude would work for him? It was like whistling in the dark. Maybe it was just his nature. Maybe he just didn't know any other way to deal with the fact that he had married a woman who thought nothing of selling her body to men, regardless of how it made him feel. Why did he stay with her? Was it his deep sense of guilt that kept him bound to her? The feeling that he owed her? That was part of it. A big part, he had to admit. But he did love her. In spite of it all, he loved her. As crazy as that was.

Sure, his business was failing, sinking faster each day than he anticipated, collectors calling him on his cell phone at all hours. He was three months behind on the rent at the office and about to be locked out, and had just bounced his car payment this month. Closing was inevitable. But that didn't mean she had to go back to prostitution, for God's sake. There were other things she could do. The insurance company where she worked before had paid well. Why did she give it up?

His wife was a prostitute. What did that say about him as a man? He felt like a complete failure. This was entirely his fault. If he was a better man, a better husband, bringing home a paycheck that could support them, this wouldn't have happened.

A few minutes later, he stood at the side of the bed where she lay in a half sitting up position. He reached for her hand. It felt cold. Her face was bruised, one eye swollen shut, her lip cut, and there was a thick bandage around her head. He stared at her, digging around in his mind for some words that seemed fitting but failed to conjure any. His head was pounding. The accumulation of stress from everything—his business, his finances, his daughter, the move, and now his wife—bore down on him and he wondered how much more of it he could stand.

"Are you in any pain? Can I get you anything?" he said eventually. What followed was a scene that seemed distorted, bizarre. He could only attribute it to the fact that she was on medication and wasn't thinking clearly.

She pulled her hand from his. For a long moment she gazed at him through her uninjured eye and didn't speak. He watched the tears gather in her eye and she looked away, pressed a tissue to her face.

"Are you okay?"

"Do I look okay?" Her voice was abrupt.

He contemplated this for a moment, and he felt his face burn with emotions he didn't understand. He cleared his throat and said, "No, you don't look okay, Pam."

"I suppose you think this is funny."

"What? Funny? Why on earth would you say something like that?"

"You don't seem so surprised by this. Were you expecting someone would beat me up one day?"

"Pam, what are you talking about?"

"Please, I'm not a fool. I know you were behind this. I hope you're proud of yourself. How much did you pay the guy? I hope it was more than five hundred bucks, because that's what he gave me before he fucked me. Where did you get the money to pay him, anyway? You better not have taken it from my stash."

Brett took a step back from her, flinching at her words, pressing a hand to his forehead. "You think that I did this to you? Have you lost your mind?"

She winced as she tried to move, clearly suffering.

"Pam, you don't know what you're saying, you've suffered a—"

"Go on. Admit it, Brett. You planned this and carried it out to get me to stop. To make me afraid."

"For God's sake Pam, I love you. I would never do anything to hurt you and I don't know what would make you think such a thing. Haven't I always been here for you? Haven't I always been supportive? I know we don't have a perfect marriage, that we've had our share of fights. But who does have a perfect marriage anyway? All I know is that I love you, Pam. I love you no matter what. And...and we'll get through this. Together, we'll get through this like we always do. As long as we're together, we'll be fine."

"You're a liar!"

"Pam, don't be this way. This is crazy, I—"

"You're such a fucking asshole. And you're a fool. Don't know which side your bread is buttered on. All you're good at is screwing up, isn't that right? Isn't that right?!"

"I guess you really got a good whack on your head because—"

"Go away! Get out of here and leave me alone! You're nothing but poison in my life. You ruin everything you touch. Everything!"

"Jesus Christ—"

"I should have left your ass years ago. When Allison died. I'm the fool for staying with you. I'm the fool! I'm the fucking fool! For marrying you in the first place. It was the single biggest mistake of my life."

"Let me get a doctor in here—"

"I don't need a fucking doctor! I just need you out of my life!"

"Pam, I think—"

"Get the fuck out!" She picked up a water bottle from the bedside table and hurled it at him, missing his head by inches. It exploded on the floor behind him. "Get the fuck out of my life you bastard! I fucking hate you! I hate you!"

Brett backed out of the room and bumped into someone who was entering. It was a woman; tall, lanky with a severity about her that said she was all business. A man followed her in, appearing as if he'd come from the same mold. Brett knew immediately they were cops.

Chapter
THIRTY-TWO

"Let's talk outside," the male cop said, eyeing him with a steely gaze. His mouth was a flat line etched in a fleshy, sunburned face.

Brett tried to laugh off his wife's comments, which the cops had obviously overheard, but it was painful to laugh. The hallway was busy with people, some slowly pacing, others—nurses and medical staff—hustling past. Brett was suspended in dread, gazing worriedly at the disconnected faces made harsh by the fluorescent lights. What was to become of him? His marriage, his future?

"I'm Detective Richard Slatery." He handed Brett a business card. "And you are Mr. Jameson?"

"Yes, I'm Pamela's husband."

"Your first name?" he asked, flipping open a small note pad.

"Brett. Brett Jameson."

Slatery proceeded to ask some perfunctory questions, his address, phone numbers, and place of work. Brett answered them as best he could, his concentration splintered. He knew he'd failed her again somehow, like he always had. How were they going to get beyond this? It seemed impossible.

"Can you tell me what your wife was doing at the hotel this afternoon, Mr. Jameson? She was not registered there as a guest. Was she visiting someone?" The cop asked, his eyes squinting, sizing him up.

"I don't know."

"She didn't tell you she was going there today?"

"No, she didn't say anything about it to me."

"Well, does she know someone who works at the hotel?"

"Not that I'm aware of."

"Did she give you any kind of explanation as to why she was there?"

"She didn't say anything about it."

The detective brushed thick fingers over a cleft chin, the shadows under his eyes suggesting he hadn't experienced a good night's sleep since entering the police academy. "Perhaps she was visiting a guest staying at the hotel, then."

Brett shrugged and looked down the hall. What was he suppose to tell this man? That his wife was there with a trick? How could he expect anyone to understand? He felt his face burn with shame.

Then Brett began to chuckle as the weight of all their secrets seemed to fall away. It was only a matter of time before they figured it out. And what then? What would they think of that?

It had been a mistake to leave Manhattan, to think they could live out here in the country. To think that Justine would be happy out here. That it would be good for her and the baby. How had he let Pamela convince him this was a good idea? He felt himself collapsing inside, afraid of everything. Afraid of all the choices they had made. Not knowing what to do now. Everything around him was falling apart—his business, his marriage, his home and security. All of it crumbling at the very foundation.

The cop gave him a quizzical stare. "Look, Mr. Jameson, I'm sure you're not going to like what I'm about to ask you, but I have to ask it anyway because it's my job to get to the bottom of this...Was your wife having an affair?"

Brett felt himself sinking as he wondered if Rory Madden had done this. Fatigue pulled at his limbs, making him feel awkward. He seemed to be moving through a haze, as if in a dream.. His vision began to blur. There had to be something he could do. There had to be something the police could do for his family, to protect them.

"My wife is not having an affair," he said, swallowing against the tightness in his throat. Should he tell the police what he thought? Maybe he should call that cop who had come to their house the other day. He knew Madden, after all. Maybe he could do something, put him in a line-up or something, and Pam could identify him.

"Okay, I'm going to go in and talk with my partner and see if you're wife can explain things to us then. Mind waiting out here for a bit?"

"Sure, no problem."

Brett slumped against the wall as the cop entered the hospital room. Then he began a slow, directionless prowl up and down the hallway, as if walking through a dream.

A few minutes later, both cops emerged and approached him.

"It appears your wife is suffering some sort of memory loss," the female cop said. "Claims she has no idea who assaulted her and has no memory of even being at the hotel. So for now, we'll try our best to piece this together with the limited information we do have. Here's my card. Call us if your wife remembers any of the details of the attack. We'd like to get this guy off the streets."

Brett took the card and wondered if he should buy a gun.

Chapter
THIRTY-THREE

Justine paced the living room floor, gazing out through the window every few minutes. The evening sun broke through dark clouds as a flock of sparrows swooped and dipped between the branches, and then took to the sky, only to swoop toward the ground and swing up again in wide arcs. To Justine, it seemed like a mad dance. It was hypnotic. She gazed at one bird longingly, thinking, *There goes my spirit.*

Tears welled in her eyes as she thought of the baby birds dead in the nest above the front door. She'd just checked on them. All three. Dead. Stiff like they were stuffed. The mother bird gone.

Her mind was in a panic. She didn't know what to do. She watched the leaf buds on the trees as they waved in the breeze. She watched the shadows between the trees, the dried ferns and underbrush from last season, swaying every few moments. She watched a bunny dart across the grass. In the living room of the house she scanned the furniture, the spaces beside the furniture, the walls, the wood grain pattern in the floor, and the texture of the ceiling. She watched Duke sleeping on his pet-bed by the window, baking in a square of golden light, his little round belly rising and falling. She wished she could absorb his peace. But she felt her breath quicken. Her blood pounded in her ears.

Pamela's face burned in her mind. She was a demon disguising herself as a human being, the proverbial wolf in sheepskin, trying to blend in, and waiting all the while for her opportunity to strike. She was a calculated predator with one diabolical purpose—like a virus infiltrating an unsuspecting host: to slaughter, consume, and ultimately, annihilate. Justine knew her intentions. It was why she wanted to move out here in the middle of nowhere; to isolate them and then take control. She wanted the baby. There was no denying it. That had been her plan all along. She was going to kill Abigail.

A face in the window startled Justine and she let out a short scream. It was one of the gray people staring in at her with their hollow eyes. She backed up and looked down at her baby in the swing. When she turned back to the window, it was gone.

"You know what you have to do."

She needed to get out of the house. Her heart thumped as she loaded the baby bag with supplies. She changed the baby, dressed her, and bundled her into the baby carrier. Before she left, she let Duke out for a pee and then locked him in his wire crate in the kitchen. With the baby, she headed out to her Jeep in the garage.

Justine saw the same face again, silently gazing in at her, when she reached for her seatbelt. She jumped, threw the car in reverse and hit the gas. She peeled out of the driveway, looking for the gray people in the rearview. But they were gone. It's like they were closing in on her. What did they want?

The edgy mood from earlier had come along for the ride. Images of her early teenage years emerged like a scratchy film reel; wrists strapped to a chair, staring at blank walls, an oxygen-starved scream trapped in her lungs, feeling like she had landed in purgatory. Most of that year was a void, obliterated from her mind like a hole in a map or the pages of a book torn out. The years prior to being institutionalized were like disconnected remnants of a dream. She wanted to forget the hospital, even though memories of it always rose up, like bitter bile in her throat, if she didn't keep swallowing them down.

But the thing that puzzled Justine, the most ironic thing about the psych ward, was the fact that none of the patients asked for help or reported anything wrong to the staff. The only goal was to get out; to mention side effects from the meds or negative feelings was to risk having extra days tacked onto your stay by the psychiatrists who all but controlled your fate. So she had earned not to complain, to be cooperative, dependent, to smile, to speak optimistically, in hopes that they would see she had adjusted, improved and could be released back into the world.

Much of what was labeled as mental illness, Justine had learned over the years, was behavior that was simply not understood. She considered how Native Americans who heard voices were given the title of shamans of their tribe. So how was it today in society if you heard voices, you were quickly institutionalized and fed drugs to silence those voices? She thought of how at one time homosexuality was considered a mental illness and gays were locked up and given experimental treatments. One psychiatrist she was forced to see when she was a teenager was an openly gay man. He wore a wedding band and displayed a picture of himself and his lover on his desk, their tanned faces youthful, happy. Interesting how yesterday's madman could become today's therapist.

Justine took a few deep breaths, attempting to slow her heart rate. Doctors; the biggest drug pushers on the planet, she mused. How was it adults told their children that drugs are bad while they swallowed mass quantities of their own happy pills? What a sick and twisted world we live in while we practice hypocrisy and self-righteousness, spewing forth our bullshit and expecting the next generation to learn from our mistakes when we couldn't even learn from them ourselves. Here we were like a bunch of mindless sheep, swapping the simple gifts of life for some prepackaged illusion of bliss forced on us by the pharmaceutical industry in TV commercials and slick magazine ads with smiling, happy people, all the while treating side effects like they were a choice of garnish on a burger. It was just like that Vincent Price voice-over from Alice Cooper's "Black Widow."

. . . It attacks the central nervous system, causing intense pain, profuse sweating, difficulty in breathing, loss of consciousness, violent convulsions and, finally...death.

There was no way she was going to let her dad take her to see some stupid psychiatrist. There was no way she would fall for their tricks, walking innocently into that appointment like a stupid rabbit into a trap. And there was no way she would let them take her baby and lock her up in some psych ward. She would die first.

A plan. She needed a fucking plan. But what? Where could she possibly go and how would she survive? Her thoughts felt fragmented, like they were being split in two and jumbled together so they didn't make any sense. As soon as one thought entered her mind and she grasped at it, it vanished and another thought or image replaced it, rushing in at the speed of light. She looked at her daughter in the car seat beside her, her eyes blinking against the evening sun spilling across her face.

Abigail was so innocent and helpless, just like those baby birds. How could they be so cruel? How could they want to harm Abigail? She needed to think. She needed to develop a plan. She should fast for a few days and meditate. Then the answers would come.

Justine switched on the radio as they traveled along East Lake road toward her grandmother's house and tuned it to a classic rock station. Bob Seger's deep voice enveloped her as she drove. The hills that surrounded the lake were beginning to turn green. Their sloping rock faces fading into the steel blue of the lake, washing together with the sky heavy with slate clouds. Already there were a couple of boats on the water, a fishing boat and a yacht.

She wondered what it would be like to own a boat, to live, sleep and eat with the rocking foundation of a floor that constantly moved. Maybe it would suit her. At least for a time. She found herself longing for something. Something concrete that seemed indefinable. She felt weightless, tumbling. She thought of Rory. Maybe she would go see him; maybe it was he for whom her heart was searching. He gave her the reason to believe that her life might change for the better. She wanted so much to believe that it was possible. That there was something more for her in the world than this.

When she pulled up in front of her grandmother's house a few minutes later, an ambulance was in the driveway. Had her grandmother taken a fall? Maybe they had gotten to her, too. Maybe they were carting her off to a psych ward. She parked on the street across from the house and hurried up the front steps with Abigail in her carrier. Inside, she found her grandmother strapped to a stretcher with an oxygen mask over her face. Her sightless eyes gazed up at the ceiling, tears streaming down the sides of her skull.

"Oh, my god, what's happened? Where are you taking her?" Justine looked from the paramedics to the nurse.

The nurse said, "They think she might have pneumonia. They're taking her to the hospital."

Justine watched helplessly. She knew, somehow, that this was the end. Once her grandmother went inside that hospital, she would not be coming out. At least not alive.

Back at the house Justine lay on her bed, feeding her daughter, trying to calm her mind with thoughts of Rory. What latent force had he awakened in her?

She had stopped by his apartment again on her way back from Gran's but left disappointed when she didn't find him there. The phone was ringing as she wandered down the stairs a few moments later. She wondered if it was Rory calling. A smile came to her face at the thought. He would protect her and the baby.

"Justine, how are you?" Her dad's voice greeted her on the line. "I'm on my way home. They're going to keep Pam overnight so I'll come back for her tomorrow."

"Well, what happened to her, Dad?"

"Just a fall. She had a fall," he said. "I should be there in about half an hour. Are you and the baby okay?"

"Sure. Of course, Daddy."

"Everything's okay?"

"Everything's fine."

"Hey, you keep the doors locked when you're home by yourself, okay Sweets?"

"Yeah, Dad."

"Okay, just making sure. Listen, you would never open the door to anyone you didn't know right?"

"I'm not five years old."

"Of course, I know that."

"What's wrong? You seem upset. Is there something you're not telling me?"

"No, it's just...I worry, you know? With that break-in and my car being vandalized. I just worry about you and Abigail. I just want to know that you're safe at all times, okay? It's funny, I think I felt safer living in the city." He laughed and Justine thought it sounded odd, like it was a release valve for stress.

"I drove out to see Grandma this afternoon Dad," she said. "An ambulance came and took her to the hospital. They said she stopped breathing. Something respiratory."

"Jesus, that's not good news. I'll be home soon and we can talk about it then. Can you do me a favor, Sweets? Can you just go around the house and check that all the doors and windows are locked? And turn on the outside lights?"

Justine released a breath. "Sure, Dad. No problem."

"Hey, I love you." he said and hung up the phone.

A fall. Weird, Justine thought.

Chapter
THIRTY-FOUR

The next day Brett was up early. He headed into Rochester in the morning and returned late-afternoon with Pamela. Justine stood with the baby in her arms and stared at her stepmother as she came through the front door, shocked by the damage to her face. Pamela didn't even look at her or acknowledge her or Abigail in any way. She simply kicked off her shoes and quietly went up the stairs.

"She's okay, just upset and a little tired," Brett said, trying to smile. Justine could see the fatigue on his face, a shadow of pain reflected in his eyes.

"Hey, Abby-girl," he said, taking the baby from her arms. Abigail squealed in delight and kicked her pudgy legs.

"You look like shit, Dad."

"Funny, that's just how I feel. A little Grandpa-and-baby time will chase it away."

He lifted the baby up high in the air and laughed.

"I'm going to step out for a while," she said.

"Okay, where are you going?"

"The hospital. Check in on Grandma. And then I'll get some groceries."

"That's a good idea. I know Pam's worried about her, but she doesn't want to see her with her face the way it is."

"What happened to her, Dad?"

"She took a fall," he said turning away from her, and Justine knew he was keeping something from her.

"Must have been some fall." She made a face.

He didn't respond, just babbled to Abigail and moved over to the windows.

"Leave the baby with me, then," he said. "We'll hang out and get caught up."

She hesitated and glanced up the stairs. "I don't think that's a good idea."

"Why not?"

"She needs me. She needs to stay with me. I have to protect her."

"Justine, I'm quite capable to taking care of my granddaughter for an hour or two. Go on, get out of the house. You need a break yourself once in a while. You don't need to be hovering over her every minute."

"I don't hover over her."

"Yes, you do, Justine. Every second. I think you need to lighten up a bit. She's not made of glass, you know."

"She needs to stay with me, Dad." She held out her hands, reaching for the baby. Brett turned away and Justine felt a raw panic surfacing within her.

"Let me take care of her. She'll be fine. Go out and get some fresh air, Justine. Don't worry about her."

"Give her to me."

"Sweetheart, calm down. Abigail is hanging out with her Grandpa. She's fine. Stop worrying about her."

"Give her to me!"

Brett turned from her.

"Dad!"

"The baby's fine. Go out and do something for yourself for a little while," he said walking up the stairs.

Justine held her breath and then finally said. "Don't let Pam near her. Promise me you won't let her near Abigail. Whatever you do, keep her away from my baby."

"She's going to want to rest. She took a couple of Valium." He gave her a quizzical look and asked, "Are you feeling all right?"

"I'm fine."

"Are you sure?"

"I'm trusting you Dad, okay? You understand? I'm trusting you with my daughter. Keep her safe. Keep her away from Pam."

She grabbed her keys from the table by the front door and headed out to the garage. But she didn't go to the hospital. She drove into Penn Yan.

Chapter
THIRTY-FIVE

"I've got about two hours before I turn into a pumpkin. I swear, living at home with my parents is like being twelve years old again," Justine said when he let her into his apartment.

Their clothes were off before they were barely inside the door. Leaning her against the wall, he pushed up her blouse and unsnapped her bra. Without hesitation he pulled off her jeans until she was completely naked in his arms. Moving into the bedroom, they lay down on his bed, their bodies entwined. The evening sun flooded through the curtain, caressing their skin as they made love, hurriedly, passionately, their rhythm and movements perfectly in tune with each other.

Afterward, Rory flicked his Zippo and lit himself a cigar. He lay with his head propped up against a pillow and Justine's head on his shoulder, the sweat drying from their bodies.

"Look at you with your cigar," she said and laughed. "You're like Clint Eastwood in *The Good, The Bad, And The Ugly*."

She removed the cigar from his mouth and took a puff.

"Me and Clint? We're like this." He crossed his fingers and held them up for her to view. "I think I liked him best in *Dirty Harry*, though. He had better hair and a really cool gun."

Rory recited the movie lines, doing an Eastwood impersonation. "I know what you're thinking—did he fire six shots or five? Well, in all this excitement, I've kind of lost track myself. But, being that this is a .44 Magnum, the most powerful handgun in the world and would blow your head clean off, you've got to ask yourself one question: Do I feel lucky? Well, do ya, punk?"

"Hey, that's pretty good. You sound just like him, except for the accent. Kind of look like him too, in a sexy, rough-around-the-edges sort of way. I like that in a man."

"He's getting old now, Clint. Makes me sad to see him turning into some old geezer."

She handed him back the cigar and stuck out her tongue. "These things are gross."

"They're good for you. They've got vitamins and stuff."

"Yeah, not to mention cancer. Just because you don't inhale those things don't mean you can't get cancer, you know."

"Well, they haven't hurt Harry Callahan any, now have they?" He blew out a mouthful of smoke and grinned. "So, how's your wee puppy?" he asked, changing the subject.

"He's good. Getting fat."

"Has he still got his puppy smell?"

"Yes, he's still got it. Right behind his ears. That's where I smell it the most."

They laughed, and then she said, "I'm going to look for a place of my own, so I have to find somewhere they allow dogs."

"You mean you want to move out of the house?"

"I have to. I can't trust my parents. They want to put me away again, Rory. I just know it." The pace of her voice accelerated. "My dad set up an appointment for me with some shrink, and I'm sure he's going to build a case against me to put me back in the hospital and take my baby away. I know that's what they want. I just know it. I've got to save myself."

"But you're not crazy."

"I know I'm not. They treat me like a child. It's unbearable." She sat up, wrapping her arms around herself, her long hair falling across her face, and continued. "They walk around, acting like they're so perfect, so much better than everyone else. My stepmother, especially. She's always looked down her nose at me. Thinks my music is worthless, a waste of time. But you know, they've got the most fucked up marriage. It's like it's not even a real marriage. It's just for show, like everything else in their lives."

"How is your stepmother, anyway? You said she was in the hospital. What happened to her?"

"I don't know. My Dad said she had a fall, that's all he'd tell me. But her face is all bashed up," Justine said. "Looks like she went through a fucking windshield or something."

Rory sucked his teeth and then drew on his cigar in silence.

"And you think your parents want to put you back in the psych ward?" he said after a moment.

"They've been plotting against me for weeks," she said, flipping her hair back from her face. She rubbed her eyes and turned to stare at him as she continued, her voice angry. "They put me on pills just because I had a panic attack about Abigail. I stopped taking them, and they fucking know I stopped, and now they're talking like I'm crazy. And they want me to go talk to some shrink? So that's why I have to leave. I've got to take Abigail and move out. I was up all last night thinking about it. I've thought it through. I'm not even going to tell them where I'm going. I've got a bit of money in the bank. I'm just going to pack up when they're at work and I'll be gone when they get home and they won't be able to find me. I've got to save myself and Abigail while there's still time."

She lay down again, clinging to him suddenly. She seemed on the verge of panic. He could feel her heart racing. She was like a frightened bird in that moment. Utterly vulnerable. Innocent. He found himself wanting to protect her, to take care of her. She brought out a compassionate side in him, a longing to connect with something more than his own misery.

Rory kissed her forehead and stroked her hair. "It's okay. I won't let anything happen to you, girl. I won't let them take you away."

"I wish they would just disappear sometimes, you know? Like the earth would open up and suck them down inside and put them out of my misery. That's what I wish. That the earth would just swallow them up so that they didn't even exist."

Rory felt something dawn inside of him. A spark igniting, lighting a fire. He took a slow drag on his cigar, studying the darkening sky through the window. After a moment of consideration, he said, "You could kill them."

She sat up on her knees, naked, her eyes like tiny stars looking sideways at him. She laughed for what seemed like an unusually long time, until he thought that perhaps she actually was nuts, or maybe on her way there.

"Yeah? But isn't *that* crazy?" She shook a finger at him, grinning.

"Perhaps," he said. "Perhaps it's not."

"Are you serious? You really think that's an option? Like I could do that? Could I really do that?" She shook her head, a smile on her lips as if she just tasted something new and wonderful. She inclined her head and looked toward the window, the shadows lengthening across her face. "It never even occurred to me before, killing them. I mean I've thought about protecting myself. Like self-defense, you know? If they came at me, I would fight. But killing them? Maybe that's it! Maybe I need to get them before they get me!"

He took another drag on his cigar and blew out a long stream into the air. "You know, it's not like you're going to change them and they're not going to change you. Life is all about choices, girl. What you decide to do and what you decide not to do. That's what shapes you, leads you in different directions. It's a matter of what kind of results you want to achieve. How you want to live your life. You've just got to be more self-directed if you want to get anywhere. What is it that you want, Justine?"

"What do I want?"

"How do you want your life to be? It's a pretty simple question."

"I want it to be free. I want to be free to make my own decisions. Free to be who I am." Her eyes were wide, staring at him, glinting in the remaining light from the window.

"And what's stopping you? Your parents and the decisions they want to make for you?"

"Yes."

"Then how are you going to overcome that? Are you going to let them dictate to you? Are you going to take orders from them?"

"No, no, I'm not."

"Then what do you want to do about it, girl?"

"Well, I want to be free of them," she said, her brow furrowing in anger. "I want to get away from being under their microscope. I've got to save myself, that's what I've got to do. I have to save my baby and myself. It's not too late."

"How will you do that?"

She ran her fingers over his stomach and then she stopped and gazed down at him in silence, watching as he took a drag of his cigar.

After a moment she asked, "Have you ever killed anyone, Rory?"

"Aye. Many," he answered without hesitation.

"What was it like?"

"Like nothing. Like changing your socks. It's not as difficult as you might think." He butted out his cigar in a teacup saucer beside him. Lifting a hand, he twisted his fingers in her hair and kissed her.

"Didn't you feel bad afterwards, or regret it later? Isn't it inherently wrong, like, in the eyes of God?"

He shook his head and frowned. "God did not give us laws to live by. Man made those up and assigned them to God via some storybook. People believe it as absolute truth, following along like nothing more than lambs to the slaughter. But if they had half a brain they'd be able to see it was a work of fiction."

He pulled her down beside of him and moved his body, entwining it with hers. Leaning on one elbow, he gazed down at her, touching her face, tracing his fingers across one breast.

"You're so soft."

"That's 'cause I'm a girl, as you're always reminding me." She smiled sweetly.

"Is that why? ...Girl." He began to tickle her until she squealed and begged him to stop.

A moment later, he became serious.

"I've something to show you," he said, standing up and pulling his jeans on.

"Okay, what is it?"

"It's about your father and your stepmother. I wasn't going to tell you, but given what they're trying to do to you and how they're treating you, I think you should know."

He watched her dress, a look of concern on her face as she flipped her hair back from her shoulders. "You make it sound like I need to prepare myself for some bad news or something."

"Well, sort of. You're not going to like it."

She followed him into the living room and sat down cross-legged on the wood floor in front of his laptop, as he instructed. In jeans and bare feet he crouched down and hit a key on his laptop. The light from the screen glowed softly around them. He accessed the Internet and clicked on the saved Web sites. Stephanie of New York flickered over the screen.

He turned the screen toward her, stood up and moved into the kitchen, where he flipped on a light, and fetched a soda from the fridge. The sound of it opening echoed off the walls. He tipped it toward his mouth, took a long drink, feeling it fizz in his nose, making his eyes water.

She was staring at the screen when he turned back to her, her face stone like, betraying no thoughts. She was sitting very still. He studied the way the light fell across her features waiting for her response. She gazed up at him, expressionless.

"This is fucking sickening." She shook her head, standing up.

"I'm sorry to have to show you."

"No, it's good that you did." She folded her arms and stared at the floor, her body appearing rigid.

"What about my father? You said you found something out about him."

He accessed his email and clicked open the pictures. Justine let out a little cry as they came into view and she covered her mouth with her hand. She took in a breath and folded her arms around herself. Then she stood up and burst into laughter. Rory chuckled as he watched her, and then he was quiet, studying the way she bowed and raised her head, shrieking, with tears running down her face.

"I knew it! I fucking knew it!" she said, moving into the kitchen. Her eyes were wide and crazed looking. She laughed again, and slapped her hand several times, hard, on the counter beside him. Her reaction seemed exaggerated. He wondered at her behavior, certain that it was true; her parents must know her better than he did. Maybe she really wasn't all there. She did spend some time in a psychiatric hospital, after all. Maybe she really was a wack-job.

"He was seeing her a year ago, and I found out about it." She rubbed the backs of her fingers at her eyes and sniffed. "God, this is so ugly. He promised me that he'd stop if I didn't breathe a word of it to my step-mother. It appears that I'm the only one who's kept up my end of the bargain. God, this sucks! I shouldn't know these things about him. About her, too. Why do I have to know about this shit? Who are these fucking people?"

Rory moved toward her and encircled her in his arms when her laughter turned to tears. She rested her head on his chest and he felt the convulsions of her body as she sobbed. After a moment, she took the soda can from his hand and sipped.

"If I wanted to kill them, how would I do it? What would be the best way?" she asked, moving over to the window in the living room to look out at the street.

"You don't really want that, do you? You don't want your parents to die."

"Yes, I do. I want them dead!" she said, her face suddenly angry. "I want them out of my fucking life for good. They're trying to put me back in the psych ward and steal Abigail away. I can't let them do that, Rory! I've got to stop them!"

"Okay, okay. It's okay," he said, placing his hands on her shoulders to calm her.

"As soon as you mentioned it, I knew right away it was the answer I've been searching for."

"Are you sure? Are you absolutely certain that you want them dead? That you want them to die? It's not as if you can change your mind afterwards. Once they're gone, they're gone. You can't undo it."

"It's the only way. Now all I've got to do is figure out how."

She wasn't even looking at him. He got the feeling she was in another world.

"That's not something you should concern yourself with, girl. Leave it up to me; I'll take care of it for you."

"You would do that for me?"

"Aye. I would do that for you. But you've got to be absolutely certain you want this. Maybe you need to sleep on it for—"

"No! No! No! It's what I want! I don't want to wait any longer. I don't have time for that. There's no fucking time, Rory. It's got to be done right away, before they get the baby."

Rory stared at her, studying her face, wondering what he was dealing with here. Did this woman really understand what they were talking about? She seemed paranoid, on the edge. He didn't know if he could trust her. She might actually be completely psycho. That could be a dangerous thing. For him.

He'd known other people who were crazy, like Psycho Willy from the UFF. An image of the man licking the blood from a knife after he'd slaughtered his victim appeared in his mind. One time, Rory watched in disgust at he gouged out a man's eye and slipped it into his pocket as a souvenir. He didn't dare say anything to Psycho Willy. Nobody did. He was dead now, hung himself in the Maze years ago with bed sheets. It was the best thing to happen to him.

"I've been so worried about what they've been planning for me," she said. "And what they would do to my baby once they took her away from me. I can't sleep anymore. I wander around the house all night like a fucking zombie, not alive and not quite dead. It's been a nightmare for me. I don't want them to suffer Rory, that's not what I want. It would have to be quick."

"Aye. I won't make it painful. It will be over very fast."

"Sweet. Will you do it soon? Right away?"

"As soon as I can."

Justine took a deep breath and smiled. Her entire demeanor seemed buoyant. "All right, I feel better. I feel like a huge weight has been lifted from my shoulders."

"But if you have a change of heart—"

"It's got to be done," she said. "There's no other way. This is the best solution for Abigail and me. It's got to be done."

"All right then, if you're sure it's what you want."

"How would you do it?" she asked, her eyes looking suddenly excited. "Shoot them? Make it look like a break-in or something?"

"Now, that I won't tell you. How and when is not something you're to know. That way, if you're ever questioned by the police you won't know anything about it. I want you to find out their schedule for the next week. Where they are going, times, dates, etc. and let me know."

"They're leaving for Rochester on Monday morning. My dad told me. Seven a.m. sharp they're leaving. Pam has an appointment with the doctor who treated her at the hospital. They always leave right on time too. I could set my watch by it. They're both very punctual people, very organized."

"Okay, good. What you also need to do is go home and just behave like nothing is going on. Can you do that?" he asked, his hands on her shoulders.

"Of course."

"Don't let your dad know about the pictures you've seen. Or let on what you know about your stepmother. Just act normal, go about your normal routine. And we should not see each other for a little while. Don't phone me or anything. I'll come by and see you when I think it's safe, but don't phone me, all right? Only if it's an emergency or if your parents change their schedule. Make sure you let me know of any change in their schedule. Can you do that, girl?"

"Sure, I can do that." She nodded.

"Okay, so seven a.m. on Monday they're leaving together? And will they take your Dad's car or your stepmother's?"

"They'll go in the Lincoln, for sure. My dad hates driving Pam's car, and he'll want to drive. He hates her driving, too, so they'll take his car."

"All right. Good. Just be patient. You won't have to move out of your house, after all."

"Sweet. You will move in with me when it's done," she said smiling, as if there was no question, as if it's something that was not up for debate.

"Sweet," he repeated and gazed down at her, knowing that his plan was unfolding before him. He kissed her and dragged her back to his bed.

Chapter
THIRTY-SIX

The wind picked up and whistled around the sides of the house. The trees swayed ominously in the gathering gloom. Brett lay fully clothed on top of the bedcovers beside his wife, watching them though the window.

"Pam?" He touched her hand to see if she was awake.

She cracked open her uninjured eye and stared at him.

"Can I get you anything? Are you hungry?"

She shook her head and closed her eye.

"You should eat something. I could make some grilled cheese or soup."

"I'm not hungry."

He looked over at her glass of wine on the bedside table. He had refilled it twice for her now. "You probably shouldn't be drinking while you're on the painkillers. How about a cup of coffee and some cookies, then?"

"I don't want anything."

"We should have told the police the truth, Pam. Regardless of what they might think of the circumstances of how you met that guy. I mean he called you, so you would have a phone number right? Maybe the police can find him if—"

"I don't want to talk about this."

"Pam, I..." He searched for the words to convey his feelings, to try and make peace with her. "I know we've had our problems. I know that I haven't been the man you wanted me to be but—"

"Can we not do this, please?"

"I think we need to talk, Pam."

He watched her sigh, resign herself to it.

"I don't know why you think I would ever hurt you," he continued. "I love you. I don't want to lose you, Pam. I've got too many years invested in you. I think if we both try a little harder we can get through this."

He studied her face in the dying light, hoping for a glimmer of something that would give him the encouragement he needed. She turned away, her gaze on the wall. He sighed, his heart heavy, and said, "The idea that I would hire somebody to go to a hotel room and beat you up is just ludicrous. I would never in a million years think of doing something like that to you. Why would you even think that?"

"Because of what he said to me." She turned to him, fixing him with a worried look suddenly.

"What? What did he say?"

"He said something about you playing ball. It was clear that he knows you and—"

"What? Playing ball?"

"Yes."

Brett sat up. "What did he say exactly?"

"I don't remember. It's all just a blur. Just something about Brett not playing ball and then that's when he hit me over the head with the bottle and I blacked out."

"Shit." He stood up and paced beside the bed, hands in his pockets.

"What?" she asked.

"Nothing. I just…did he have an accent? "

"Scottish or Irish, something like that. I think it was Irish… what?"

"It's nothing. I'll leave you to rest."

"Brett?" She paused, and he could see the anguish on her face. "I'm sorry. I shouldn't have lashed out at you, I know you didn't have anything to do with this. I'm sorry about everything."

"It's okay," he said, sitting back down. He stroked her hair and her face tenderly.

"I love you." She squeezed his hand and started to cry.

"I love you too. We'll be okay, Pam. We'll get through this." He smiled and kissed her forehead. "Rest now. I'll check in on you in a little while."

Had Madden called her and posed as a customer? Is that how he got her out to the hotel? He knew right away as this thought entered his mind that Rory, in fact, had set them up. Somehow, he'd found out that Pamela was working as a prostitute. How he'd gotten this information was a mystery, but he'd found out nonetheless, and he'd used it to his advantage. Rory wanted to strike fear into their hearts, make them afraid to live in their new home, make them want to move back to where they'd come from. Well, it was working. Goddamn it was working!

Anger rose within him, but then it subsided into sorrow before it had even ignited. He felt tears in his eyes. How was he going to make this right? How was he going to protect his family against this maniac when he felt so helpless himself?

Downstairs he found Justine standing by the windows overlooking the back yard.

"Do you think we'll ever find him?" she asked as he appeared beside her.

"Find who?" His mind was filled with thoughts of Rory Madden.

"Duke."

"Yeah, he'll come back. He's probably just out there exploring the woods; he'll come back when he's hungry."

"I hope so. I hope he's not lost, or coyotes have got him."

"It's only been a few hours," Brett said. "I'm sure he'll find his way back."

"There's a lot of trees out there, Dad. He could easily get lost, and it's dark now. He's just a little guy. A coyote could get him. You should have put him in the kennel when you let him out, especially at night."

He watched as she twisted her hair with both hands, pulled forward over one shoulder like a rope.

"Don't worry. He'll come back, Sweets. Dogs are tough, he can handle the dark."

"It's so windy out there. I can actually feel the house moving."

"Looks like a storm is coming." He studied her face, the worried expression, the nervous energy wafting from her, and asked, "What would you think if we sold this place, moved back to the city?"

For a moment her expression didn't change, as if she had to sift through a horde of different answers for the one that felt right. Eventually, she turned and looked up at him.

"Could we actually do that? I mean, we just bought this place."

"I don't know. I'm just thinking out loud," he said and looked at the sun setting through the trees on the horizon, the shifting colors moving fast across the sky.

"You know, I love the house. I love the property and the scenery and all the stars at night," she said. "But, you know that sense of peace and solitude that we first liked about this place? I don't feel it anymore; it feels scary to me now. I don't feel safe out here. We're not safe here."

Brett contemplated the look in her eyes, the way she continued to twist her hair like she wasn't even aware that she was doing it. He felt a sense of guilt, thinking about how they took her away from everything that was familiar, her friends, and her support system. Were they too eager, too certain about what they wanted that they were blind to their daughter's needs and wants? He'd been excited, too hopeful to believe this could be anything but wonderful. And it was wonderful, for the most part. But these days he witnessed a glint of something in her eyes that worried him; fear like you'd see in the eyes of a captured animal. He'd try again to ask her about getting back on her medication but she'd only resist, and he knew that if he pushed her, she would fight him. She could be so stubborn.

Maybe they had been in too much of a hurry to move out here and just believed that she would adjust fine without really considering if it was true. This was Pamela's dream, not Justine's and not his. He worried about his daughter out here by herself with the baby when he was out of town. It was time he closed the business, got a job. He could get a sales job somewhere. The idea of working for somebody else after owning his own business for so many years was painful. But what choice did he have now?

The name Rory Madden pierced his thoughts again.

"If you don't want to play ball that's your choice. But you're not going to like what's coming next, buddy."

He thought about that phone conversation with him yesterday. Did the guy really think he was just going to hand him the keys to their home and walk away? If he thought the pictures of him and Lorena were so damaging, then he was wrong. Pamela wasn't a fool. She knew about his affair. It was something they never talked about and it certainly wasn't something he wanted to rub in her face. But he wasn't going to allow himself to be blackmailed. If Pamela were to see the pictures, then so be it. She would be angry, of course, to have the evidence of it paraded before her eyes, and he would be embarrassed. But it didn't matter. He loved Pamela, in spite of everything, he loved her. That had always been enough.

Brett had phoned an alarm company days ago and made an appointment for a sales person to come out and discuss their choices. From there, it would take another week before an alarm could be installed. Maybe he should report this whole blackmail thing and his suspicions to the police.

"Pamela and I are leaving for the doctor in the morning," he said.

"I know, you told me. At seven a.m., right?"

"Yeah. You and Abigail should come with us. We'll drive to Manhattan after."

"I'll think about it."

"Actually, Sweetheart, your appointment with Dr. Hill, that psychiatrist I was telling you about, has been moved up to tomorrow afternoon. He phoned me today because he had a cancellation so I said to put you down, so—"

"Dad, I'm not interested in seeing some fucking shrink. I've told you this already." Her eyes darkened. She stopped twisting her hair and folded her arms, glaring at him.

"Do it for me? Please? Just go one time, see if it helps. Do it for me, Justine." He put a hand on her shoulder.

She rolled her eyes. "Dad, I—"

"Just an hour of your time," Brett said. "Then you can spend some time in the city and see your friends. We can go pretend we're tourists and go to all those places we've seen a million times living there but have never been. Like the museums, the Empire State building, catch a Broadway show."

"You've never been to the Empire State building, Dad?" She chuckled.

"Never."

A loud crack from outside startled them, and they both turned to look out the window as a tree fell in the shadows of the yard in front of the deck.

"Shit!" Brett said.

"Wow. That almost hit the house!"

"Yeah, damn I hope no more trees come down in this wind. I've got to clean out the garage and start parking the car in there," he said. "I just had that windshield replaced."

Brett opened the door to the deck and stepped out to take a look.

The wind gusted, swooping down into the trees with a violent force. The tree that lay on the ground was a big maple, broken in half, its white flesh exposed in the gloomy light. He would have to take a chain saw to it.

Brett came back inside the house. "Shit, that's a big tree."

In the next moment, the lights flickered and went out. The house was immersed in darkness.

"Oh, my God," Justine gasped.

"What's happened?" Pamela yelled from upstairs.

"Power lines must have gone down," Brett called, watching the outline of her figure come down the stairs like a ghost. "Do we have candles?"

"There's some in the drawer in the kitchen beside the fridge. There's matches in there, too," Pamela said, crossing the room, the wine glass in her hand. Brett took his phone from his hip and turned on the flashlight application. It cast a soft white light into the room. He could see the bruises on Pamela's face.

"I hope this won't be a long power outage, considering the fact that we have electric heating in this place," he said as he went to search for the candles. "But you know, I have a feeling we should get used to this. Bet it happens more often than in the city. We probably need a generator out here."

He walked into the kitchen and found a dozen or so taper candles and a box of matches. He knew there was a flashlight around somewhere; problem was that things like flashlights never seemed available when they were needed. Likely it was in the garage still packed in a box with all the other crap he would never find. He pulled out a number of candles and looked around for something to put them in. Then a piercing scream from the living room startled him, and he dropped the candles on the floor.

"What? What?!" He ran back over to where his wife and daughter stood at the window.

Justine was backing up, staring at the windows.

"Something's out there!" she gasped.

"I didn't see anyone." Pamela shrugged.

Justine gripped Brett's shirt.

"Where?"

"Outside. It went around the side of the house."

Brett rushed to the door and wrenched it open.

"Brett, no! Don't go out there!" Pamela warned.

"Be right back." He slammed the door behind him.

Chapter
THIRTY-SEVEN

Justine stood beside Pamela in the darkness. The wind wailed so loudly that it shook the windows, and Justine was sure it would lift the roof. Could it be Rory outside? Was this it? Was it going to happen now?

She peered out the window, trying to see into the shadows cast by the full moon. She thought of how dependent they were on moonlight, living out here in the country. Whenever there wasn't a moon in the sky, it was impossible to see anything outside but blackness. That's what unnerved her about living here. She folded her arms tightly across her body. Was this power outage Rory's doing?

Maybe she should light some candles. She felt her way into the kitchen like a blind person. She found the drawer next to the fridge and fished around for the matches. Retrieving a small square book of matches, she fumbled to light one. Her hands shook as a tiny orange flame burst to life. She was able to see the candles on the floor. Lighting one, she extinguished a match and then reached for the crystal candlesticks in the cupboard. Within a few moments she had lit nearly a dozen, sticking some in empty wine bottles and melting others to plates.

"Oh, for God's sake, Justine you're going to burn the place down. Did you really need to light that many? It's not even fully dark out yet." Pamela scowled, entering the kitchen. "The baby's crying. Can't you hear the baby crying?"

"Yes, I can hear her."

"Well? Go and get her! What's the matter with you?"

Looking at Pamela in the glow of candlelight, Justine contemplated her impending death, wondering if maybe it should be a little slower and more painful.

She turned from her with a candlestick and went upstairs, thinking about her father out there in the dark.

"Hey, Abigail, sweetheart." She smiled at the baby in her cradle and set the candle on the bedside table. Abigail was crying furiously, her little face red and angry. Justine had fed her some pureed chicken and sweet potatoes earlier, so she couldn't be hungry. She probably wanted to nurse out of comfort, as was her growing habit.

Justine lifted her out of the cradle and lay down with her in bed, offering her a breast. She devoured it, the crying coming to a stop. Justine sang to her baby, stroking her face and head in the soft glow of candlelight, willing herself to relax.

The gray people inside the walls began to whisper and she knew suddenly what she had to do to protect Abigail. She sat up, burping the baby, and then leaving her on the bed, she retrieved the knife she'd stashed in the bottom of the baby bag. She used the knife to unfasten the screws in the square vent at the bottom of the wall in her bedroom. It was just big enough inside. Carefully she wrapped Abigail in a baby blanket and tucked her inside the wall. Abigail gurgled and looked at her with those innocent eyes glittering in the shadows, but didn't cry. Then Justine screwed the vent cover back in place. She would be safe now. The gray people would protect her until Rory got rid of her parents.

Justine put the knife back inside the baby bag, and went downstairs where she found Pamela and her dad by the door. Brett held Duke in his arms and looked at Pam, who was standing with a hand pressed to her mouth, her eyes wide open as if she'd had a fright.

"I found the little devil." Brett turned and grinned when he saw Justine approach, holding up Duke. He set him on the floor and the dog immediately ran back to the door, pawing furiously at the bottom of it to get out again.

"He had something—" Pamela began, but Brett shook his head at her, placing a hand on her shoulder and then giving her a one armed hug, comforting her.

"What? What did he have?" Justine asked.

"Nothing," Brett said.

Justine moved past them and peered out the darkened windows, scanning the deck. Then she saw it.

"What the hell's that?" A dead animal? A squirrel, perhaps. She shooed the pup away from the door with her foot. "Is that what he had? What is it?"

"You don't want to see it Justine, trust me," Brett said.

"Why not?"

"It looks like a...a hand," Pamela said, her voice shaking. "It's partially decomposed, like he's dug it up from somewhere,"

"A hand? What do you mean a hand?"

Justine opened the door and stepped out onto the deck.

"Don't go out there," her father said but she ignored him.

In bare feet she stepped over the cold wood, the wind lifting her hair and whipping it around her head, and gazed down at the object on the deck, just at the top of the steps. It was definitely a hand—a human hand—shriveled, discolored, pieces of bone exposed in the fingers. The fingernails were blackened. She felt her stomach lurch at the sight and took a step back.

Then an image of her father lying on the ground covered in blood came to her. It sent a shock wave through her mind and body. She tensed at the thought. She paced back and forth, staring at the severed hand, her heart hammering in her ears. She felt dizzy suddenly, nauseous like she was going to be sick. In the dark, she ran back inside the house, into the bathroom, and stood over the sink. Her stomach heaved and she retched, and coughed up it's undigested contents. She sobbed and splashed cool water on her face, and then a sharp clarity dawned on her. Her mind stabilized, as if a curtain had been raised to reveal the mechanics behind the performance.

She thought of Rory and those scars all over his body. She thought of him lying there on his bed with a gun in his hand, talking about how killing someone was like changing his socks. Is this who she was? Is this who she had become? Was she like Rory; cold, calculating...a killer? And she knew in that moment she had been walking around impaired for weeks, her judgment influenced by erroneous thinking, her mind fragmented as if it had been damaged somehow, rendering her incapable of making sound decisions. No, she was not like Rory. And she didn't *want* to be like him.

With a towel, she wiped her face and looked at her reflection in the mirror. And it was then she realized what she had set in motion. The horrible plans she had made. Plotting her parent's deaths. How could she? *What had she done?!*

"Justine!" Brett called from behind the bathroom door.

Brett looked at her with worried eyes once she opened the door. "Are you okay?" he asked.

Justine nodded and said, "We need to call the police."

Chapter
THIRTY-EIGHT

"We still have that policeman's card. The one that came by the house," Pamela said. "It's in the kitchen. Give him a call."

"Good idea," Brett said. Justine caught his arm before he walked away.

"Did you see anyone when you were outside, Daddy?"

"No, nobody's out there."

"Are you sure? You didn't see a man? A man outside the house?"

He paused and looked at her sideways. "Are you all right, Sweets? You look pale."

"I...I don't feel well...I feel like I'm going to be sick again. Something's wrong. I—"

"What is it?"

"Come sit down on the sofa," Pamela said.

"I don't know. I...I just...I feel like I've been dreaming or something. Nothing feels real to me." Her eyes darted around the room.

"You're shaking, Justine." He directed her by the elbow to the sofa and sat down beside her.

"You'll be okay. You just had a shock, seeing that horrible thing outside." Pamela sat down on the other side of her on the sofa.

"No," Justine said. "I mean yes, it was a shock, but that's not it."

They both gazed at her, waiting for her to explain, and it was then she realized the gravity of the situation. It was then she understood that they were not her enemies, that they truly loved her; in spite of all their strife, and their secrets, they had her best interests at heart. They weren't bad people out to harm her or her baby. Hadn't they taken her in when she was pregnant and allowed her to stay and have her baby? Hadn't they supported her, emotionally, financially? Granted, there was no shortage of issues, but had they ever once done anything intentionally to harm her? Even when Pamela picked up the phone and called that cocaine hotline, resulting in Justine's commitment to that psych ward, even that was not done with malice. It was with the purpose of helping her. Justine knew that. She knew that now. Of course. They loved her. How could she possibly have thought they deserved to die?

She felt incredibly guilty in that moment for all the horrible plans she was making. Plotting their deaths? What was wrong with her? The idea was insane, and yet she knew she had embraced it, thought of it as a choice. But it was as if someone else had been plotting it, not her. As if she had been standing outside of herself watching herself do all of these things, making all of these plans. She felt completely stunned.

Oh, my God, what had she done?

"I think...I think I'm losing my mind." She gasped and burst into tears. She turned to her father and cried on his shoulder as he held her.

"It's all right, Sweets. It's going to be fine. Don't worry about anything, okay?"

"I...I don't know what's wrong with me, Daddy. I've...I've been thinking such horrible things. Crazy things. And...and I've been hearing voices telling me horrible things about...about the baby. That...that you guys were going to take her away from me."

She broke down again in heart-wrenching sobs.

"We'll take you to see that doctor tomorrow, okay? We'll get you some help. It will be okay," her father said, rocking her. "Don't you worry, Little Spark. It's going to be fine. I'm here for you. I won't let anything happen to you. It's going to be fine."

"I...I know, Dad...oh, God!"

"What?"

"Rory...Rory, he's—"

"What?"

"He's planning something. He wants to hurt you and Pamela."

"What are you talking about?"

"He told me he's going to kill you. I can't believe I went along with it, I'm so ashamed to even admit that I was—"

"Justine, do you know this man? Have you talked to him?"

"He's been here at the house when you guys were out. I let him in and, oh Daddy, I've just been so lonely up here all by myself, it's so far from everything and I just felt so fucking isolated all the time, and he talked to me and he was so interested in me and for the first time I felt—"

"Oh, my God! Did he, did he hurt you? Did he touch you?"

"No, he didn't hurt me," Justine said, sniffing, wiping her nose on her sleeve. "He was really nice to me and I think that I really have genuine feelings for him, you know? But he said he's going to kill you and Pam. I can't let that happen. I've got to call him and tell him that I don't want to do this anymore. I think if I just explain things to him then he'll listen to me. I really think he cares about me, so he'll listen to me."

Her father stood up without a word and turned away from her.

"I'll be back in a little while," Brett said and rushed out the front door before either of them could protest. Pamela said she was going upstairs to check on Abigail.

Justine felt completely exhausted, worn out physically and mentally. She lifted Pamela's wine glass from the table and stared at it's contents wondering, were these her tears?

"Justine?" Pamela called from upstairs, the alarm in her voice echoing through the dark. "Where's the baby?"

The baby! *Oh, God, she'd put her inside the wall!*

Chapter
THIRTY-NINE

From the trunk of his car, Brett pulled out a tire iron. As he turned the key in the ignition, he slid the tool underneath the seat.

The wind whipped tree branches onto the road, which was slick from the downpour. Brett turned the car onto East Lake road and headed into town. He set the wipers to a fast speed so he could see through the drops that pounded the windshield, and then turned them up again to the highest setting. He gripped the steering wheel tightly, leaning forward, trying to see the road in the dark. His heart pounded wildly.

Brett passed only one other car on the way to town. A crack of lightening flashed in the sky and lit up the road and the trees in a blinding white. A raccoon darted out of the darkness and did a wobbly dash across the road, but it was far enough away that he didn't have to brake.

His thoughts were laser-focused, the emotion so intense that it was alarming. All the more frightening was the knowledge that he couldn't stop himself. There was a vague thought somewhere in his head of this being wrong, and he wondered if what he was about to do would be something he might regret. Brett was not a violent man. He could count on one hand the number of physical fights he'd been in since kindergarten. But even though he considered himself a peaceful person, he also knew there were times when you were forced to take a stand. And tonight, he wasn't taking counsel of rationality; he was only mindful of his rage and following through with the course he was on—the course of protecting his family and all he held dear.

The rain intensified as he turned onto a deserted Main Street. Chen's Chinese Food. Rory has an apartment above that place, the cop had said. Brett scanned the buildings and found it just up ahead on the other side. He did a U-turn and parked on the side of the road. He emerged from the car in the downpour, not caring if he got wet. The tire iron was in his hand, held flat beside his pant leg.

Brett found the door beside the restaurant that led up a narrow staircase. The stairwell was dark and smelled of insecticide and decay. He hurried up the stairs, trying to keep his feet quiet on the wooden steps. A strip of light glowed faintly underneath the door at the top of the small landing. There was a broom in the corner. From behind the door, he could hear a television. Brett took a deep breath and then knocked firmly. He waited only seconds before knocking again, more insistently. The energy was so intense within him that his legs were shaking. The tire iron felt ice cold in his grip.

"Rory?" he yelled. "Open up. We need to talk."

Nothing. Brett took a step back and then kicked as hard as he could beside the door handle. Wood splintered and cracked as the door flew back. He stepped into the darkened room, which smelled of marijuana. The dull glow of a small television cast a weak light into the room, flickering across the sparse furnishings. *South Park* was playing. The place was empty. Maybe he wasn't home. What time was it? He checked the time on his cell phone. It was 10:35. Perhaps he was out somewhere. He moved further into the room until he noticed a thin ribbon of smoke coming from a crushed cigarette on a plate sitting on the coffee table. Beside it was a glass of something with ice inside. Just as the knowledge that Rory must be here dawned on him, he heard the distinct click of a gun being cocked behind him

"Drop the weapon and turn around very slow," a man said. He recognized the accent and knew it was Rory.

Brett felt the solid metal of the tire iron in his grip. He was not about to give in. He didn't come here to get terrorized by this thug. He was done with standing by and letting this asshole stomp all over his life, his home, his family, his sense of peace and security. He was done with feeling powerless and afraid. Brett was taking back his life.

Without another thought, he reacted. His body exploded into action. He bent at the knees, swinging around with the tire iron extended outward like a baton, aiming it low. It connected dully with bone—a knee or a shin, he wasn't sure. Rory let out a painful groan and crumbled. Brett swung again, bringing the tire iron down as the man was backing up, struggling for balance. The weapon hit him on the wrist, knocking the gun from his hand. He swung with a back-handed motion like a tennis player, and struck him in the head. Rory fell backwards onto the floor. His face was a mask of pain as he went down. Another crack to his jaw and blood spurted forth. One more blow to his ribs. Then Brett took his boots to Rory as he lay dazed on the floor, turning over in a slow-motion attempt to shield himself from the blows that landed on his ribs, his kidneys, his legs, his ass.

Brett stopped. He didn't want to kill the man or permanently injure him. As beatings went, this one probably wouldn't put him in the hospital, but he would likely be pissing blood for days and feeling pain for a lot longer.

Brett paced beside him, his breath coming in gasps. Then, leaning over the man, he studied his face distorted with pain, the veins like fat worms on his neck thick with agony. Their eyes met.

"Stay the fuck away from my family and my house. You hear me?" Brett spoke low and angry.

Rory spit a stream of blood and saliva on the floor, as he lay with his eyes shut tight. He panted, and retched, clearly in agony.

"You come anywhere near my wife or my daughter again, I'll kill you. You understand what I'm saying here, cocksucker? I'll fucking kill you." Brett gave him one final kick before leaving, right in the nuts, eliciting a howl of agony from Rory's throat.

Chapter
FORTY

At five o'clock the next morning, the alarm sounded on Rory's cell phone. He shut it off, and felt a searing pain rip through his chest. The Percocet he took last night had worn off. Carefully, he rose to a sitting position, wincing from the injuries to his ribs. He reached for the bottle of pills and shook three of them out. With a mouthful of water, he swallowed them and lay back on the pillows, panting from the effort.

With his tongue, he felt the broken front tooth and the fat lip he'd sustained. That son-of-a-bitch Jameson had won that round; he'd give the man that. But in a matter of hours, Rory was going to win the war.

For a few minutes, he dozed in and out of sleep, waiting for the pills to take effect. When he finally rose from bed, about twenty minutes later, it was still dark. He dressed by the light of the moon and then, limping slightly from the injury to his shin (a bump nearly the size of a golf ball), he went into the kitchen to make himself a coffee. He lifted his T-shirt and inspected his left side. The bruises extended from underneath his arm, down to his hip, and he could feel others on his thigh. They were a deep shade of plum.

Rory flipped open his Zippo and lit a cigarette, watching the coffee drip into the pot. He measured out several lines of coke on the counter, and snorted them up immediately. He needed to be completely sharp for what he was about to do. The painkillers were taking the edge off his injuries, but his mind needed to be focused.

Justine's deep blue eyes were in his thoughts. He could still smell the scent of her hair, the taste of her skin on his tongue. She was an incredible woman. Damaged, yes, but weren't we all damaged to one degree or another? Were we not all tainted by the disappointments this life afforded us, our spirits trampled, our dreams fractured, our hearts and minds beaten over and over, burned to ashes until they were no more? The choice to die or rise up and recreate ourselves was ours, alone. Lying down was never an option for Rory. He was a warrior. Always would be.

The wings that carried him to higher ground were cast from the fire inside of him, breathing into him, its cry calling out from the silent screams trapped in his soul. He could feel the beating of its wings, that great bird inside of him, pushing upward. He would be victorious. Nothing could keep him down.

After gulping his coffee, he left with his Colt .45 tucked in the back of his jeans and 1.25 pounds of C-4 in a paper bag stuffed in the pocket of his leather jacket. The streets were deserted as he turned his car south on East Lake road, with "The Bleeding" by Five Finger Death Punch blasting from the radio. Minutes later, he pulled up in front of his house. He parked the car a few yards down the road and limped along on the soft earth, soggy from all the rainfall the night before, beside the brick driveway, breathing the damp air into his lungs. The frogs were coming to life in the swampy areas of the property, their mad chirping animating the gloom. The moon followed him, casting light across the lawn, its presence pressing into him. He wished he had waited until there was no moon for this. A cover of total darkness would have been better.

Rows of solar lights planted along the driveway and walkway up to the house cast circles of ocher light. They appeared cheap to him, unworthy of being on such a superb piece of property with a house this luxurious. He pictured himself removing them when he moved back, and tossing them straight into the trash.

Rory stepped across the bricks of the driveway to the back of Brett's Lincoln. He crouched along the outside of the car, and then finding the right spot, he carefully lay down on his back on the ground, mindful of his injuries. From his pocket he removed the explosives with the electronic detonator attached and a timer set to 7:30 a.m. The faint odor of the C-4 brought back memories of the UFF. He recalled one time he was lying on the street, attaching a bomb to a car owned by an IRA member, much like he was doing at the moment, when he heard a car door slam and the driver pulled away before he could finish the job. Someone spotted him, and he was chased down the Falls Road, bullets whipping past his head. He narrowly escaped.

He never imagined, years later, living over here in America, that he would once again be attaching a bomb to someone's car. Strange, the way life worked.

Rory reached under the car and fixed the C-4 high up in the undercarriage, just in front of the gas tank, making sure it was secure. When he was satisfied, he stood up, brushed himself off and made his way back to his car. He parked the car further down the road on a dirt lane, where hunters sometimes parked in the fall.

Rory lit a cigarette and touched the bump on the side of his head. He checked his broken tooth in the mirror and inspected his injured face. His nose was swollen and he couldn't breath through it. No matter. It would heal in a couple of weeks. The tooth would be a little more difficult. He would need to see a dentist. That was going to suck. He swallowed two more painkillers with a sip from an old water bottle in one of the cup holders. Then he popped the vertebrae in his neck and leaned back in the seat, waiting for the sun to rise.

He was lying there, dozing, when the ringing of his cell phone jarred him moments later. When he opened his eyes, it was still dark. The clock on his phone said it was six-forty-five. Who the hell was calling him at this hour, he wondered, looking at the unfamiliar number. But he recognized the Belfast area code.

"Rory, Gilmour here. I just realized the time difference and that I'm probably waking you, aren't I?"

"It's all right. How's everything?" Rory blinked sleep from his eyes and reached into his jacket for a pack of cigars.

They made small talk for a moment. He got the feeling that Gilmour was stalling; like there was something he needed to tell him but didn't want to.

"What is it Gilmour? You have an update on Frances? Did you find her diary?"

"Aye, I've got an update for you, but no diary, Rory. We didn't need it, after all. But there's an update, all right. Quite a bit, actually. That's why I'm calling you. We've solved your sister's case, Rory."

There was a tone in his voice that Rory didn't like. It was somber, not at all jubilant, the way solving a cold case should be. Rory flicked his Zippo and lit the end of his cigar, waiting for the man to continue.

"I'm afraid it's not the ending any of us were hoping for, but at the very least it gives us some closure." He sighed heavily and paused.

"What is it you have to tell me, Gilmour?"

"We found some remains a few days ago. We ran some DNA tests and compared it with the samples we took from hair follicles in Frances's hairbrush. I'm afraid it's a match, Rory."

Sitting there in his car, staring out the windshield at the moonlight shifting over the mirrored surface of the lake, Rory felt a wave rise up and move through him, pounding his soul, taking him under. He felt himself sinking down. His chest restricted painfully. He lost his breath.

"Randal Trowbridge wasn't the same Randy fellow you said she had referred to in her diary," Gilmour continued after a moment. "Trowbridge didn't know Frances. The day she didn't come home from school, he had been out drinking in a pub all afternoon and made the foolish decision to get in his car and drive home. He admitted he was driving too fast and the roads were wet. He said Frances ran across the road and he couldn't stop in time. He ran her down, and then he said he stopped the car and got out to help her. He said nobody was around, no witnesses at all. Strange that nobody saw anything that time of day and all. He picked her up and put her in his car to take her to the emergency room. But apparently, in his words, she died before he could get her there."

Gilmour paused. Rory was still sinking downward inside to a place of deep distress. His breath caught in his throat; he felt as if his heart had stopped beating.

"The guy said he panicked, and took her body out to the bogs and buried her," Gilmour went on. "Autopsy confirmed she died of severe head injury. It wasn't an abduction, as we thought. There were no other signs of trauma to the body consistent with anything other than her being hit by a car. There was no sexual interference. The body was still fully clothed. It looks like this Randal Trowbridge fellow is telling the truth. Fifteen years too late, but he's signed a confession. I think it's been eating away at him all this time. Surprised it took him so long to come forward. Would have saved your family a lot of heartache, had he the balls to face it. It was just an accident. Christ, all this time and…it was an accident."

"The wee locket was found with her, as well," Gilmour continued in a heavy voice. "I've got it here with me. I can send it to you if you give me your address."

When Rory drew a ragged breath into his lungs, the wave subsiding, there was a painful tearing inside of him. He felt his spirit rip from his body like a physical thing and wash away. Rory watched transfixed, the smoke from his cigar curling and twisting in front of his face, dancing ghostlike; the early morning light just beginning to crack on the horizon. The ashes spilled down his shirtfront. He flicked the cigar out the window.

He heard a car approaching and turned to see the Lincoln pass by.

"I'll call you later," he said and hung up.

Chapter
FORTY-ONE

Rory started the engine and felt his heart pick up speed. He fastened his seat belt, rolled up the window, and pulled out onto the road. He followed the car at a safe distance, keeping his eyes on its taillights. His mind was in a daze and he drove as if he were dreaming. Minutes later he followed the car out onto the highway and sped up to keep a close eye on it as it merged with traffic. The sun was beginning to rise on the horizon, casting light through the windows of the Lincoln, and he could see the silhouettes of its occupants.

Something didn't make sense. He could see a third head inside the car. It looked like there was a figure in the back seat.

Rory punched the gas pedal and pulled up closer. Yes, there was definitely someone in the back seat. He maneuvered his car into the next lane and sped up alongside the Lincoln on the passenger side, keeping back a few yards. Through the windshield he could see the arm of somebody in the front passenger seat, a gold bracelet around the wrist. It was the mother. He sped up a bit and peered into the back seat, and he laid eyes on Justine.

"What the fuck?" What was she doing in the goddamn car? She wasn't supposed to be in the car!

He pulled up alongside the Lincoln until his window was even with hers. He could see Abigail in her car seat in the middle. Rory's heart flipped and a sweat broke out across his hands. He lifted his foot from the gas pedal and the car fell back.

He needed to get Justine and the baby out of the car! How was he going to get them out?!

"What the hell is she doing?!" Anger coiled through his brain as he tried to think. He stepped on the gas and sped up beside the Lincoln again, looking in at her, trying to get her attention. A car in front of him was suddenly closer than he realized and he had to hit his brakes before he smashed into the back of it. He checked the next lane and swerved over behind the

Lincoln, close on its tail. Passing the car, he sped up alongside the Lincoln again, hoping to catch Justine's eye. He reached for his cell phone and dialed her number, trying to keep up with the Lincoln and keep his eyes on the road at the same time. It went directly to her voicemail.

"Shit!" He looked at the time. 7:05 a.m. He had twenty-five minutes to get her out of the car before it exploded. He must save her! How the hell was he going to do that?

Rory pounded his horn, looking over at Justine. He hit it a second time and she turned to look at him. Her eyes registered surprise, and then a look of fear came over her face.

"Get out of the car!" he screamed, knowing she couldn't hear. "Get out of the fucking car!"

He watched as a hand fluttered to her mouth and she turned to say something to her parents in the front seat. Rory took his foot off the gas pedal, allowing the car to slow. Checking his mirrors, he turned the steering wheel and cut behind them, and crossed into the left-hand lane. He pulled up to the driver's window and laid on his horn.

Brett turned and scowled at him.

"Pull over!" Rory waved his arm and pointed with his finger to the roadside.

The Lincoln sped up. Was Brett ignoring him?

"Stupid fucker!" Rory hit the gas pedal and sped up beside him again. This time, he pulled out the handgun he had stored in the console and pointed it at Brett.

"Pull over!"

Alarm crossed Brett's face at the sight of the gun. Rory watched him check his mirrors and then yell something. He looked frightened and angry at the same time.

Rory drove with the gun in his hand, his heart pounding, as he checked the time on the dash. 7:07, it read. He had twenty-three minutes. Twenty-three minutes to get Justine and the baby out of the car. The Lincoln slowed and moved over to the right-hand lane, cutting off a semi. The truck honked and pulled around Brett's car. Rory slowed his car, riding up on the Lincoln's rear end. He could see Justine turning to look at him and then back at her parents, yelling something. She looked frantic. Their car pulled over at the shoulder and slowed to a stop. Rory eased up in front of the Lincoln and hit the brakes, his wheels skidding on the gravel and fishtailing, kicking up a cloud of dust.

He put it in park and jumped out, the gun flat at his thigh. Between the cars, he hurried over to the rear passenger-side door, where Justine was sitting behind her stepmother. He yanked on the handle but it was locked.

"Open the fucking door!" He pounded the window.

Justine looked confused. What the hell was she doing? Rory thought. The driver's door opened and Brett jumped out, glaring at him over the roof of the car.

"I'm calling the police! Stay the hell away from my family!"

Rory ignored him.

"Justine, open the fucking door!"

"Did you hear what I said?" Brett yelled.

The back door opened and Justine stumbled out.

"What the fuck are you doing?" He grabbed her by the upper arm.

"Get your hands off my daughter!" Brett scrambled around the back of the car.

Rory raised his hand only waist high so the passing cars couldn't see, and pointed the gun at him. Brett took a step back.

"Give me your cell phone." He pointed with the gun to the phone on Brett's hip.

"Rory, no!" Justine said. "I don't want to do this anymore. Rory, please I—"

"Shut up!" Rory said. "Get the baby out of the car!"

Brett unclipped his phone and tossed it in the gravel at Rory's feet. Rory kicked it into the ditch.

"Rory, listen to me! Please! I don't want to do this!" Justine pleaded.

"What the hell do you want from us?" Brett demanded.

Keeping a grip on Justine, Rory moved around the open door and yanked on the handle of the stepmother's door. Pamela let out a little cry, staring, frightened, at the gun, and unlocked the door. Releasing his grip on Justine, he reached in and snatched the cell phone from her hands. He pressed the End button, wondering if she had placed a call to the police. Probably. He pitched the phone into the open field.

"What the fuck do you think you're doing?" Brett said, squinting against the sun as it rose above the trees.

"Get the baby out!" Rory shoved Justine toward the door.

"Why don't you leave us alone?" Pamela screamed at him, standing up. "We didn't do anything to you. Why don't you just leave us alone?"

"Get back inside the car." He pointed the gun at her chest, watching the passing cars to see if anyone was taking notice. They probably looked like a family on an outing, perhaps having missed their turn off and were now contemplating an alternate route. Nothing unusual.

Pamela let out a cry and sat back down. Justine pulled the baby carrier out of the back seat. Abigail fussed, clearly annoyed at the commotion, but she didn't cry.

"Get back in your car and drive." Rory trained the gun on Brett, still keeping it low enough to be concealed by the car.

"What are you doing? You can't take my daughter."

"Get back in your fucking car now or I'll put a bullet in her. You understand?"

Brett swallowed, hesitated for a moment and walked back around the car.

Justine said, "Rory, listen to me! Rory!"

"I want you to get in your car and drive," Rory said to Brett. "I'll be right behind you. Don't try to alert anyone. Just drive the fucking car like normal, and Justine will be fine. Don't fuck up or she'll end up dead. Do as I say!"

"What are you doing this for?" Brett asked.

"Get in the car and drive like I told you. That's all you have to do. Understand?"

Brett got into the driver's seat.

"Wait, I've got to get Duke!" Justine screamed as Rory pulled her away.

"Hurry the fuck up!"

Justine reached in and pulled the pet carrier out, struggling with its weight and the weight of Abigail's baby carrier in her other hand. Rory ushered Justine over to the Challenger and opened the back door.

"Buckle up the baby," he said. He got in and rolled down his window, waving Brett past.

"Rory, what the hell is this? How can you just pull us over on the side of the fucking highway? What's wrong with you?"

"I had to get you out. I had to save you." Their eyes locked in the rear-view mirror.

He considered the distressed look on her face and thought of Frances. She was dead. She had been dead all this time.

Maybe it was possible that we weren't all meant to live to be a ripe old age and die in our beds surrounded by loved ones. Maybe some of us were destined to live only for so long. For just a few short years before we were called home, our lessons on this earth having been learned, our journey, whatever that might be, completed. Like the cycle of birth and living, death was, after all, natural to our existence. Maybe there were no accidents in this life, and it was inevitable that Frances died exactly when she did. Just like all the people he had put in their graves. It could be that that was his purpose on this earth—to facilitate the deaths of those he had killed. Everyone had a purpose. Life in itself was its own purpose. But maybe this, too, was his purpose. And now, looking at the car in the lane ahead of him, he knew the occupant's deaths were part of a universal plan greater than all of them.

Chapter
FORTY-TWO

"Jesus fucking Christ, Rory, what is going on? What the hell are you doing this for?" Justine asked, her body shaking. Abigail was crying, her lips turned out in a frown, her tear-filled eyes appearing as frightened as Justine felt. Duke was whimpering in his pet carrier, sitting on the other side of the baby.

Rory said nothing, just moved his head from one side to the other and popped his neck, then looked straight ahead out the windshield.

"Well? What are we doing? Can you tell me? What the hell are we doing here? And what happened to your face?"

"I'm saving your ass, that's what I'm doing," he said, as he did a shoulder check and pulled into traffic behind the Lincoln.

"Saving my ass? From what? What are you talking about?"

"Your old man is what happened to my face, by the way."

Justine stroked Abigail's head, telling her it was okay, even though she didn't know if that was true. She thought of the cell phone she had discreetly passed to Pam when she reached back inside the car for the dog. Pam was probably calling the cops at that very moment. She thought of the hand Duke had dragged back to the house. The police had come out during the night and taken it away. They said they were going to send a forensics team out today to comb the property for any more remains.

Rory turned up the stereo. The heavy beat of a metal song pulsated in the air.

"Are you going to tell me what the fuck's going on?" she said.

"What the hell were you doing in the car, Justine? Why didn't you tell me? Isn't that exactly what we discussed? You were going to let me know of any change in plans, remember?" His voice was angry, and Justine felt her own frustration kick in.

"Well, I was going to phone you this morning and let you know that I wanted to call the whole thing off, but I didn't think you'd actually be up before the fucking sun carrying this thing out."

"You thought it was all a joke? Is that it?"

"Maybe the last time we talked I was just mad, or fed up, I don't know. To tell you the truth I think I was out of my mind." She thought of how she'd put Abigail inside the wall of her bedroom. She had to be mad to do that. It seemed ludicrous today. But she'd done it, thinking it was right. Pamela had frantically unscrewed the vent and pulled Abigail out and then taken her into their room for the night, locking Justine out. "It was crazy, what I was planning. But I guess I came to my senses. I love my parents. I do love them and I just can't do this to them. I can't go through with this and—"

"Oh, that's just fucking great isn't it? When exactly did you have your little moment of repentance, Justine? And why the fuck didn't you bother to let me in on it right away? Are you that fucking stupid?"

"Look," she said, taking a breath and lowering her voice. "You're right. I'm sorry. I should have told you right away. I took a couple of Valium last night and I passed out early, so I—"

"You're damn straight you should have told me!"

She looked at her daughter, who had stopped crying and was staring at her transfixed. Justine mustered a smile for her, aware of the danger they were in. Duke's whimpering had also subsided. Through the windshield, she could see her parent's car a few car lengths ahead.

"Okay, you're right. You're absolutely right," she said.

"There's nothing I can do about it now." He glowered at her in the mirror.

"What do you mean there's nothing you can do? What's going on? What have you done, Rory?"

"There's a bomb attached underneath. At seven-thirty their car will blow sky high. Good fucking thing I stuck around and saw you in the back of the car, now isn't it? You and Abigail would be blown to bits."

She felt the blood drain from her head. Her heart hammered against her ribs like it was trying to break free of its cage. A cry escaped from behind the hand she pressed to her mouth. The digital clock on the dash read 7:21 a.m.

"Oh, God! We've got to stop them! We've got to get them out, Rory. Drive up to their car. We've got to get them out of the car!"

He didn't answer, and she could feel that he had taken his foot off the gas pedal. They were slowing down.

"Fuck! Rory, please, please!"

"It's too late to change your mind, Justine."

"No! Wait! Please, Rory, don't do this, please don't do this!"

"You know they're just going to put you back in that hospital. You know that. I thought we had this all planned out. I thought this is what you wanted."

"I changed my mind," Justine said, clutching the back of his seat, digging her nails into the soft leather. "I don't want this anymore. I don't want them dead. They don't deserve this, Rory. They're good people. They don't deserve this. Please, let's just stop, okay?"

"Like I said, there's nothing we can do about it now. It will all be over in a few more minutes."

"No! There's…there's still time. We can tell them, we can get them out!"

She wracked her brain for some sort of way to save them. This was all her fault. She had set this in motion. She had to do something.

"Rory, listen. I've got a better idea, Rory. My parents…they have a life insurance policy and there's a clause…a…a double-indemnity clause. So… so what that means is if they die in an accident I get twice the money, Rory. So we've got to think of another plan, okay? A…a way to make it look like an accident, okay? Then we'll get all the money. It's like a million or more. More I think. More like two million from the both of them. We could end up with over two million dollars, Rory. Over…over two million, so let's think of something else. Let's plan this thing out better. A bomb will only look like murder and…and I just don't want to raise any suspicion or risk not getting the insurance, so let's—"

"I told you, it's too late."

"But, that's a lot of money, we should think about this for a minute, Rory. We should—"

"Didn't you just tell me you'd changed your mind about killing them?" His battered face was in the rearview, his eyes narrowed at her.

"Yeah, but then I remembered the life insurance. I would kill them for that. I…I would do it for all that money. Who wouldn't want all that money? Two million dollars if they die accidentally. There must be a way we can figure this out so we can get the money and not raise any suspicions. Let's be smart about this, Rory, let's not throw this opportunity away."

She watched as he shook his head, and she knew she wasn't going to persuade him.

"It's too late."

"But I—"

"Forget it! It's almost over now."

A rage came over her—fierce, violent, bigger than her. She struck him hard on the side of the head with her fist. "Fuck you, you son of a bitch! Fuck you!"

She cuffed him again and he reached back, grabbing her hand. It slipped from his grip and she started beating him on the head with both her fists, screaming at him. The car swerved into the other lane and slowed down. Rory got hold of her hair and pulled.

Justine groaned, aware in that moment of her baby's crying, aware that she needed to try and stay calm for Abigail. She could see the diaper bag on the floor at her feet. The knife! She remembered she had hidden one of the kitchen knives inside. While her hair was painfully being yanked, she reached down and grabbed the bag. She unzipped it and thrust her hand to the bottom. Her fingers touched the smooth handle of the knife and she pulled it out.

With the knife griped tightly in her fist, she stretched out her arm and swung it forward. She let out a wail as she plunged it into his flesh. From her position in the back seat, with her head pinned down as he yanked on her hair, she couldn't see exactly which part of him she had struck. But he let out a sudden cry. The car lurched to the right and slowed down. Justine raised her hand and struck him again. He released her hair. Again, she plunged the knife into him and this time she felt it go deep. His hand knocked her arm away. She lost her grip on the knife. She could see the handle was sticking out the front of his neck.

He lost control of the car and they careened to the side of the road, heading for the ditch. She flung her body across Abigail's car seat and hung on as the car jolted and slammed into the ditch, coming to a stop. Duke's pet carrier tumbled. The dog let out a pathetic cry.

Quickly, she undid the seatbelt on Abigail's car seat, noticing the drops of blood on her forehead like some gruesome baptism in a horror movie. She felt an incredible sense of guilt, mixed with her fear.

"It's okay, baby. It's okay," she said and grabbed the baby bag, opening the back door.

Rory was lying on his side, slumped over the console between the seats. He released a soft moan. She could see the time on the dashboard. 7:24 am.

The door was heavy as she pushed on it, realizing the car was on a slight incline. She leaned with all her weight on the door and forced it open.

Abigail stopped crying and was now just whimpering as Justine pulled her from the car by the handle of the carrier. With her other hand she latched onto the pet carrier and dragged it out awkwardly, bumping and banging it, jostling the pup inside. She fell to the ground on her ass as she tried to scramble away. Then she managed to get her feet underneath her and hoisted herself up. A car stopped behind them and a man got out of the driver's door, hurrying toward her. But she had no time to talk. She needed to get to her parents.

She could see their car ahead on the side of the road. It was about four or five hundred feet away. It was backing up toward her. From behind her, she heard a siren approaching fast.

With the baby carrier in one hand and the pet carrier in the other, she ran up the side of the road. She heard the man behind her call out to her. She ignored him.

"Dad! Dad! Get out of the car!" she yelled and realized she was sobbing, terrified she wouldn't reach them in time.

She cast a look behind her and shuddered. Rory was emerging from the car, stumbling forth like some mad man on a mission. One hand was pressed to his neck to stop the blood as he careened toward her. She could see the front of his shirt was soaked dark red. In his hand he held a gun. She turned toward her dad's car, which had stopped. But he and Pamela had not emerged from it.

Then she tripped, and her hands shot out. Abigail's baby carrier went down with her and turned over on its side. Duke's carrier skidded out in front of her. The dog let out a howling cry. Justine sobbed. Abigail was screaming.

"It's okay, baby." She choked out the words, her voice quivering. "Mommy's here."

Lifting both the carriers again, she struggled to her feet, knowing only that she had to keep going. She felt like she was in a dream, trying to run, but moving in slow motion. Why was this so difficult?

She wasn't going to save them in time. She would fail, and they would die, and it would be all her fault. She was responsible for all of it. Their blood would be on her hands. The only two people in the entire world who truly loved and cared about her. She felt as if her heart had been cut from her chest.

She twisted her head backward and saw Rory advancing on her. Behind him, a car came to a skidding stop. She could see police cars coming up fast. Then a crack split the air. A hot pain tore into her back and she felt both her knees smack against the ground as her body thrust forward from the force.

Chapter
FORTY-THREE

Justine heard his gasping breath before she saw him. She lay on her back, trying to get up, trying to reach for her daughter. The baby carrier was turned away from her and Abigail was screaming. The puppy's carrier had tumbled over on its side. The dog was howling. Then Rory's sweaty face lurched into her line of vision.

She tried to speak, to plead with him, to make him understand that he couldn't do this. She was a mother. Her baby needed her. She couldn't die. Not yet. Not here. Not until her daughter was all grown up. Please God, not yet!

"You stupid bitch," he said, weaving before her like a boxer who'd lost the fight and was ready to do a face plant on the mat. The hand at his neck was wet with blood. "You and I could have had everything…everything!"

He raised the gun toward her and cocked it.

Justine let out a scream. Then she heard shots. Rory's body jerked forward and a look of surprise crossed his features. In the next second, he collapsed on the ground beside her.

Justine struggled to a sitting position and that's when she saw Linden, the old cop who'd come to their house, ambling toward her with a gun in his hand. He was limping and looked about ready to keel over, himself.

He kicked the gun from Rory's hand and then reached for the baby carrier, turning it around so they could see Abigail. Justine felt as if she were hypnotized, waiting for the snapping of fingers to wake her.

"Paramedics are on the way. Don't try to move," he said.

"The car…the car has a—"

The next thing Justine remembered was the force from the blast knocking into her as the car exploded behind them. She lay on her side, and watched the mushroom of black smoke rise into the air. Both of the back doors swung open with the blast. The entire car was engulfed in flames. A giant bonfire at the side of the road.

Justine's face was wet with tears and mucus, and she coughed. The sobs flowed out at the realization that she'd killed her parents. She'd done this. She was responsible. She'd killed them!

A sharp pain stabbed through her as she tried to move. She managed to get to her knees and crawl across the gravel toward her baby.

"Abigail!" she sobbed, afraid her daughter might be dead, too. This couldn't be happening! "Abigail!"

The baby's face was red, wet with tears as she screeched. And Justine sobbed harder with relief. Her hands were shaking as she undid the buckle on Abigail's carrier and struggled to lift her out. She held Abigail's warm body tightly to her chest and rocked her, sitting at the side of the road, chocking on her tears.

The old cop was down on one knee retching, like he was trying not to throw up. He was gasping for air. Rory lay motionless on his back, staring up at the sky.

Her entire body vibrated and she clung to Abigail's tiny body as the realization dawned on her that she was alone in the world. Her parents were dead. How was she going to live with that knowledge? How was she going to go on, knowing that she was responsible for their deaths? The very people who had loved her and Abigail, cared for them, protected them. And in her delusions, she had thought they were the enemy. She had helped arranged this entire thing! It was all her fault! What had she done?

She felt her mind breaking wide open, severing down the middle. She was crazy. She belonged in the psych ward. She didn't deserve to be a mother to Abigail. She would surely destroy her, too, with her madness.

"I killed them! I killed my parents!" She turned to the cop, sobbing.

He was looking beyond her, the morning sun reflecting in his aging eyes. Without a word he nodded, motioning toward something behind her.

Justine turned to see her father and Pamela walking toward her. She sucked in a breath and scrambled to her feet with Abigail.

"Daddy!" she screamed and ran on weak legs toward them. She could see the tears flowing down Pamela's battered face and the unhinged look on her father's face, and she felt the most joyful sensation that they were still alive. It was like a dream—a nightmare—the whole ordeal. As if she had just imagined it all.

"Justine, oh, my God!" her dad said, embracing her and Abigail. "Are you okay?"

"You're bleeding!" Pam said.

"It's okay," she said, wiping the tears and grit from her face. "I think it just hit my shoulder."

Justine sobbed as both her parents held her. They would be all right. Everything would be all right as long as they were together. She checked Abigail and rubbed at the drying drops of blood on her head with her sleeve. The baby squinted up at her in the morning sunlight and smiled. Justine laughed and then sobbed, kissing her daughter's soft head.

A small army of police and paramedics descended on them. Another cop was scolding Linden about being on duty with his injuries, talking about how he was lucky they found him in that ditch when they did.

"Yeah, yeah," he said waving a thick hand in the air. "I'm not on duty, don't worry. I was just released from hospital and heard the call on my scanner. Wasn't far away so thought I'd swing over, see if I could help. Just in the nick of time, I'd say."

Then he nodded at Rory, lying on the roadside a few feet away and said, "Besides, I had some unfinished business to take care of."

Chapter
FORTY-FOUR

Rory lay on his back at the side of the road. He felt detached as he listened to the commotion surrounding him; the blast from the C-4 a moment ago, the sound of metal hitting tarmac as something was blown from the vehicle; car tires screeching on the road as people came to a stop; the yelling; the screaming; the sirens.

There was an odd peace inside of him as he lay there, feeling as if he were inside the eye of a tornado. His entire body was vibrating, and yet he felt no pain. He could no longer feel the wounds in his neck, but he could sense his blood flowing out, and knew it was also emptying down his throat, filling his stomach.

He thought of Frances, with her soft flowing hair, shimmering gold in the sunshine as she cart-wheeled and walked on her hands. He wondered if she had stopped and turned in time to see the car barreling toward her before it knocked her down. Did she have a moment of abject terror, or did she not feel anything, her mind simply fading to blackness? Maybe if he had been a better brother he would have walked her home from school like he was supposed to. He might have stopped her from crossing the street, or seen the car coming and pulled her out of its way. He might have saved her.

Perhaps. Perhaps not. What the hell did it matter now, anyway?

Rory gazed up at the sky, amazed at how blue it appeared. He felt himself awakened to everything around him, and yet he wasn't even high anymore. The sound of the wind blowing through the trees filled his ears like music, and it sounded so sweet, as if he were hearing it for the very first time. He was aware of the warmth of the rising sun on his skin, the birds singing, the ants crawling in the ground, the earth awakening to spring, coming alive all around him; the plants, the flowers, the trees, the animals, the insects. How was he so heedless to all of this before when it had been right here with him the entire time? It was all so simple. All of it sufficient and complete within itself.

He thought of the idea of an immortal body, and how horrible it would be to live forever in the same body. What would be the evolutionary purpose of living forever? He thought of the vampires in the Anne Rice novels, how after centuries of remaining the same, Lestat became bitter and unhappy existing in the same form while the world around him changed with the natural cycle of everything. The idea of immortality, while it might seem desirable, in practicality it was not so sublime. But perhaps this was just a quality of our spirit, that timelessness we all cherish and cling to as a lover, fearful of being abandoned, fearful of our own loneliness. Our nature therefore must be immortality. And our existence must continue on after death.

If Rory was to die today, he was ready. He had heard somewhere that the soul actually chooses the time and circumstances of the body's physical death, and it chooses its own experiences and events in its lifetime, trapped in this flesh and blood between birth and death. If reincarnation exists, then death is just another event, a transition from one form to the next, a butterfly shedding its cocoon. He wondered if he just let go in that moment if it would bring him to Frances.

He felt the wings of the great bird within him pulling at him; breaking free; climbing upward; expanding into the vast, blue sky; soaring beyond the realm of the physical; carrying him home. And he realized the bird was himself, the wings were his own, and he was free.

Also by Julia Madeleine: Scarlet Rose

When a wealthy Toronto business man is found tortured and murdered in a hotel room, his 22-year-old stepdaughter, Fiona Dalton, must help police find the killer. Forced at the age of 16 into the adult entertainment industry by her own mother, Scarlet Rose; a washed-up alcoholic burlesque queen from the 1960s, Fiona navigates her way through the dark recesses of her family's history, uncovering shocking secrets that threaten to destroy her. All the while her mother becomes fixated on the only thing that truly matters to her: getting her hands on her dead ex-husband's money.

ISBN: 978-0980887402
published by Black Heart Books

www.ingramcontent.com/pod-product-compliance
Lightning Source LLC
Chambersburg PA
CBHW020617260626
47157CB00003B/1053